BRAVER THAN
You Know

KATIE ARDEA

Leaf Rain Books

Chapter 1

A twig snapped. Something was moving, and it was close.

Knife in hand, Kimberley Colter froze, her heart skittering. How had she become so unaware? So immersed? Hadn't she learned that the wilderness, no matter how deceptive its appearance, could exact a heartbreaking price for inattentiveness? She spun toward the trail she'd followed into the forest. *Fight...Flight...*

Suppressed laughter jolted her gaze to a tall man, a teenaged girl, and a young boy peering at her from within a stand of aspen trees thirty feet away. If she'd been a portrait photographer, she would have wanted to capture the trio just as she saw them then—the bubbling merriment in the girl's eyes, the lazy amusement in the man's, the piercing intensity in the boy's. Sticky with sweat, she folded the knife blade into her multitool and slid it into her pocket. Moments before, she'd used it to scrape off an army of ticks crawling up the exterior of her cargo pants. "Hello."

"Hi." The girl approached, clad in green shorts and a yellow T-shirt, her limbs tanned.

At close range, Kimberley decided she was perhaps

seventeen or eighteen. Blonde curls framed an oval face dominated by unadorned, smoky green eyes. She was fresh and lovely, poised at the edge of womanhood.

"There are a few ticks on the back of your shirt. I'll get them for you." The teen smiled with easy charm. "You were so focused on your camera, we wanted to see how close we could get before you noticed us. Sorry if we startled you."

"Good thing you don't eat oblivious lenswomen." Kimberley lifted her heavy ponytail off her nape for the tick removal and then let it fall. Mid-May heat permeated the southern Manitoba air, carrying earthy scents of sun-drenched foliage and decaying forest leaves. Spring had arrived early on the Canadian prairies, and Turtle Mountain Provincial Park was every bit as hot and dry as Calgary had been a week ago. At her feet, forest plants formed a three-dimensional carpet of textures and colors. *A safe subject*, the voice inside her head taunted as she collected her tripod-mounted camera. *And only a stone's throw from Adam Lake beach and your brother.*

The other two strangers stepped forward in unison, the man moving with the smooth grace of a cat while the boy approached hesitantly, a little behind. Kimberley met the child's probing gaze and smiled the reassurance he seemed to need. He looked to be seven or eight, his eyes dark blue, his red hair trimmed short under a Toronto Blue Jays baseball cap.

"Ah, an explorer."

"I beg your pardon?" Kimberley looked up at the man.

She guessed his age to be late twenties or early thirties. Dressed in a snug white polo shirt and black shorts, he had an athlete's wide shoulders, tight abs, and muscled limbs. Like the girl, he was blond, his straight hair neatly styled in a classic short masculine cut. His face was all regular planes and angles, clean lines accented by a straight nose and the hint of dimples in his cheeks. Still amused, his eyes were neither the green of the girl's nor the blue of the boy's; instead, they were a clear, pale amber.

"There's a tick on the verge of descending into territory you'd probably rather it didn't explore. Would you like us to check for others?" Laughter lit the stranger's eyes.

Kimberley swept the blood-sucking pest from her blouse's lapel. At twenty-seven, she'd had plenty of experience quashing overtures made by male clients during the wildlife photography tours she and her fiancé had led. It looked like she'd have to do it again. "No, thanks." She injected frost into her voice and tossed the stranger her "professional photographer quashing a male client look." "I'll do a thorough search later."

The girl broke into a mischievous grin, yet the boy continued to study Kimberley intently. Family was written all over the trio. The man's coloring mirrored the girl's, while his facial features were repeated in the boy's. He looked too young to be the girl's father, but it was certainly possible he was the boy's. Heaven help his wife if he was married. The kind of flirtation he indulged in could tear a marriage apart.

Bryan...Eleven months ago, the man she'd planned to

marry had scooped her into his arms and danced a crazy waltz around piles of gear they'd assembled for a last shoot in the Rockies before their wedding. She'd curled her arms around his neck and laughed for sheer joy, her heart in danger of splintering from happiness. Two days later, he was dead and she was in hospital, fighting for her life.

She pushed the memories aside. *Different place. New life.* Perhaps this stranger didn't know the riches he possessed. She glanced at her watch and gave an involuntary start. "Excuse me. I'm late for a barbecue."

"What were you taking pictures of?" The words exploded from the boy. Tensed, he stared at her, his expression a mixture of painful shyness broken by curiosity.

The man and girl looked at him in surprise.

"Patterns in the leaves." Kimberley was as unable to resist the child's overture as she was to resist the kids at the recreation center where she volunteered in Calgary. The old saying about helping yourself by helping others had certainly proven true in her case. "Some of the leaves look like hearts."

"The violets!"

"That's right. Others look like starbursts or spear tips, and there are so many shades of green it's as though the forest wove a carpet and laid it out for us to walk on."

The child nodded, his eyes shining. "Is your job taking pictures?"

"Yes. I'd love to stay and chat, but my brother will think I'm lost if I don't get back to the beach. Bye."

As she began to turn away, the man stepped toward her, his eyes filled with a rich warmth that stopped her in her tracks. Every trace of teasing had disappeared. "Thank you." He nodded toward the boy.

He really was a striking man, switching from word games to straight-out appreciation in little more than a heartbeat. "It was my pleasure," she told him. "I've been known to talk the ears off people interested in photography. Excuse me."

She'd taken several steps along the path when she heard the boy's excited voice behind her. "Dad, did you see how she used her knife to get rid of those ticks? When can I have a knife?" So, the man *was* the boy's father.

She hurried through the forest, mentally snapping photographs. Family of black-capped chickadees. *Click.* Red squirrel pulsing its way up an oak tree. *Click.* The trio of strangers intruded into her thoughts. The child had been so intense, as though something was trying to break free inside him. The girl had been direct and charming, the kind of personality she'd enjoy in a friend. And the man? Was he even aware of his masculine presence? An unexpected pang of disappointment surfaced at the realization that she'd likely never see the three again.

She stepped onto the beach and waved to her brother, Gary, and his wife, Wendy, seated on lawn chairs near a fire in a barbecue pit. The day-use area of the Adam Lake campground was filled to capacity, with children romping on the beach and shouting from shallow water warmed by weeks of unseasonable heat. She joined Gary and Wendy in shade cast by a grove of aspens near the barbecue pit. "I hope the sausages aren't burned to a crisp."

"Just done. Get any interesting pics?" Wendy forked a half-dozen sizzling sausages onto a plate. She'd tied her brown dreadlocks back with a green scarf that matched her maternity dress.

"Nothing riveting." Kimberley set her tripod on a level patch of grass as Gary lounged back in his chair, his bare legs crossed at the ankles. Anyone seeing the two of them together would immediately note the family resemblance— the same black hair, vivid blue eyes, and golden-hued skin that tanned effortlessly into warm brown.

Wendy handed out plates, and the three of them tucked into sausages, salads, and buns, pausing frequently to gaze out over the lake and forested hills. They burst into laughter at the sight of a toddler racing away from his mother's grasp, his torso clothed in a T-shirt and his bottom as bare as the day he was born.

Out of nowhere, grief slammed into Kimberley, tearing her breath away.

* * *

If the photographer lived locally, she was new. Lincoln Steele scanned the park's day-use area. Otherwise, he would have heard about her. The Steele Cattle Company had a lot of connections.

He'd almost refused when Matt had asked to come to the park. With the early spring, ranch work was piling up. Still, as tied to the land and seasons as he was, his son was his top priority. So he'd said yes, and in one of those godsends occasionally tossed onto his path, he and the kids had encountered the gorgeous woman peering through her camera lens in the forest. After he'd teased the lovely stranger, her striking eyes had chilled him with sky-blue frost, yet they'd shone with warmth for Matt. There'd been an instant connection there.

If he did see her now, what excuse could he make to approach her? *Excuse me, miss. You're the first stranger my son has spoken to in years. Normally, he's afraid of people he doesn't know, especially women. Do you live somewhere nearby so that he might see you again?* It sounded weird, like a really bad pickup line.

Then he spotted her crying. A man, presumably her brother, held her hand while a pregnant woman leaned toward her, features sympathetic. The lovely photographer's shoulders shook as she wiped tears from her face. This was definitely not the time to make a move to meet her.

"Dad, she's crying." Matt's voice sounded squeezed.

Lincoln looked at his son, whose eyes were focused on the weeping woman, and then at his sister. Terri had picked up on the black-haired woman's cool response to him and had whispered, "Not everyone shares your sense of humor."

"Terri."

"I've got it." Her eyes met his, poised confidence clear in their depths. "Leave it to me."

* * *

"Excuse me?"

Kimberley looked up from packing leftovers into a cooler. She'd shooed Gary and Wendy off on a stroll, needing time to gather her composure after going to pieces at the sight of the toddler. "Oh, hello again." She immediately recognized the teen and boy who stood near her.

"Hi. I'm Terri Steele, and this is my nephew, Matthew Steele."

So, the teen was the striking man's sister. *Interesting.* The boy again studied Kimberley intently, his gaze laced with something she couldn't quite place. "I'm Kimberley Colter. Pleased to meet you."

"We're pleased to meet you, too. You mentioned to Matthew that photography is your work. Do you have a website? We'd love to see some of your photos, wouldn't we, Matt?"

The red-haired boy nodded, his gaze searching.

"I do have a website. If you search for Colter Wilderness Photography, you'll find it."

"Is that C-O-L-T-E-R?"

"Yes. I have a business card in the car, if you'd like one."

"I would."

"Just a sec. I might as well carry this cooler to the car while I get it."

"Do you have other things to carry? We can help."

Words shot from Matthew, "Yeah, we can help."

Kimberley paused, studying Terri and Matthew Steele more carefully. The teen exuded sunny warmth while her nephew stood tensed. "All right. Thanks."

She handed the cooler to Terri and a bag of buns to Matthew before hoisting the second cooler and walking toward Gary and Wendy's sedan. "I like this part of Manitoba. I've visited northern parts of the province before—Churchill in particular, to photograph polar bears—but this is my first time in the southwest corner. Do you live in the area?"

"Yes. On the north slope of the mountain. Where do you live?"

Having resided near the foot of the Rocky Mountains all her life, Kimberley smiled at the reference to the gently rounded hills that comprised Turtle Mountain. "I live near mountains, too, in Calgary."

Disappointment flitted across Terri Steele's face. "I've been to the Rockies. They're amazing. You're lucky to live so close to them. Matt and I were thinking that it would be great if you lived around here. We're both interested in photography and maybe we could discuss it with you."

"Sorry. My brother and his wife and I are ready to head back to Brandon, and I'm flying home this evening." Kimberley removed a business card from her wallet in a pack on the car's rear seat and handed it to Terri. "But feel free to contact me if you have any photography questions. My e-mail address and cell phone number are on this card. You, too, Matthew."

"Thank you."

"Yeah, thanks."

Kimberley accompanied her new acquaintances back to the beach as Gary and Wendy approached, hand in hand, the soft radiance of love enveloping them. Terri turned to her. "If you're ever here again, why don't you look us up? My mother owns the Steele Cattle Company. You can find it online, if you're interested."

"Thanks for the invitation. I'll keep it in mind." She made introductions, and after the quartet exchanged handshakes and hellos—Matthew's barely audible—Gary asked Terri, "Did I hear you say your mother owns the Steele Cattle Company? I'm an engineer. Last year, I drew up plans for an indoor riding arena for Lauren Steele."

"That's my mother."

"Are you the daughter who rides dressage?"

"I am, and Matt's learning to jump." Terri stepped away. "It's been nice meeting you, but we'd better go. My brother—Matt's dad—is waiting for us." After walking a few steps with her nephew at her side, she paused and turned to speak to Kimberley. "I'm sorry if my brother's remarks offended you. When he said them, I thought they were clever, but I realized afterward that they might have made you uncomfortable."

Before Kimberley could respond, the two Steeles walked away.

"What an extraordinary girl!" Wendy whispered, following Terri with her gaze. "So poised and polite. Her eyes had me itching to paint her. And the boy could hardly tear his eyes off you. You've made a conquest."

Gary's face tightened. "What did her brother say?"

Kimberley kept her voice low. "He was just flirting, Gary. I brushed him off."

Wendy nodded to where a tall blond man strode across the beach to meet Terri and her nephew. "Is *he* the one you brushed off?"

"Yes." The moment Kimberley replied, Terri's brother captured her gaze, his expression of male interest laced with the same unidentified emotion as his son's. As he stepped toward her, the look in his eyes held her riveted to the sand, her heart racing in her chest. An instinct, an almost overwhelming feeling, urged her to walk to him.

"At the risk of sounding like a smitten teenager, I'm going to say 'Wow!'" Wendy murmured.

"Let's hit the road." Dislike laced Gary's voice. He turned away from the beach and walked toward the sedan.

Kimberley forced herself to step back and raised a hand in greeting toward the man on the sand.

He dipped his head in an acknowledging nod before turning his attention to his son and sister.

"Do you suppose he sent the kids to talk to you?" Wendy whispered to Kimberley as they walked to the car.

"I have no idea." Kimberley's mind raced. *What's happening?* She and Bryan had worked together for five years. In that time, their respect and liking for each other had deepened into friendship and blossomed into love. Yet, when this man, whose first name she didn't even know, stared at her across a Manitoba beach, she'd experienced a nearly irresistible compulsion to cross that sand and stand within the circle of his arms.

Wendy raised her eyebrows. "Sure you want to return to Calgary today?"

"He's probably married."

"No man who looks at a woman the way he looked at you is in love with another woman."

Kimberley slid into the sedan's rear seat and ignored Gary's questioning gaze in the rear-view mirror. Then it came to her—what the trace emotion was she'd seen in the eyes of Matthew Steele and his father. It was compassion.

Chapter 2

"Linc, Matt, I've got Kimberley's website up." Terri stared at her laptop. "I'm impressed. Her work is fabulous. Mom, come and have a look."

"Who is Kimberley?" Lauren Steele asked.

Lincoln watched his mother stand from the floral-patterned sofa in the living room of her open-concept log house. At forty-nine, she looked more like Terri's older sister than her mother. A person would have to look hard to notice the few gray hairs in her short wavy blonde hair.

Terri spared her mother a glance. "A wildlife photographer from Calgary. We met her in the park today. Matt got her to tell us about her photography."

Lincoln saw his mother control her surprise at Terri's last statement. She threw him a questioning look, and he nodded. She asked, "What was she photographing, Matt?"

"Patterns of leaves in the bush. Their shapes and colors."

"I see. Let's have a look."

Lincoln joined his mother and son at the oak dining table where Terri sat. He was unprepared for the spectacular vistas and wildlife close-ups that appeared on the screen as his sister clicked through a slide show. One exquisite image was replaced by another: the Rockies, the Arctic, Australia. Africa, mountain goats, Arctic wolves, crocodiles, polar bears, giraffes, grizzlies, a flock of flamingoes. Beside him, his mother leaned in closer to better view the screen. "Why, they're stunning! What talent she has."

"It turns out that her brother designed our arena," Terri said. "Small world."

"Gary Colter? That's intriguing. Didn't you recognize him? No, of course not. Neither of you were present when he and I discussed the arena details." Lincoln's mother turned to him. "You didn't meet her?"

"If you mean introduce myself, no."

Terri grinned. "She didn't like it when he teased her about a tick that was about to crawl down the front of her shirt."

"I see."

"I'm going to e-mail her." Terri clicked her computer mouse, leaving Kimberley's website. "I have a couple of composition questions."

Lincoln stepped away from the computer and motioned for his mother to accompany him. Matt and Terri remained glued to the screen, Terri's blond curls dancing as she turned to ask Matt, "Which photo was your favorite? I want to tell Kimberley."

"So," his mother teased *sotto voce* as she and Lincoln strolled into the living room, "you liked her enough to tease her but didn't introduce yourself?"

He led his mother through open French doors onto a plant-draped patio grayed by dusk and then closed the doors behind them. *Is this idea racing around in my brain just plain crazy?* "I need to bring her here."

"Well, perhaps 'liked' was too mild a word."

"For Matt."

"*What?*" All traces of his mother's teasing disappeared. "What do you mean?"

"Something tells me she's the person to help Matt."

"But you know nothing about her. Darling, you can't simply pluck a woman out of her life in Calgary and bring her here. She could be married and have children."

"She wasn't wearing any rings."

"That doesn't preclude a committed relationship."

"But if often does. Tell me, when was the last time you heard Matt talk to a stranger out of his own volition?"

His mother shrugged. "Not for years."

"Exactly. Today he talked to Kimberley because he didn't want her to leave after I annoyed her. The words burst out of him. And he was torn up when he saw her crying."

"Crying?"

"Yes, after we got back to the beach. Matt and Terri did a little sleuthing for me, and Matt not only spoke to Kimberley again, he also said hello to her brother and his wife. That's the most unprompted talking he's done in a situation like that since..." Ugly memories flooded Lincoln's mind.

"You need to say it."

He turned away so his mother wouldn't see the pain that still ravaged him when he thought of what his son had endured. "All right, I'll say it—the abuse. Matt broke through the darkness, and that's a huge step. I don't know why he was so taken with Kimberley, but it seemed as though he saw her there in the forest—ticks crawling all over her while she took her pictures—and instantly fell in love with her."

"I see."

Lincoln turned back to his mother. "You always say so much with just those two words. Okay, yes, I was attracted to her. No, I didn't fall in love with her, but my son might have. I'd like to see where things could lead for him."

"How can you be so sure she would be good for him?"

"I can't, but I know what I saw. She reached out to him as though she instinctively understood him, and he responded. Terri's in full agreement."

"I see." His mother looked deep into his eyes, her own the same smoky green as Terri's. "Well, perhaps if she's willing to exchange emails with Terri—maybe even with Matt—that might open some possibilities." She placed her hand on his arm. "Talk to the Big Guy about this. I know your marriage with Gayle soured your outlook on life, but God is good."

Lincoln stepped away. "Is he?" he asked softly. "Tell that to Matt."

* * *

Kimberley draped an arm around her father's shoulders as

he reviewed a legal brief in his two-story Calgary home. "I've been mulling over something for the past month and want to ask your opinion."

Elliott Colter hugged her briefly before pointing to a chair beside his desk. His blue eyes, so similar to hers, studied her alertly as she seated herself. "I've noticed you've been preoccupied lately. Shoot."

"I'm thinking of moving to Manitoba."

His eyebrows lifted. "How did you come up with that idea?"

"Gary and Wendy." Her bout of tears after seeing the bare-bottomed toddler in the park had sparked her brother's suggestion, which his wife had enthusiastically endorsed. "They think I need to get away from Calgary, that living somewhere else would help me to move on."

"It's been a year since Bryan died."

"I know." One spring day in the Rockies, her life had overflowed with happiness and the promise of a joyful future. The next, she was in hospital and Bryan was dead. In a few horrifying minutes, her future had become a painful void stretching before her. Only the unconditional love and support she'd received from her father and Gary and Wendy had pulled her through the post-traumatic shock and depression. Her father had insisted she return to his house after her release from hospital, and she'd been glad to do so, but now she needed to step out on her own again.

"What do you think?" her father asked.

She lifted a shoulder and let it fall. "At first I didn't take the idea seriously, but then I got excited. If I move, I'd only be an hour's drive from Gary and Wendy and the baby."

"So, you have a particular area in mind."

"Yes. Turtle Mountain, in the southwest corner of the province." Home of the Steele trio who refused to leave her thoughts—charming Terri, her handsome and intriguing brother, and Matthew, who despite being anxious and nervous had reached out to her, touching a place in her heart. "Gary said there's plenty of wildlife in the area and that the consolidation of small farms into larger holdings left a lot of older farmhouses vacant. He suggested I look into renting one of those."

Her father's gaze sharpened. "You're ready to head back into the wilds?"

"I have to try, Dad, as difficult and painful as it might be. Turtle Mountain is a lot tamer than the Rockies, so it could be the perfect place for me right now. And I'm intrigued by the idea of experiencing rural life first hand, rather than as a photo backdrop. I've spent a lot time in the outdoors, but I've only ever lived in Calgary."

"Then you should do it." Her father nodded briskly. "Life is full of challenges and risks, Kimmie. You—better than most people—know that. So, follow your heart on this."

"Thanks, Dad." Kimberley dropped a kiss on his salt-and-pepper hair. She climbed the stairs to the house's upper level and, in a room that had been hers as long as she could remember, sat at her desk and typed an e-mail to

Terri Steele. The teen had contacted her several times with photography questions, and Kimberley had received three brief, hesitant queries from Matthew.

```
Hi Terri. We might be able to talk
photography in person after all. I've
decided to move to southern Manitoba. I'd
prefer the Turtle Mountain area if I can
find a house to rent. Ads going out
tomorrow. Cheers, Kimberley
```

After shutting down her laptop, she hurried down the stairs to the house's large entry. "Go for a walk, Lexi?" Her young female husky sprang from its pillow and pranced around her, the dog's plumed tail brushing her legs. Because she'd flown to Manitoba to visit her brother and sister-in-law, she'd left her pet with her father. Now she ran a hand through Lexi's soft black-and-white fur and then clipped a leash onto her ecstatic canine's collar and walked through the warm darkness of a Calgary summer night.

* * *

"I've got news. *Very* interesting news." Terri set her laptop on the oak table. "Kimberley is planning to move to Manitoba. In fact, she'd like to move to Turtle Mountain if she can find a house to rent."

For several seconds, Lincoln stood frozen in his mother's dining room, incredulity sweeping through him. Snapshots from the park flashed through his mind—an unknown black-haired beauty crouched over her camera, Matt's words bursting out, tears trickling down Kimberley

Colter's face, his own gaze locked with hers across a stretch of sand. For the past month, he'd relived that look and every move the woman taking photos in the forest had made. He'd listened to Matt's excited conversations with Terri about the shutterbug tips Kimberley had shared. And he'd mulled over possible ways to entice the lovely stranger to Turtle Mountain but had come up with no clear plan.

"Do you want to read the letter she sent?" Terri's voice broke into his musings.

He moved to stand behind Terri, his mother joining him. As he read the letter over Terri's shoulder, he was struck by the fact that his mother had stood by him through whatever life had thrown at him—the good, the bad, the ugly. She looked up at him before saying, "How very interesting."

In her eyes, he caught a glimpse of the same idea that had leapt into his mind. "The old Steele place. Would you consider renting it out again? I know you had problems with the last tenants."

Terri looked up from her laptop, poised to act. "She's sending out ads tomorrow. Do you want me to e-mail her?"

His mother drew in a deep breath and released it slowly. "No." She rested her hands on her daughter's shoulders. "However, tomorrow morning I want you to photograph the old house—inside and outside. I'll write to her myself."

Again Lincoln met his mother's eyes, hers now

unreadable with her special brand of mystery. She seemed about to say something to him but instead addressed Terri. "Time for bed. You have a riding lesson first thing in the morning."

He settled his Blue Jays baseball cap on his head. He had an early morning ahead, too. "If the sales run on time, I should be back from Winnipeg by seven to pick up Matt." His son was already asleep upstairs in his mother's guest room.

"That's fine. The cows listed for auction look like excellent prospects."

"I'll do my best to bring them home." The fifty head he would be bidding on were purebred Aberdeen Angus from one of the best Angus breeders in the province. The fact that their calves had already been weaned was an additional draw this year, since the lack of rain during the past three months had drastically reduced pasture quality. No calves at foot meant that the cows—a major investment for the ranch—should be able to maintain their condition despite the less-than-ideal grazing.

As Lincoln strode to his pickup, the sweet balminess of a June prairie night enveloped him. Fireflies bobbed through the darkness, and faint breezes caressed him. He stared up into the star-studded darkness. *She's coming.* Before he'd figured out a way to bring Kimberley Colter to Turtle Mountain, that puzzle, already solved, had dropped in his lap.

Chapter 3

"Almost there, Lexi." Kimberley patted her husky's shoulder. In the town of Seton, northeast of Turtle Mountain, she gassed up and bought groceries and a land ownership map, as per her new landlady's suggestion. On a late June Monday, the small town seemed hunkered down on its grid of streets. Heat bounced off the sidewalks. Blocky stores and houses stood bare under the scorching mid-day sun. Street trees hung dusty, wilted leaves that fluttered in a strong breeze.

The day after she'd e-mailed Terri, Kimberley had received a message from the teen's mother, accompanied by photographs of an elm-shaded, older farmhouse situated on a rise overlooking a ravine. Lauren Steele had written that the house was known as "the old Steele place" and was situated on Steele Cattle Company land about a half-hour's drive from the nearest town, Seton. With a sense that God was prodding her shoulder, Kimberley had arranged to rent it.

During the past ten days, she'd tied up loose ends in Calgary, sorted through her belongings, and packed her Ford Ranger with necessities to live for an undetermined length of time in a farmhouse in Manitoba. She'd stretched the drive from Alberta into a leisurely three-day excursion, her express purpose to once again immerse herself in the beauty of the natural world and the solitude of being alone.

Dry summer heat cast a tawny shawl over the prairies, yet views of rugged river valleys, sun-scorched grain fields, and rangelands dotted with cattle and pronghorns had inspired her. With Lexi by her side, she'd cautiously hiked river-eroded badlands east of Calgary, her heart pounding at the sight of old wolf tracks, her nerves jumping at the sharp whistle of a ground squirrel. In the Cypress Hills straddling the Alberta–Saskatchewan border, she'd stood trembling in a clearing and then forced herself to walk into a forest that loomed like a wall in front of her. After five minutes—her senses screaming at her to run from the shadows—she'd hiked back to her truck, her legs shaking. Then she'd driven across southern Saskatchewan's bald prairie and entered Manitoba's southwest corner.

Can I really do this again? Do I have the courage? During the months following her physical recuperation, she'd barely gone through the motions of photography; however, the drive from Alberta, even with its terror-infused moments, had birthed a reawakening of her desire to record images of landscapes and wildlife. Whether she could cope emotionally with capturing those images, and whether her desire for photography would grow to the point where it continued to provide her with a livelihood, remained to be seen—as did the length of her stay in Manitoba.

Rolling prairie merged into parkland as she turned off

Highway 3 and drove south on Sanderson Road. Ahead, big round hay bales rested in long rows in a field on one side of the gravel road. On the opposite side, paddocks filled with cattle surrounded a complex of barns, corrals, and long, open shelters. A sign caught her eye: "Steele Cattle Company." She steered her truck into the parking area in front of a small gray building with "Office" on a sign beside the door. After opening the truck's windows so Lexi would have air, she walked toward the office, her nose wrinkling at the odor of cattle manure that wafted through the ranch yard.

"You get used to it." Attired in riding breeches and knee-high black boots, Terri Steele stood from a bench in the shade of a tall elm tree near the far end of the building. "Hi, Kimberley."

"Hi, Terri. Good to see you. Your mother told me to stop by the office to collect the key for the house."

"Yes. Mom and Linc and Matt are over at the ring. They asked me to watch for you. Matt's lesson should be almost over."

Linc. Lincoln. "So, your brother is Lincoln Steele, manager of the Steele Cattle Company?"

Terri gave her a keen look. "That's right."

"I took your suggestion and looked up the company website."

A hint of Cheshire cat appeared in Terri's expression. "Good!"

After she'd checked the website, Kimberley had sampled that name, rolling it over and over in her mind, fitting it with the image of the man who had stared at her so intently across the Adam Lake beach. Something about him had captivated her, yet she didn't understand why. One of the reasons she'd come to Turtle Mountain was to answer that question.

"Pretty dog." Terri nodded at Lexi as she walked by the Ranger. "The ring is this way." She led the way past corrals and a barn in which a tall young man adjusted a saddle on a dappled horse. "Did you have a good trip?"

"Yes. I didn't hurry, and Lexi and I did some hiking and exploring along the way."

"Do you always carry a camera with you?"

"I do, but not always the same one, and often more than one."

The teen's mischievous smile surfaced. "Do you have one with you now?"

Kimberley reached down and removed a black, palm-sized Sony Cyber-shot RX100 point-and-shoot digital camera from her cargo pants pocket. "This is my all-situation, just-in-case model. It's light and takes high quality images. I've learned that good subject material can appear anytime, anywhere."

Terri paused at the entrance of a wide building adjacent to the horse barn. "This is the arena your brother designed. The ring is beside it. We'll need to be quiet because Mom and Linc like to watch Matt's lessons without distractions."

As she and Terri stepped past the arena, Kimberley spotted Lincoln Steele standing next to a slender blonde woman. He turned and looked directly at Kimberley, his gaze locking with hers. The same adrenaline rush she'd so often experienced when photographing wildlife raced through her. Here on Turtle Mountain, she'd stepped into the territory of a man whose smooth movements and amber eyes reminded her of a big cat—a hunter. Well, she was hunting, too—hunting a glimpse of the rest of her life.

* * *

Lincoln ran his gaze over Kimberley Colter. Dressed in cargo pants and a long-sleeved blouse with sleeves rolled up to her elbows, she was every bit as attractive as he remembered. Her black mane of hair tumbled over her shoulders, and her vivid blue eyes contrasted starkly with her tanned face. She appeared tense and focused, like a runner anticipating the starting pistol.

What impact will this woman have on my son? For the past six weeks, Matt had been happier, especially since learning that Kimberley would be living practically next door. Each night when Lincoln tucked him into bed, his face had been alive with anticipation. And just now, when Matt had spotted her approaching the riding ring, his expression of anxious determination—typical during jumping lessons—had switched to joy, his entire face lighting up and his eyes shining in a way Lincoln hadn't seen for years. Lincoln's mother had drawn in a sharp breath. "You see?" he'd whispered.

Now he looked deep into Kimberley Colter's eyes as though reading his son's future in them. With his mother at his side, he stepped forward to meet the woman he'd said he wanted to bring to Turtle Mountain. "Hello." He extended his hand. "I'm Lincoln Steele. This is my mother, Lauren Steele."

* * *

Kimberley faced the tall man whose amber eyes and rich voice had slid into her mind too frequently to ignore since she'd returned to Calgary. "Mr. Steele." She reached out to shake his hand, its warmth enclosing hers lightly. Today, he wore a Toronto Blue Jays baseball cap, like his son had in the park. Apparently, father and son were fans.

"Make that Lincoln." He released her hand. "May I call you Kimberley?"

"I'm not sure that's wise. I think any stranger who offers to check a woman for ticks should be kept at a distance until his intentions are known."

Terri choked off a snort of laughter.

Wry amusement filled Lincoln Steele's eyes. "Touché! That means I'll have to earn your trust."

"You will." Kimberley turned to Lauren Steele. "Hello, Mrs. Steele." She shook the ranch owner's hand, noting the other woman's warm but intent scrutiny and striking resemblance to her daughter. "Thank you for entrusting me with your property without ever having met me."

"My dear, the old Steele place has never been home to anyone as exotic as a wildlife photographer. We're delighted to have you here, Kimberley, if I may call you that."

"Of course."

"And please, call me Lauren. 'Mrs. Steele' always sounds so formal."

"Thank you, I will."

Kimberley's gaze sought out Matthew, riding his pony to Lincoln's side. Again he was the child with the probing eyes, yet today their blue intensity seemed warmed by joy. She recalled the exquisite Ulysses swallowtail butterflies she'd photographed in tropical Australia, their brilliant blue iridescent upper wings edged with velvet black— edged with sorrow, perhaps, like Matthew's eyes. She smiled against that sorrow. "Hello, Matthew. I'm glad to see you again. I really enjoyed your emails."

"Hi." He smiled shyly. "Thanks."

"We'd better leave the ring to Sandra and Jamie." Lauren indicated a petite, dark-haired woman and the tall young man with the dappled horse Kimberley had seen earlier in the barn. As Kimberley followed the Steeles away from the ring, Matthew's red pony clopped along at her side.

Lauren paused to pat the arena's door frame. "We're so pleased with this structure your brother designed. Do you ride, Kimberley?"

"I've been on trail rides in the Rockies, but that's it." Kimberley glanced at her truck, her peripheral vision having registered Lexi moving restlessly in the cab. "Excuse me, but my dog looks like she needs to stretch her legs. It's been a long drive."

"Yes, of course. I'll get the house key." Lauren hurried

toward the office.

"Come on, Matt." Terri stepped in the direction of the barn. "Nice seeing you again, Kimberley."

"You, too. Bye, Terri."

"What's her name?" The words broke from Matthew.

For a moment Kimberley was baffled, but then she realized the child was referring to her dog. "Lexi. Her name is Lexi."

He nodded, easing up on the reins, and his pony responded by trotting smartly toward the barn.

"He likes you." Warmth filled Lincoln Steele's eyes and voice.

"Is that a big thing?"

"Yes, it is."

Gravel crunched underfoot as Lauren approached. "I'll keep that in mind. I like him, too. Excuse me."

Her new landlady handed her a key ring with two keys on it. "Turn right onto Sanderson Road and take the first right. That's the access road to the house. The larger key is for the back porch, and the smaller one is for the sun porch. Feel free to walk in the fields behind the house and on any Steele Cattle Company land you want to explore. Look for L. R. Steele on the land ownership map."

Kimberley's eyebrows lifted. "That's very generous. Thank you."

Lauren smiled a more mature version of Terri's mischievous grin. "We've seen the photographs on your website. Perhaps you can make our lowly gophers and groundhogs look as exciting as those lions and polar bears."

Kimberley laughed and held out a folded slip of paper. "I'll do my best. Here's a cheque for the first two months' rent, as we agreed."

"Thank you and welcome to Turtle Mountain."

As Kimberley reversed and turned her truck, she noted Lauren and Lincoln Steele deep in conversation. Both paused to glance at her. *Am I the topic of their conversation?*

Less than five minutes later, she parked in the yard of her new home. The one-and-a-half-story yellow farmhouse looked unremarkable but solid, with a white rail fence bordering the lawn surrounding it. From the yard, she gazed through a screen of bur oaks on the ravine slope and across a wide grassy ravine to the Steele Cattle Company pastures and buildings on the ravine's far side. She hadn't realized she would be so close to Lincoln Steele's work base, yet the knowledge filled her with an unexpected sense of security.

Released from the truck's confines, Lexi relieved herself and raced to an oak on the ravine slope. A red squirrel in the tree barked out staccato bursts of chatter, incensed at having its territory invaded.

Her dog would remain glued to the tree as long as the squirrel was present, so Kimberley took the opportunity to unlock the house and walk through it. The kitchen was sandwiched between the north-facing porch she'd entered and the house's south-facing sun porch, a fact that hadn't been clear from the photographs. She stepped from the kitchen into a rose-painted living room with a hardwood floor and a sofa and loveseat, and then looked into a small latté-colored bedroom positioned on one side of the living room. Around a corner on the opposite side of the living room, she located the full bathroom painted in shades of yellow. A set of stairs near the bathroom led to two rooms with sloped ceilings in the house's upper half-story. The smaller of the two was painted coral, and the larger, the warm green of a tropical ocean. Each was equipped with a single bed and a few other items of furniture. Both were bright and airy and would make perfect work rooms. From the outside, the house looked squat and functional; yet, inside, it exuded warmth and country appeal.

She quickly unpacked the truck while Lexi remained occupied with the squirrel. By the time dusk crept among the yard's elms, filling the spaces between the trees with diffuse gray light, she'd stored the last of the items she'd brought from Calgary—the ball glove and cleats Gary had instructed her to bring—and had eaten her first meal in the yellow house. The next thing to do was assemble her desk.

Hours later, still too excited to rest, Kimberley wandered the yard with Lexi, listening to summer night sounds and staring up into darkness brightened by stars and a waxing moon. Finally her spirit quieted. The nightmare wouldn't come. She would sleep.

Chapter 4

With Matt seated beside him, Lincoln turned his pickup onto the dirt road south of the old Steele place. Early morning sunlight cast a golden glow over drought-yellowed pasture south of the road. If they didn't get rain soon, he'd be selling cattle—a lot of cattle.

"Dad, there's Kimberley's truck." As his son pointed ahead to the red Ranger parked at the roadside, movement flashed in the oak woods edging the pasture. A figure sprinted out from the trees, the woman's camera held tight against her chest, her black ponytail swinging wildly. Seconds later, a cow moose charged out from the oaks, ears back, head down, hackles raised.

Lincoln gunned his pickup and pounded on the horn, the blaring noise puncturing the peaceful morning air. He pulled in ahead of the Ranger and revved his engine, his hand still hard on the horn. Thirty yards from the pasture fence and ten yards behind Kimberley, the moose broke its charge and trotted back toward the trees.

Lincoln shoved open the door and yelled, "You're safe. She's gone."

Racing toward him—her face white with terror—

Kimberley Colter ducked through the barbed-wire fence, took one step, and crumpled to the ground.

* * *

"*Kimberley!* Dad, what's wrong with her?"

The words came to Kimberley as though through a fog.

"I think she fainted." A strong hand shook her shoulder gently. "Are you hurt, Ms. Colter?"

Not in that place. Not alone. Her head swam as she opened her eyes. *Of course. Turtle Mountain. Lincoln Steele.* Abruptly, she rolled onto her side and vomited repeatedly, her body shaking.

"Hey." The hand rested on her shoulder again, this time offering comfort. "Here." It handed her a clean handkerchief after she'd finished.

"Thanks." Kimberley sat up slowly and wiped her mouth, her hands trembling. *Wildlife photographer faints after moose encounter—so professional.* Sucking in a deep breath, she banished her mocking internal voice. "Well, that's a first. I've never fainted before. It's a good thing it happened *after* your dad scared the moose away, right Matthew?"

A smile flitted across the boy's face, erasing the worry in his eyes. "Yeah."

As she pushed up from the ground, Lincoln Steele offered her a hand, his amber gaze searching. "Sure you're okay? You're white as a ghost."

"You'd be white, too, if you'd had a thousand pounds of mad momma moose breathing down your neck. And here I thought Turtle Mountain would be tame compared with the Rockies." She lurched to the left and caught herself. Why wouldn't the ground stay solid under her feet?

"Let me help you. You're swaying all over the place."

Her rescuer slid his arm around her waist and walked her to her truck, his strength a welcome anchor. At the Ranger, she pulled away from him. "Thanks, I'm okay now. Sorry for interrupting your day."

He stepped back. "No problem. It's not every morning Matt and I get to rescue a beautiful woman running for her life. I have to hand it to you—in less than a day you found the only moose I've seen on Steele land in four years."

"A moose I definitely did not expect to find."

"Did she have a calf with her?"

"She did. I backed away as soon as I saw them, but she came after me. I dodged around trees, looking for something to climb, but there were no low branches, so I made a run for it." Her hand still shaking, Kimberley opened the Ranger's door. "Thank you. I'll head somewhere else."

"Get back in the saddle?"

"Exactly." She smiled shakily at Matthew. "If I don't, I might never take another photo."

The boy's brow furrowed.

Lincoln Steele touched his baseball cap. "Don't rush off. Give yourself a few minutes."

"I will."

As father and son walked to the blue pickup, Matthew paused and called to Kimberley, "You're really brave…and really, *really* fast."

She waved to him. *Fast, maybe, but not brave. Not anymore.* Sobs tore at her throat as the pickup pulled away. *Bryan.* He'd stood between her and death, and for what? So she'd be afraid of the natural world they'd loved so much? She wiped a sleeve across her face, climbed into her truck, and started the engine. *Get back in the saddle.*

She drove north from the old Steele place and made herself walk through a pasture to a marshy slough, her jittery nerves gradually settling as she photographed dabbling ducks tipping their tails to the sky, and yellow-headed blackbirds singing raucous territorial songs from atop cattails. *The earth holds so much beauty.* A yearning rose within her, a yearning to once again walk in joy and confidence within that beauty, capturing its secrets and mysteries.

In late afternoon, she looked up at the rumble of a vehicle entering the yard. She closed the portrait photography book she'd been reading and ran downstairs from the coral room. Lexi romped at her side as she hurried through the living room and kitchen and opened the back porch door to Lauren, Terri, and Matthew. "Hello."

Lexi greeted each of the visitors with a sniffing inspection and rubbed hard against Matthew, pushing him off balance.

"Sorry, Matthew." Kimberley reached out to steady him. "Lexi hasn't learned all her manners yet."

Lincoln's son laughed and ruffled the husky's fur.

"That's okay. I like dogs." Abruptly, his smile died, his shoulders drooping.

Lauren placed a hand on her grandson's shoulder. "Sadly, Matt and Lincoln's dog wandered onto Sanderson Road last week and got run over."

"I'm so sorry to hear that, Matthew." Kimberley knelt on one knee and ran a hand over Lexi's back while she looked into Matthew's face. "What kind of dog did you have? What was its name?"

"He was a black Lab. His name was Trapper."

"Was he a young dog?"

Matthew shook his head. "He was older than me."

Kimberley smiled. "And how old are you?"

"Almost nine."

"You and Trapper must have had lots of adventures together."

He nodded, his hands caressing Lexi's fur. "Yeah."

"You can always treasure the memories of those adventures."

"That's what Grandma says."

Kimberley stood. "And she's right." How many times had she told herself the same thing?

Lauren smiled, gratitude in her eyes. "We stopped by to check that everything in the house is working the way it should. Are you having any problems?"

"None at all. Lexi and I are settling in."

"You've recovered from your moose adventure?"

"I have." That story was bound to get around.

"Good." Lauren smiled at her daughter. "Terri baked

you a pie."

"It's saskatoon berry." Terri offered Kimberley a ceramic pie plate holding a golden-topped pastry. "I hope you like saskatoons."

"Love them." Kimberley accepted the gift. "Thank you so much. I'm a decent hand at chocolate cake, but I've never mastered pies."

"Terri wins prizes for her pies at the fair. " Matthew giggled while Lexi licked his hands.

"Lexi, heel."

Obediently, the husky assumed a position at Kimberley's left side.

"Sit."

The dog sat.

Terri looked from the husky to Kimberley. "Do you have your camera in your pocket? I'd like to take a picture of you and Lexi there by the house, with the pie. The two of you are a perfect match for each other."

Kimberley balanced the pie plate against her torso with her left hand while digging the little Sony out of her cargo shorts with her right. She handed the camera to Terri. "Smile or no smile?"

* * *

Lincoln limped from his truck to his mother's house. He was filthy, sore, and hungry. It was time to collect Matt and head home to burgers grilled on the barbecue—a meal they'd eaten too frequently of late. He sighed. A hot shower would feel great, but the doctor had said he had to wait forty-eight hours before getting the stitches wet.

It had taken much longer than expected to move the fifty new Angus cows onto fresh pasture—as fresh as any of the ranch's pastures were in the drought. One of the cows had repeatedly bolted from the herd, leading him on a not-so-merry chase. Mounted on his appaloosa gelding, Batlock, Lincoln had directed the cow back to the herd a half-dozen times, only to have the recalcitrant bovine bolt again. The last time, the big Angus had tried to muscle through a barbed-wire fence. Not a pretty scene. After he'd cut the wires to untangle the cow, he and Batlock had driven it to the barns, where he'd corralled the injured animal and called the vet clinic.

His mother met him at the door of her home. "You're limping. What happened?"

"One of the new cows tried running the fence and tore her bag. She kicked me when I crowded her into the exam chute so Jake could have a look at her." Lincoln's longtime friend, Jake Kruger, had put ten stitches into the cow's udder.

"Is it serious?"

"The cow or me?"

The mischievous smile he so loved on his mother appeared. "Well, both."

He stepped into the house. "She's stitched up, and so am I. Is Matt ready to go? I need some grub." Then he tacked on, "It took a while at the hospital, and I left my phone in the truck. That's why I didn't call."

"Where did she kick you?"

"Side of my calf. Lucky it wasn't my shin, or I'd be in a cast."

Terri called from the living room, "Linc? Come see these pics I took of Kimberley."

Lincoln questioned his mother with a look.

"We dropped by before supper to check that everything in the house was working, and Terri asked if she might take some photos of Kimberley with her dog. Have a quick look. They're good. And there's steak, baked potato, and salad left from supper, if you want it. Saskatoon pie, too. Matt's already eaten."

"In that case, I'd love a meal. Thanks, Mom—I don't know what I'd do without you and Terri to help me with Matt and feed us."

His mother threw him a droll look as she sauntered toward the kitchen. "I'm keeping track. When I'm in the old folks' home, I'll bring out the tally book, but for now, I'll reheat that steak."

Matt slipped past his grandmother, eyes shining. "Hi, Dad."

"Hey, cowboy." Lincoln enfolded his son in a hug, stifling a groan when Matt's knee bumped his injured leg.

"What's wrong?"

Lincoln sat on a bench near the door. "Nothing much. I got kicked by a cow, but I'm okay." He wrapped an arm around Matt's shoulders. "What have you been up to?"

"Terri and I went for a bike ride, and then I helped her bake pies. We took one to Kimberley, and I had fun playing with Lexi for a while." His son's eyebrows drew together. "There's blood on your pants."

"Like I said, I'm okay." Lincoln eased his left boot off, wincing when his stitched calf complained about the tugging. "How's Kimberley?" All day, he'd had flashbacks of her sprinting toward him—her face white with fear—and then, her body—strong yet enticingly female—encircled within his arm. Was there more going on with her than just the moose scare? Her reaction had been extreme. Still, as she'd said, a thousand pounds of angry moose breathing down a person's neck would probably terrify anyone.

"She's fine, I think." Matt's words broke into his reflections. "She had a little camera in her pocket and let Terri use it. She smiled or did whatever Terri wanted."

An intriguing scenario. "I'll wash my hands and then have a look. Why don't you go help Grandma get my supper ready?"

"Aw, do I have to?"

"You know the answer to that."

After washing up and combing his hair, Lincoln limped into the dining area to where Terri was seated at the table with her laptop in front of her.

"I hear you got kicked by a cow." His sister looked up at him, her eyes assessing him as though she was composing a photograph in her mind.

"News travels fast. Where are these pictures?"

She clicked a key and rose from her chair. "Have a seat. That one's my favorite."

He sat, wincing again, and then forgot all about his

injury. On the screen before him, Kimberley smiled straight into his eyes. Her black hair and tanned skin, along with her rumpled pink blouse and baggy green cargo shorts, painted rich colors against the backdrop of the yellow house with its white trim. Her vivid blue eyes nearly matched the eye color of the young husky resting on its haunches beside her. She held a pie in her hands, and although Lincoln knew she hadn't baked it, the warmth of her smile suggested she might have. An incredible yearning welled up in him—a yearning to be on the receiving end of that smile, to be the man to take Kimberley in his arms, to come home to her.

"What do you think?" Terri asked.

"It works, Terri. It works real well."

"*Real* well? Don't let Mom hear you say that, or we'll get the grammar lecture again."

Lincoln grinned and clicked the forward arrow icon, wanting more images of the bewitching woman he'd first seen in the park. The next photo showed a serious Kimberley, her eyes measuring him. In the third, she smiled down at the pie she held, her body in a position of absolute symmetry. In the fourth, she laughed at her husky—its ears pricked up and its head lifted as the dog fixed its complete attention on her.

Terri leaned over his shoulder. "Kimberley gave me some pointers. She said she might branch out into portrait photography and asked me if I'd like to model for her next week or the week after. She's going to buy a backdrop screen so she can try indoor and outdoor shots."

"Sounds like a plan." He rose from the chair, his gaze lingering on Kimberley's image on the laptop screen. Her eyes—so vivid and lit with curiosity and energy—drew him to her in the same way that a clear pool draws thirsty stock. *Irresistible.*

Chapter 5

Each morning for the rest of the week, Kimberley rose before dawn and walked Lexi north of the yellow house past a windbreak of Manitoba maples and through a cut hayfield. After retracing her steps, she attached the husky's long leash to a clothesline in the yard and ran her hands over her dog's soft ruff. "Back soon." She slung a bulging daypack and telescoping tripod into her truck cab and placed a top-of-the-line Nikon D4 digital single lens reflex camera equipped with a telephoto lens on the passenger seat. Then she spent hours exploring the grid of rural roads as she acquainted herself with grain fields, hay fields, and patches of forest and native prairie on the gentle slopes of Turtle Mountain.

Excitement—sometimes trepidation—raced through her as she photographed a white-tailed deer and fawn, a wary coyote skulking along a pasture edge, turkey vultures feeding on a cow carcass, and prairie sunsets that bathed evening sky with pink fire before shading into deep blue darkness. Each day she paused in her travels for a few words with at least one member of the Steele family, Matthew peppering her with questions. Did she get any pictures of the moose? Had anything else chased her? Was she scared of snakes? Was her pack heavy? No, no, no, and yes. His interest was like a spring bud unfurling and carrying her into its green promise.

On Friday, the last day of June, she turned right at the end of her access road and drove Sanderson Road until it intersected with the dirt road she'd parked on the day the moose had charged. She drove past the pasture she'd sprinted across, periodically easing off the gas and glancing at the land ownership map she'd placed in her lap. When she reached the parcel of Steele Cattle Company property she'd chosen to explore, she geared down and parked in an overgrown access lane barricaded by a metal gate with a no trespassing sign on it.

With the smoothness that comes from countless repetitions, she fastened the tripod to the exterior of her daypack, attached a portable blind to her belt, and slid her arms into a camera harness. She clipped the Nikon to the harness, hoisted her pack onto her shoulders, and slipped between strands of the barbed-wire perimeter fence beside the gate, careful to duck low enough to give her pack clearance.

Beyond the fence, early sunlight gilded an uncut meadow prematurely tinged with late-summer yellows. Kimberley studied the golden expanse for subject possibilities and potential dangers, the fresh dawn air laced with a bouquet of prairie scents including the honeyed fragrance of sweet clover. All was still and peaceful. The moose would be long gone. *New day. New challenges.* Tall grasses swished against her cargo pants as she followed a rough lane that led through the meadow toward bur oak woods. At the sound of a vehicle on the dirt road, she looked back over her shoulder.

A familiar blue pickup with an extended cab pulled to the side of the road and stopped behind her truck. Its engine died, and Lincoln Steele, dressed in jeans and a black polo shirt, exited the cab, his Blue Jays baseball cap shading his amber eyes. He strode to the fence and swung his long legs over it with the ease of years of experience.

Kimberley waited for him, enjoying his smooth movements in the early light. No plaid shirt for this rancher, and no Stetson. He didn't fit her image of a cattleman, although she'd noted that he wore a scuffed pair of cowboy boots. She called out, "Good morning, Mr. Steele."

"You're up with the birds, *Ms. Colter.*"

She smiled at his emphasis. "On a clear day, the best light is in the early morning and evening. It's warmer—more golden—and the shadows aren't as strong."

He stopped a few feet from her. "Looking for anything in particular?"

"No, just exploring."

He swung a hand toward the gate. "In case you missed it, there's a no trespassing sign on the gate. You might want to ask the landowner for permission to walk on his land."

"*His* land? Do you mean this isn't Steele Cattle Company land?"

"That's right."

"But I checked the land ownership map." Kimberley's hands fumbled as she pulled a plastic bag from her cargo pants pocket. Trespassing was hardly the way to make a good impression. She removed the map from the bag, unfolded it, and pointed to a block of land outlined on the map. "Is this where we are?"

He stepped beside her to look at the map. "It is, but take a closer look at the owner's initials." He placed his left index finger next to the small print on the map. His ring finger was bare, with no indentation to signify that he'd worn a wedding ring, yet he'd fathered a son. *Who and where is Matthew's mother?*

Kimberley forced herself to squint at the fine print on the map. "Oh!" She lifted her eyes to those of the man at her side. "It says L. *A.* Steele, not L. R. Steele."

"Lincoln Andrew Steele at your service."

"I'm sorry I trespassed." She folded the map and returned it to her pocket. "It's good of you to not be angry."

A smile etched laugh lines in his face. "I've never come across a beautiful woman in my meadow at first light before. There's a hint of magic in that. Why ruin it with anger?"

Her hand itched to pull her point-and-shoot camera from her pocket. Lincoln Steele had a heart-throb grin if ever she'd seen one—the dimples, the white, slightly uneven teeth, the warmth in his eyes. That smile could make a woman walk straight into his arms—at least mentally. Abruptly, she stepped away from him, suddenly wary. *Would you talk about magic in the morning if you knew...?* "You're gallant, Mr. Steele."

His gaze took on the intent, probing quality she'd seen in his son's eyes. "No, honest. You're not the first person to make that mistake with the map. If you want to walk on my land, all you have to do is ask."

He'd talked of magic in the morning, and she sensed it all around her—Steele magic. The whole family nearly glowed with it, and this man most of all. He stood before her, tall and handsome and one of the best things she'd seen at first light anywhere. "May I have permission to walk on your land?"

"I'm not sure that's wise. I think any stranger who trespasses should be kept at a distance until her intentions are known."

"Touché!" She laughed. "I believe the correct response is that I'll have to earn your trust."

"Let's start by dropping the formality."

"All right. May I have permission, Lincoln?"

He took his time answering, his gaze holding hers. "You have it. Enjoy your outing." He turned and strode toward his truck, lifting a hand in farewell.

Kimberley stared after him, peeling apart layers of meaning in his voice and eyes. When he reached the fence, she turned on her heel and walked on through the meadow and into the oak trees. For five minutes, she committed a wildlife photographer's cardinal sin of being oblivious to her surroundings. When she realized her distracted state, she forced herself to transfer her focus from Lincoln to the forest around her. Bryan's words flashed into her mind, haunting her: *Be alert, Kimmie. Always be alert. It could save your life.* Being alert hadn't saved him.

* * *

"One more thing before you head out," Lincoln told the three men striding from the office kitchenette toward the door. "A reminder that the photographer renting the old Steele place has permission to walk on Steele land—mine and the company's. If you haven't seen her driving around or walking on the property, you will. Black-haired woman. Kimberley Colter. Drives a red Ranger."

His foreman, Alf Goodon, nodded. "Seen her parked with a big camera sticking out the window."

"That's her."

Goodon, Phil Johnson—the company's stock whiz, and Dale Peters—an agriculture student Lincoln had hired for the summer, all filed out of the office.

Black-haired woman. The simple description said nothing about the way Lincoln's mind dwelled on how Kimberley's hair had fallen in a thick ponytail below her shoulders earlier that morning, the way her eyes—such a vivid shade of blue—had changed with every emotion she'd expressed, the way she'd laughed at his teasing. She'd been a black-haired angel in his golden meadow—an angel who could have asked for anything, and he would have had a hard time turning her down.

"Lincoln?"

He jerked his focus back to the office.

Seated at her desk, his mother studied him. "You were staring off into the blue."   .

He tugged his baseball cap brim down. "Sorry. What did you want to discuss?"

"The next shipment of feeders to go out. Is everything in place?"

Lincoln envisioned the eighty grain-fed yearling Angus steers in the ranch's feedlot. "Yes. A week from Tuesday at seven a.m."

His mother tapped a pencil on her desktop. "Do you think we did the right thing?"

"I think the timing is perfect."

Her gaze searched his face. "I'm talking about Kimberley."

"So am I." He touched his cap again. "I'll pick Matt up from your place and take him with me to check the crops."

"Good. That will give Terri a little time to herself."

Lincoln strode to the door. Without a doubt, offering the old Steele place to Kimberley had been the right thing to do. Since her arrival, Matt's face had radiated joy at bedtime, and the kid couldn't stop talking about her. Lincoln wanted to see that joy on his son's face for a long time to come.

He drove the half-mile from the ranch office to his mother's log house and spotted his son and sister throwing a Frisbee in the yard. With school out for the summer, Matt spent as much time at his grandmother's house as at his own. Lincoln braked to a stop in the driveway and opened the passenger window. Heat poured in like a wave. "Hey, cowboy, let's go check the crops."

"Okay, Dad." Matt dropped the Frisbee, ran to the pickup, and scrambled into the passenger seat.

Terri picked up the Frisbee and spun it on one finger as she approached the truck. "You're stealing my buddy away."

Matt grinned.

"I'll have him back in a couple of hours," Lincoln told her. His sister earned her horse's keep and money for university by babysitting Matt, mucking out stalls, exercising the boarders, and pumping gas in Seton. It meant a lot of juggling, but she was a born organizer, plus, she didn't have a boyfriend. It had looked like she wasn't even going to attend her senior prom, but at the last minute she'd announced that she'd be going with a friend, emphasis on *friend*, and his mother had whisked her to Winnipeg to buy a prom dress—short, purple, with a ruffled skirt. The "wow" look on Terri's escort's face had been priceless; Paul Engbrecht might never be the same.

With Matt at his side, Lincoln spent the next two hours driving the grid of roads that provided access to ten sections—ten square miles—of Steele Cattle Company property. A mix of pastures, grain fields, and pockets of forest and native prairie, the ranchland bore witness to four months with almost no rain. Pasture grasses were short and tinged with yellow, a sure sign that forage quality had deteriorated. Thin crops of oats, barley, and wheat stood barely knee high. Again and again, he and Matt exited the pickup and walked into fields for a close-up look at stunted grain stalks that grew from bone-dry soil cracked into irregular gray polygons. It was painful to guess how few bushels per acre the crops would yield. His mother had said she'd never seen such a hot, dry spring and early summer in the twenty-five years she'd lived on Turtle Mountain. Alf—Lincoln's foreman—had told him it might be the kind of drought that came once in a lifetime. Heeding their comments, he'd ordered Phil Johnson to assess the stock with a view to selling half.

"Dad, there's Phil." Matt pointed.

Speak of the man. Phil's green pickup was parked at the roadside ahead. Standing inside a tawny pasture, the stockman spat out a stream of tobacco juice before casually walking into a herd of a hundred Angus steers, each of which could have bolted and crushed him, although none did. Instead, they formed a circle around him, heads up and curious. Phil dipped his head to the left, and steers on his left shuffled to the side, creating a clear path.

"How does he do that?" Matt asked, his voice filled with awe.

"I don't know. It's a gift he has." The first time Lincoln had seen it happen had been at a cattle auction in Brandon. Without whip or cattle prod, a red-haired man with a paunch had walked into a series of holding pens filled with restless, bawling cattle and simply gazed at the animals. In each of the pens, the cattle had ceased bawling and shoving, instead standing calm and curious. And, in each of the pens, the herd had parted when the red-haired man had dipped his head, creating a path he'd casually walked. Lincoln had offered Phil a job on the spot.

Now, as Phil strolled through the herd of steers, his lips moved as he checked the animals' condition, and he occasionally reached out to lightly scratch a steer's forehead. Lincoln shook his head in wonder. His employee, who also happened to play left field on the Seton slow-pitch team Lincoln played on, was sometimes crude and awkward with people, but never with cattle. During the three years he'd worked at the ranch, Lincoln had never had reason to rebuke him for his work— although he'd had to lay down the law about Phil's use of filthy language on the job.

Out of nowhere, an image of Kimberley appeared in Lincoln's mind. His eyes narrowed. What would Phil's reaction be when he encountered Kimberley?

Three days passed before Lincoln saw Kimberley again, and then for no more than a few seconds as she drove past the ranch yard and waved to him. For the rest of that week and the next, he found himself watching for the red truck, unexpected elation coursing through him each time he and Kimberley shared a wave or a few friendly words.

Two weeks after he'd seen the photos of Kimberley, Terri told him, "I'm going over to the old Steele place tomorrow evening to model for Kimberley. I suppose I'll cycle or walk because Mom and Matt are spending the evening with the Stewarts."

"I'd forgotten that." His mother was scrupulously fair about ensuring that Matt's other grandparents had access to their only grandson. Rose and Paul Stewart had never forgiven Lincoln for his separation from their daughter and had berated him for not standing by her. Trouble was, they didn't know the whole story. "I can pick you up, if you want."

His sister gave him a quick kiss on the cheek. "Deal. Thanks, Linc."

His offer was an excuse, another chance to see Kimberley. When was the last time his heart had soared like this? *When I was in love with Gayle.* Angry sorrow knifed through him as he dismissed his former wife's image. *Look how that turned out.* Was he even ready to try a new relationship?

Chapter 6

Kimberley switched off two spotlights, casting her experimental studio in the living room of the old Steele place into shadow. After snapping a series of outdoor portrait shots, she'd taken more shots indoors.

"Do you sell a lot of photographs through your website?" Terri rose from a stool positioned in front of a greenish-blue screen.

"Yes, it's my main sales venue. I also submit photographs to a photo stock agency and sometimes receive commissions. Here's an example." Kimberley selected a slim book from a set of shelves and handed it to Terri. The book contained thirty photographs of baby animals ranging from featherless robin nestlings to delicately spotted deer fawns.

While her model eagerly paged through the book, Kimberley set the backdrop screen near a wall for safe-keeping. The shoot had gone better than expected—at least the technical process had gone better than expected. The final proof would be in the prints. Terri's natural poise and expressive personality had provided plenty of poses to work with; however, a good portrait went beyond an accurate representation to offer glimpses into a person's soul. In one of the indoor images, after Terri had been distracted by Lexi barking at a squirrel outdoors, her expression had shifted from confidence to unguarded curiosity. Along with three of the outdoor poses, that impromptu shot held exciting promise.

"How did you ever get close enough to take such good photographs?" Terri held up a full-page spread of a mother skunk leading a parade of five kits through a hayfield.

"Persistence, patience, and the power of a telephoto lens. For some of the shots, I used a blind."

"Have you worked on other books?"

"Not yet, but I've submitted proposals for a children's picture book that would feature endangered animals."

Her smoky green eyes suddenly sober, Terri frowned. "It can be dangerous photographing wild animals, can't it?"

Kimberley hesitated before setting the spotlights near the backdrop screen and then answered the question calmly, "It can be. I once rappelled down a cliff while shooting nesting seabirds, but I didn't fall."

Terri closed the book, its glossy leaves slithering into a neat pile before the cover descended on them. "I remember hearing that a grizzly killed a wildlife photographer in the Rockies last summer. How would you do that anyway—photograph a grizzly bear?"

"Very carefully." Kimberley walked quickly from the living room into the kitchen, her heart suddenly pounding.

"Would you like a cup of peppermint tea? I'm going to have one."

"No, thanks." Terri followed her into the kitchen. "You photographed baby bears and wolves and lions for that book. Wasn't it dangerous getting close to them?"

Tension knotted Kimberley's insides. She breathed in deeply to dispel it, yet her fingers trembled as she filled her electric kettle with water and switched it on. She turned to Terri and answered the question in the same matter-of-fact way she'd answered it countless times during interviews and workshops. "There's always a risk in photographing predators. The most important thing is to know the habits of the animals you're photographing—including bears and wolves and lions—in order to minimize the chances of having a dangerous encounter." She leaned back against the kitchen cupboard. "And don't push your luck. Wild animals are unpredictable. That extra close-up may not be worth it. In Africa, I took most of my predator shots from vehicles."

"What would you do if a dangerous animal suddenly realized you were there?"

She pushed away from the counter, her heart thudding. *I can do this. I'm here, not there.* She kept her voice steady. "That depends on a lot of things: what kind of animal it is, how good its eyesight is, which way the wind is blowing, whether you have any protection available. You might be able to simply leave the area, or you might be forced to climb a tree. Running from predators isn't a good idea, because it triggers attacks—but running from a moose can work, especially if someone comes along and scares it off." She flashed a quick smile at Terri before turning away, as much to hide her face for a moment as to remove a mug from a hook screwed into the underside of a cupboard. "As a last resort, you might have to fight back or play dead."

"It sounds like you've had experience, other than with the moose."

"Most wildlife photographers have, at one time or another." She caught a flash of evening sunlight reflected onto the living room floor from a vehicle. *End of conversation.* "Your brother's here to pick you up." She stepped from the kitchen into the back porch and jerked the door open at Lincoln's first knock, startling him.

The surprise in his tawny eyes changed to piercing scrutiny. "Hi. Everything all right?"

What could she say? She had the urge to tell him what had happened that day in the Rockies. Their encounters during the past weeks had created a neighborly bond, and right now, he looked so strong, so good standing there on her doorstep, in black chinos and a white, short-sleeved shirt. His hair was neatly combed, and the baseball cap was nowhere to be seen. In fact, it looked like he had a date. Kimberley stepped back, realizing that she knew absolutely nothing about his personal life. "We just finished."

Terri appeared beside her. "Kimberley showed me a book illustrated with her photographs and told me how to deal with dangerous animals."

Lincoln shot Kimberley a keen glance. "What kind of

dangerous animals?"

She shrugged. "All kinds."

"And what advice did you give Terri on the subject?"

"To avoid close encounters at all costs."

"What do you do if a close encounter is unavoidable?"

Kimberley did her best to banish that scenario from her mind, its power over her far too real. "Ask Terri. She can tell you all about it." She turned to the girl. "Thanks for modeling."

"I enjoyed it. Let me know if you want me to do more."

"I will. Bye now."

Lincoln nodded to her. "See you later."

After he and Terri disappeared around the house corner, Kimberley slumped into a kitchen chair, nausea coursing through her. *The past is gone. That conversation is over. I'm here, now, in this place, in this moment—cling to it.*

* * *

"How was the visit with the Stewarts?" Lincoln asked when he dropped off Terri.

His mother looked up from a gardening magazine. "Fine. Rose and I talked art and horses, and Paul and Matt set up a new model train track and worked on landscape miniatures."

Matt hurried past with a DVD case in his hand. "We painted lichens green to look like trees. Is it okay if I watch *Nim's Island* with Terri? It's Friday."

"You've seen that movie at least five times."

"I know, but I like it."

Lincoln looked at his mother. "Is that all right with you?"

She waggled her eyebrows. "I rather like Gerard Butler."

"Okay," he told Matt and then added to his mother, "Since I'm not nearly as fond of *Nim's Island* as the three of you are, I'll come back in a couple of hours to pick up Matt."

His mother cocked her head. "You're all spruced up. What's the occasion?"

"No occasion." *Just going for a visit.*

"Hmm. See you later, then. Gerard's calling."

* * *

Kimberley drank her peppermint tea without enthusiasm, rinsed the cup, and sought the peace of the outdoors before darkness set in. The leaves of bur oaks on the slope below the house rustled in a restless wind. Cattle bawled in the Steele Cattle Company feedlot across the grassy ravine. She breathed in a surprisingly cool wind that blew away some of her anxiety. She and Lexi followed the now-familiar dirt track through the hayfield north of the house and then wandered through a wild prairie meadow. Cloud obscured the setting sun, casting a brooding moodiness over the rolling landscape. She pulled the little Sony from her thin jacket pocket and framed a composition of wind-angled prairie grasses tossing beneath billowing periwinkle clouds.

Alone under the turbulent sky, she turned in a complete circle to test her reaction to the expansive view. Farmland stretched in a gradual descent to the north, and a patchwork of pasture, fields, and forest lay to the south on Turtle Mountain's northern fringe. Although the upland jutting out of the prairie lacked the Rocky Mountains' spectacular majesty, it called to her in a subtle way. She'd read that the French Canadian explorer La Verendrye had referred to Turtle Mountain as the "blue jewel of the prairies," and she was beginning to understand why.

Dusk settled in as she and Lexi returned to the yellow house. Indoors, she poured bath soap beneath the tub faucet and soaked amid a froth of shimmering spheres to counteract the wind's chill. When the bubbles began to dissipate, she abandoned the tub, dried herself, and pulled on a zip-up satin robe.

In the living room, she chose a classical guitar CD, hoping the instrumental music would soothe her spirit. During the past year, aided by regular sessions with a therapist, she'd painstakingly constructed an emotional barrier against her traumatizing memories. One component of that barrier was music. As the mellow guitar strains spilled into the old Steele place, a brisk rap sounded on the porch door. She glanced down at her robe, its high-necked, ankle-length cut far more conservative than most of the clothes she wore every day. Barefoot, she entered the kitchen's darkness and looked through the window. Lincoln stood on her doorstep.

* * *

"May I come in?" Lincoln stood in the illumination cast by the exterior porch light and waited for Kimberley's answer. She wore a figure-hugging blue robe sewn from a smooth fabric with a sheen that picked up on the color of her eyes. With its long sleeves and high neck, it looked too warm for a summer night, but then he noticed her damp hair pinned loosely on top her head and realized she'd been bathing. "That is, if it's not too much of an imposition."

She leveled her measuring gaze at him, the one he'd seen in the second of Terri's photos. "Your date didn't work out?"

"My date?"

She nodded to his clothes.

"I didn't have a date. Matt, Terri, and my mother are watching *Nim's Island* for the sixth time, so I decided to check the stock and stop by to visit you. I hope that's all right."

Her look was still measured, but she backed away from the door. "Come in. I was about to make myself a cup of ginger tea. Would you like something?"

He entered the porch and closed the door behind him. Kimberley's dog sniffed at his chinos and then, at Kimberley's command, lay on the kitchen floor. "Coffee or tea is good, but not herbal. To me, it all tastes like grass."

"Tea, then. Have a seat." She waved a hand toward a

kitchen chair. "Two years ago, I backpacked over a wilderness trail on the island where *Nim's Island* was filmed. It's off the coast of northern Queensland in Australia. It's real name is Hinchinbrook Island."

He pulled the wooden chair to him and sat across its seat, resting his arms on the top of the chair back. "And is it a tropical paradise?"

"It is. Jungles, gorgeous beaches, mountains, waterfalls, lace monitors—big lizards—basking in the sun, even crocodiles in some of the rivers."

"Judging from the photographs on your website, you've traveled a fair bit."

"It goes with the job." She placed teabags in two mugs and poured in boiling water.

Her voice was calm, but her movements were edgy, as if she was agitated about something. Maybe he could take her mind off whatever it was. "Turtle Mountain is hardly an exotic destination. What made you decide to move here?"

Her back stiffened and then relaxed. "I'd lived in Calgary all my life and figured that a change of scenery would help me decide what my future should hold."

Bingo. That statement had heartbreak written all over it. "The way you say that implies there was a man in your past."

She met his eyes squarely. "Yes, there was a man. Milk or sugar?"

Intense energy emanated from her, as though a storm was about to break loose. She was holding something back—something big. "Just milk," he told her. "Does that mean he's out of the picture now?"

She removed a carton from the refrigerator and poured a generous amount of milk into his mug before placing the cup on the table within reach of where he sat. "Yes, he's out of the picture. Now it's my turn." She sat in a chair on the opposite side of the table and swept a hand in a graceful curve. "This is called 'the old Steele place.' Did you live here as a child?"

Lincoln picked up his mug. "No. I was three when my mother and I moved to the area. She's an accountant. She worked for Terrence Steele for five years before they married. Terrence grew up here. They built the house she lives in now, which is where I mostly grew up."

"And your father?" Kimberley's vivid eyes still measured him.

"I never knew him. He died of a brain aneurysm when he was twenty-five. I was just a baby."

"How terrible for your mother!"

"It must have been." Memories of his earliest years flashed through his mind. Just the two of them, he and his mother—laughing, playing, crying together. Every night at bedtime, she'd cuddled him while they'd looked at a photograph of a young bearded man holding a baby in his arms, the man's face alight with joy. That photograph hung on a wall in Lincoln's living room. "His name was Andy Janes. Terrence adopted me, almost from the time I showed up, and legally after he and my mother married. He was the only father I ever knew."

"*Was*. So he's gone as well?"

"He died in a road accident eight years ago. Terri was only ten at the time." And he'd been in Florida wiping the sweat from his face with a towel after a sixty-yard dash when he'd received the call from his mother. Shock and regret had left him standing dazed in the dugout. Instantly, he'd made a decision, and with that decision, the future he'd dreamed of and sweated for had crumbled into pieces around him.

"Again, how terrible for your mother, for all of you."

He pulled himself back to the present, knowing he would make the same decision again, even knowing the consequences. "Terri was shattered, and I know my mother was devastated, but she's an amazing woman. She has an unshakeable faith. I think it sustained us all." Not once had he heard his mother rail against God for the loss of two husbands. Instead, she'd counted blessings when he and Terri couldn't.

Kimberley wrapped both hands around her mug, as though gaining comfort from its warmth. "From what I've seen, your family is very close. Are there just the four of you?"

"Just the four of us."

"And Matthew's mother?"

He took a long drink before replying. Was it time to put his brief, heaven-and-hell marriage behind him and clear the path for someone else? "Gayle and I separated after four years of marriage. Two years later, she died when she drove her car off a bridge into a river."

Shock flared in Kimberley's eyes.

"It was an accident. She got caught in a freak ice storm. What about your family? Is it a big one?"

She shook her head. "No. Just my father, my brother, and me. My mother died of cancer when I was seventeen."

"So, we've all been scarred by death."

A haunted look swept into her eyes.

Time for a change of topic. "Here's something you might be interested in. A Conservation Officer I know has been monitoring a family of burrowing owls a couple of miles east of Seton."

Quick interest replaced the haunted look. "They're endangered. Do you think I'd be allowed to set up a blind?"

"You'd have to ask Jack—the CO—and the farmer. I'll run it by Jack and get back to you if you want to pursue it."

"I do, definitely." She leaned toward him. "As soon as possible. Thanks for the tip."

"A pleasure." A man would keep on coming up with possibilities just to watch the play of emotions in her eyes. They seemed lit from within. When she laughed, they blazed with joy. This evening, their light flickered through some kind of darkness. "By the way, thanks for indulging Terri's interest in photography."

For the first time since he'd arrived, a smile curved Kimberley's lips. "It was fun. I'm used to working with a partner, and she has a keen eye."

"The pictures she took of you are good."

"They are." The smile lingered. "I'm impressed with her knack for composition."

He recalled the warmth of Kimberley's smile in the first photograph, the smile that had drawn him to the old Steele place that evening. "She said you're thinking of getting into portrait photography."

Kimberley raised her cup to her lips and studied him over its rim. "Yes. I've always been intrigued by faces and expressions." Without taking a drink, she set the mug on the table and drew in a deep breath, the measuring look returning to her eyes. "Speaking of expressions, I'd like an explanation for the way you stared at me on the beach at Adam Lake."

No beating around the bush. Lincoln set his mug on the table. It looked like a chess piece facing off against hers. "Is that why you came?"

"It's one of the reasons I came."

"You're very honest."

"You sound surprised."

"I suppose I am. I discovered belatedly that what I thought was honesty in my marriage was one-sided."

Her eyebrows lifted. "So, you distrust women, yet you looked at a complete stranger like you wanted to glue her to you."

He laughed at her description. "I don't distrust all women."

"Oh, not *all* women. And the look?" She pinned him with her vivid blue eyes.

"I wanted you here."

"Why?"

He'd known that question was coming. Already, he'd shared more than he'd expected. How much more was he willing to tell? He figured that with Kimberley, it would have to be all or nothing. "Matt's had a rough time. You're the first woman he's talked to out of the blue since he was three. Both Terri and I recognized something special in that."

"And you would do anything for your son?"

"Maybe I would, but there's more to it than that. You know what I mean, Kimberley. We both felt the attraction in the park, and we both feel it here."

Her gaze dropped. "I'm not sure what I feel."

"Then let's find out." He rose from the chair, walked slowly around the end of the table, and held out his hand to her. When she hesitantly placed hers in it, he gently tugged her to her feet. Awareness flooded between them. "See?" A storm roiled in her eyes, a turmoil he didn't understand.

She stepped back, removing her hand from his with a jerky movement. "I don't even know you."

"But you're getting to know me." Hoping to put her at ease, he teased, "Are you backing off slowly, hoping I'll lose interest?"

A startled gasp escaped her. "I see you milked Terri."

"I did, and I have to say that I like the idea of a close encounter." When he took a step toward her, she backed against the edge of the cupboard and darted a look past him, as though searching for a means of escape. "No trees to climb here."

"That's not funny."

The storm continued to rage in her eyes, a flash of anger dancing with other emotions he couldn't place. She looked as wild and magnificent as the landscapes she'd photographed. "Let's see, what are your other options? I think playing dead was one of them."

Her lovely eyes looked deep into his. "Lincoln, there's something you don't know." She sounded breathless.

"Are you married?" He made his voice gentle.

"No."

"Engaged?"

The breathlessness deepened into huskiness. "No."

"Then, when the time comes, I'll learn." Unable to resist, he kissed her.

She stood absolutely still within his embrace but didn't play dead, her lips pliable beneath his. He shifted his weight in order to embrace her, but she broke the kiss and pushed past him.

"Running isn't a good idea," he teased.

She turned to face him, her eyes filled with agony. "Please leave."

His amusement died. "What's wrong?" He stepped toward her, instinctively wanting to ease her pain, as he'd so often wanted to ease Matt's pain. "Hey." He took her shaking hands in his. "You're okay. Whatever it is, you're okay."

She seemed unable to speak.

"Come here." He took her in his arms to comfort her.

While she rested her head against his chest, he gently rubbed her back and shoulders and then kissed the top of her head, his hands lingering on the smooth fabric. He lifted her chin and looked into her eyes. The agony had dimmed. "Want to talk about it?"

"Just kiss me."

Her answer wasn't what he'd expected. He searched her gaze and then kissed her. She shocked him by molding her body to his and meeting his lips with wild desire. The fabric hugging her body was like sleek skin beneath his fingers. "You're so beautiful," he whispered before tugging the robe's zipper down and kissing her neck.

She froze in his arms.

"What is it?" He looked into her shocked eyes and then down. Exposed above the top of the zipper, white diagonal scars marred her chest.

"My God!" He stepped away and stared into her eyes. *What have I done?* The parallel scars were the result of an injury inflicted by claws. Kimberley had been mauled.

Bitter hurt flooded her face. "Pretty, aren't they? There are more. Would you like to see them, too?"

"No!" He recoiled, filled with revulsion at himself. He'd gone too far in his teasing and in his actions—way too far. He'd suspected something was bothering her, so why hadn't he followed his gut feeling instead of pushing her into acknowledging the chemistry between them? His teasing must have seemed like the height of insensitivity to her, mocking her with lessons in the case of an attack, and then he'd exposed her scars. They meant nothing to him, but he'd stepped over the line in sliding her zipper down. "Kimberley, I didn't know. I can't believe I—" He gulped, his mind flailing for words. "I never would have—"

"You need to leave." Trembling, she pulled up the zipper.

"Kimberley, wait. I'm—"

"Just get out!" She ran from the kitchen, her husky barking wildly at him.

In turmoil, Lincoln backed away from the bristling dog and strode out of the house.

Chapter 7

Kimberley clutched the blanket in her hands and squeezed her eyes shut against the expression on Lincoln's face. Shock. Revulsion. Why had she told him to kiss her? *Because I wanted to escape. Because I wanted him to take me away from the memories.* Hoarse sobs broke from her. Even now, she couldn't escape. As she lay in the darkness, the bear returned, its fetid breath stinking, its teeth and claws ripping into her body. And Bryan was there…staring at her lifelessly, his neck a lake of blood.

When Lexi's nose touched her elbow, she screamed and bolted upright, ready to lash out. Her dog shrank back, whining. "Sorry, Lexi. Sorry, girl." She buried her face in the husky's soft ruff and felt Lexi's steady heartbeat beneath her hands. Forcing herself to breathe long, slow breaths, she willed the terrifying memories to leave her.

How long she sat like that, with her arms around Lexi, she didn't know. Finally, she released her dog and turned on the bedside lamp. Its warm light flooded the room, chasing away shadows. She glanced at her watch. Two-thirty. Lexi licked her hand before prancing to the door, tail waving. "Good idea. Let's get some fresh air."

She followed Lexi through the house and opened the back porch door. Five hours ago, Lincoln had stood on the step in a pool of light, tall and handsome, dressed for a date he didn't have, his amber gaze capturing hers. Now, she walked barefoot among the huge elms, their trunks like pillars, their leaves whispering in the summer night— whispering of touches and kisses and togetherness, of a child's sweet laughter. She stared up into the night. *God, have you forgotten me?*

In the morning, pale and gritty-eyed after a sleepless night, she donned sunglasses and locked the house. She was slated to teach three workshops at a weekend wildlife photography conference in Winnipeg. The timing couldn't have been better—she couldn't face Lincoln.

Lexi romped around the yard and bounded onto the truck's passenger seat, tongue lolling. "Lucky you." Kimberley patted her husky's shoulder. "You get to spend the weekend with Gary and Wendy, and if I know my sister-in-law, she'll spoil you rotten."

At the end of the access road, she checked for traffic and spotted a blue truck to the south, driving toward her. Heart pounding, she accelerated onto Sanderson Road and sped north past the Steele Cattle Company yard, leaving a screen of dust behind her.

In Brandon, she pulled into the driveway of her brother's home with its attached studio, and removed her sunglasses. Wendy waved at her through the studio windows and met her at the door, greeting her with a hug.

"Hi. Come in. Gary has an early meeting with a client. He's sorry to miss you." She searched Kimberley's eyes. "Trouble sleeping?"

"Just last night." Kimberley glanced at a half-finished watercolor on Wendy's easel. "Adam Lake?"

"Yes." Wendy bent around her swollen abdomen to pat Lexi and then straightened. "How are things going? We'd like to visit you two weekends from now, if that's okay? Probably Sunday afternoon, after Gary's ball tournament finishes."

Kimberley forced a smile. "I'd like that. I'm still not accustomed to the fact that my nearest neighbors are a mile away."

"Those neighbors being...?"

"Lauren and Terri Steele. They live a mile to the north."

Wendy regarded her closely. "And the boy and his father?"

"Two miles to the south, according to the land ownership map."

"Do you like the farmhouse?"

"Very much. It oozes character. The solitude takes some getting used to, but I don't mind it, and Lexi loves the place. She has a squirrel in the yard to entertain her."

Wendy's raised her eyebrows. "Any more riveting looks?"

Kimberley dropped her gaze to her wristwatch. "I have to go. The conference registration ends at nine-thirty. I'll see you tomorrow around six if the workshops end on time."

"I'm planning to cook lasagna, so it won't matter if you're a few minutes late."

Kimberley ran her hands through Lexi's soft fur and caressed her dog's ears and face. "Thanks a million for taking care of Lexi for me."

Wendy patted the husky again. "I'm looking forward to it. I'll do some sketches of her."

"Don't let her tire you out. You still need a few weeks to put the finishing touches on that baby."

Radiance lit her sister-in-law's face. "Gary's already nervous about the birth. Promise me you'll be there? Then you can catch him if he faints."

"I wouldn't miss it." Kimberley slipped her sunglasses on and drove away with a raw ache inside her. If Bryan hadn't died, she might well be sharing pregnancy anecdotes with Wendy and joyously anticipating the birth of her own child. But Bryan would never again hug her to his stocky body, never again light up her life with his soaring laugh and kindness. In a terrifying flash of remembrance, he screamed her name, his blood spattering onto her face. She gasped and forced herself to focus on the highway. *Oncoming vehicles. Fields of grain beside the pavement. Manitoba prairie. Conference in Winnipeg. My new life.*

Lincoln's face replaced Bryan's, and a different pain tore at her as her mind replayed his expression of shock and revulsion after he'd seen her scars. He couldn't have made it plainer that he couldn't stand the sight of them.

* * *

"They must be gone somewhere," Matt said, looking at Lincoln across the bench seat of the pickup. "Kimberley's brother lives in Brandon. Maybe she went to visit him."

"Could be." She was definitely not at the old Steele place, nor was the dog. Lincoln drove away from the house of his stepfather's youth for the fourth time. He'd checked fruitlessly the same number of times the previous day. He'd seen Kimberley's Ranger pull onto Sanderson Road early Saturday morning, but the yellow house had stood empty for two days, looking forlorn without the red truck parked beside it.

On Friday, he'd driven to the old Steele place in search of the captivating Kimberley he'd seen in Terri's photos. He'd found her, but he'd also kicked open the door on a trauma he hadn't known existed. It explained the high-necked robe she'd worn that evening and the long pants and modest blouses with sleeves rolled up to the elbows she'd worn on hot summer days. Not for the first time, he castigated himself for his behavior.

"What do you need to talk to Kimberley about, Dad?"

"I need to apologize to her for something I did."

Anxiety leapt into his son's voice. "Do you think she went away because of what you did?"

"I hope not, Matt. Like you said, maybe she's visiting her brother."

"I really like her. She's…special. She's not scared to go out in the bush, and she's kind."

"That she is." *And I messed up everything.* "She made a big impression on you the first time you saw her, didn't she?"

His son looked down, his fingers fidgeting with a Spiderman comic book. "She seemed like…" He shrugged.

"Like what?"

"Well, like…" Matt looked up "You'll laugh at me."

"No, I won't. Tell me."

"An angel."

Lincoln stopped the truck at the end of the driveway and gazed into his son's eyes. They were the same deep blue as Gayle's had been but possessed none of the wild boldness hers had. That boldness had thrilled him as a young man, fueling his passion until he'd claimed her as his wife. Trouble was, once he'd claimed her, she'd started casting that bold look elsewhere. Matt's eyes held only vulnerability and yearning. "You're right—Kimberley *is* special. She'll be back, cowboy. Don't worry."

Matt's face brightened. "Can we get a husky pup, Dad? Lexi is so much fun!"

"I don't see why not, but it might take a while to find one." As he listened to his son's puppy chatter, Lincoln knew he had to make things right with Kimberley, no matter the cost.

* * *

"Almost there, Lexi." The instant Kimberley spoke the words, she was sure she'd spoken them before while driving this stretch of highway. Or maybe it was a different stretch. *Am I lost?* Her brain was in a fog, beaten into submission by exhaustion. She'd been revived temporarily by Gary and Wendy's good company, the veggie lasagna, a slice of chocolate cheesecake, and a cup of coffee. Gary's brow had wrinkled into a frown when she'd asked for coffee because she never drank coffee. "It's only an hour's drive," she'd told him. "See? I'm awake."

A road sign bearing a vaguely familiar name appeared, and she turned onto a gravel road. When she pulled into the driveway of the old Steele place, tears stung her eyes. She parked beside the house and allowed Lexi to romp unleashed in the yard before calling her inside. Then she stripped and lay naked in her bed, staring into the darkness like she had the past two nights. She focused on her sleep therapy exercises, but each time she closed her eyes and drifted to sleep, she woke up paralyzed with fear and screaming soundlessly in terror.

In the morning, her hands trembled as she drank orange juice and forced down half a bagel. At nine, she telephoned the Seton medical clinic for an appointment and received one for eleven. To test her driving reflexes, she tried backing her truck out of the parking area, but her head swam and her body moved like it belonged to someone else. *There's no way I can drive like this.*

Tears trickled down her cheeks as she walked back into the yellow house. She didn't know anyone except the Steeles to phone for a ride, yet her mind shied away from Lincoln. She flipped through a phone book left by a previous tenant and punched Lauren's home number into her cell phone. No answer. She stared at the number for the Steele Cattle Company. *What if he answers?* Her fingers trembled as she entered the number.

* * *

Relief pumped through Lincoln at the sight of Terri and Matt walking Kimberley's dog along the edge of the gravel road between the old Steele place and his mother's yard. He slowed his pickup to a crawl and honked his horn. His sister and son looked around and waved. He stopped the pickup and opened the window. "Want a ride?"

"No, thanks." Matt's eyes shone. "We're giving Lexi some exercise."

Terri handed the dog's leash to Matt and crossed the gravel to the truck window. "But I'd like you to take this." She wriggled out of the pack straps and handed the pack to Lincoln. "It has her food and dishes in it."

He frowned and took the pack in through the window. "Why are you looking after the dog?"

"Because Kimberley's sick. Well, it's more like she hasn't been able to sleep for days because of nightmares. Mom took her to see the doctor, and she's at our house. She's sleeping now." Remorse filled his sister's eyes. "Do you remember hearing about a grizzly mauling a photographer to death in the Rockies last year?"

"No." But his mind connected the dots.

"Well, I do. On Friday, I even mentioned it to Kimberley. It turns out that he was her fiancé and she was with him when he was killed." Terri spread her hands wide. "I feel so stupid! I kept bugging her about photographing dangerous animals. That's what triggered the nightmares."

"No, it isn't."

His sister frowned. "What do you mean?"

"*I* triggered the nightmares, so stop blaming yourself." He checked his rear-view mirror. "There's a semi coming up behind. You and Matt get off the road until it passes. And watch that car up ahead. I'll see you at Mom's."

Terri glanced in both directions down the road and hurried to Matt's side. As Lincoln hit the gas, he saw her urging his son and the husky off the road and into a stand of white-blossoming sweet clover growing in the ditch.

He drove the half-mile of gravel to his mother's driveway and pulled into her yard. In many ways, the log house and its yard, with the fruit trees and flowerbeds his mother and Terrence had lovingly planted, still seemed more like home to him than the house he'd shared with Gayle, where he and Matt lived.

As he turned off the ignition, his mother opened the side door of the log house and stepped into a breezeway between house and garage. She strolled from the breezeway's shade into the afternoon sun. "Did you see Terri and Matt?"

With the pack in one hand, he stepped down from the truck and closed the door. "They're halfway between here and the old Steele place." He walked to meet his mother. "Terri told me Kimberley's here, that's she's been ill."

His mother lifted a hand to shield her eyes from the

bright light. "Yes. She had the good sense to know she was in no condition to drive, so she called me to ask for a ride to the clinic. When I dropped her off afterward, she cried so hard, I thought she was on the verge of a nervous breakdown. Quite frankly, I was frightened for her, so I brought her here. She's sleeping peacefully now after taking medication."

"You're not going to like what I have to tell you."

His mother had a way of looking at him where she seemed to consider all sorts of possibilities before she put her thoughts into words. After studying him for several seconds, she swept a hand toward a half-dozen brightly-painted Adirondack chairs on the lawn. "Then I suggest we sit down."

He turned a chair away from the sun and set the pack on the grass. "Terri told me Kimberley's fiancé was killed by a grizzly."

"Yes. He was also a wildlife photographer. A mother bear charged them and killed him." Sympathy etched lines in his mother's features. "Kimberley's had nightmares about it for the past three nights. Terri thinks a conversation she and Kimberley had about photographing dangerous animals triggered the nightmares."

"It didn't."

His mother tilted her head. "Why do you say that?"

"Did Kimberley tell you that the bear mauled her?"

Blank shock spread over his mother's face. "No. She told me her fiancé was near her when the bear killed him, but she didn't say the grizzly had attacked her. How would you know that?"

"Because I saw the scars."

"When was this?"

"On Friday. When the three of you were watching that movie, I went to visit her."

"I've never noticed Kimberley having any obvious scars. Are they on her arms or legs?"

Lincoln looked directly into his mother's eyes, his gut tightening with the knowledge that he was going to disappoint her. "The scars I saw weren't on Kimberley's arms or legs."

"Lincoln Steele, what did you do to that poor girl?"

"What did I do?" He removed his baseball cap and ran a hand through his hair. "I tormented her with what she'd told Terri about dealing with dangerous animals. I treated it like a joke, when every word I said must have felt like a kick in the gut to her. I could tell she was agitated about something—maybe it *was* talking with Terri—but I had no idea she'd been mauled until I saw the scars."

"I take it you and Kimberley did a little spooning."

His mother's voice held no accusation. It should have. Lincoln envisioned the hurt on Kimberley's face and her disintegrating composure. He raked a hand through his hair. "I messed up. I tried to apologize, but she was too upset to talk."

His mother's gaze fell to her clasped hands. "Darling, I think you should leave her alone. She needs to heal." After a few seconds, she looked up at him. "You told me you wanted to bring Kimberley here for Matt, and I've seen the chemistry between them. He lights up when she's around, and she seems to see right into his heart. Maybe they can heal each other."

"Without me complicating things, you mean?"

"Give it time. Be still and listen for God's guidance." She looked past him. "I hear the kids coming."

His mother's wisdom was sometimes hard to bear. Lincoln twisted in his chair and spotted Matt and Terri crossing the gravel road. The instant they stepped onto the driveway, Matt sprinted ahead with Kimberley's dog bounding beside him, his sweet laughter ringing out over the yard as Terri raced to catch him. Lincoln closed his eyes and drank in the sound. *If I could, I'd bottle that laughter and take it with me into eternity.* He turned to his mother. "I'll stay away from Kimberley. Let her heal." Then he reached out and caught Matt in his arms.

Chapter 8

Kimberley sat up. The shadows were gone. She'd slept.

In the muted light of Lauren's guest room, she checked her watch and discovered she'd been oblivious to the world for sixteen hours. Hunger pangs cramped her belly as she slid out of bed and opened the room's drapes. Beyond the windows, drizzle streaked the sky and intensified the colors of roses, flowering shrubs, and four large apple trees growing in the brown lawn. Lexi bounded into view, followed by a barefoot, laughing Matthew. Both were drenched. Matthew appeared to be giving her dog a tour of the yard, although from the way the husky tugged at the leash and pranced around him, it looked like Lexi was running the show.

Kimberley showered quickly and donned the yellow pullover top and green dressy version of cargo pants she'd worn to her medical appointment the previous morning. Then she hoisted her daypack onto one shoulder, opened the guest room door, and stepped into a wide hallway. She'd been so distraught when she'd arrived at Lauren's home the previous day, she hadn't paid any attention to her surroundings. Now she did. At the end of the passage, a wrought-iron railing bordered a landing beneath a vaulted ceiling. From the landing, she looked down onto an open-concept living room and adjacent dining area. Light spilled through a wall of windows that invited her to look over the yard to a windbreak of aspens, oaks, and evergreens.

So this is the house where Lincoln grew up. Her mind shied from the thought, her painful experience with him on Friday evening still too fresh. As she descended the stairs, two sounds reached her ears: Lexi's excited barking outdoors and the faint, voice-on, voice-off conversation of Lauren speaking into a telephone somewhere out of sight.

She wandered through the living room to the wall of windows and spotted Matthew and Terri at the edge of the windbreak. An apple tree had hidden them in her view from the landing, but now, at ground level, she observed the pair struggling with something—Lexi. Her husky lunged at a dark shape in the grass under the windbreak trees.

She dropped her pack and ran for a set of French doors, glancing through the wall of windows as Terri yanked backward on Lexi's collar. Determination played over the teen's face, and she screamed something to her nephew, the words lost over Lexi's snarls and yelps. Matthew turned and ran toward the house, giving Kimberley a clear view of her husky rearing against Terri's hold, Lexi's muzzle bristling with white needles—*porcupine quills!* She dashed out of the house and sprinted across a stone patio onto the lawn, heedless of her bare feet.

* * *

Harsh bawls rasped against calm morning air. The hot, pungent smell of manure and crowded cattle filled Lincoln's nostrils as he and Alf guided eighty Angus steers, one at a time, into a portable loading chute positioned to direct the animals onto a stock trailer. The metal chute rattled and clanked as thousands of pounds of beef trod its incline.

Despite the dry summer, the steers looked sleek and meaty. The crunch would come later, when hay supplies dwindled. He and Alf had taken off a first cut in late May, but with no rain, the second growth was poor. If the drizzle dripping from the sky this morning was a harbinger of more rain to come, they might get a second cut. Still, the fact that the ranch was already feeding hay was a sure sign that even a second cut wouldn't last the winter. The time to sell was now. When the last steer had entered the trailer, he punched his mother's contact number on his cell phone. "Steers are on the truck. No problems."

"Thanks for the report."

"Is Kimberley still asleep?"

"I heard water running upstairs a few minutes ago, so she must be awake."

"What's Matt up to?"

"He and Terri are outside with the dog." Loving indulgence filled his mother's voice. "Your son is crazy about that husky. In a way, it'll be too bad when Kimberley goes home. It's been wonderful to see Matt laughing as much as he has yesterday and tod–"

Lincoln heard Matt's stricken voice in the background. His heart leapt. "What's wrong?"

"No human emergency, but we need your help. The dog has a face full of quills."

"On my way." First, the nightmares; now, the quills. Kimberley might be ruing the day she'd moved to Turtle Mountain.

He ran for his truck and sped to his mother's home. In the yard, agonized snarls ripped the air. He sprinted behind the house to where Kimberley was wrestling the husky to the ground, attempting to pin the dog between her thighs. His mother and Matt were doing their best to stop Lexi from scrabbling backward out of Kimberley's grasp, and Terri stood nearby holding pliers. The dog's muzzle looked like a pincushion.

He dropped to his knees beside Lexi and caught a glimpse of relief washing into Kimberley's tense face. "You sit on her," he said. "I'll hold her jaws." He grasped the husky's muzzle and pried its jaws open. Blood trickled onto his hands, the dog's gleaming fangs nearly touching his fingers. "Go to it, Terri."

Her brow furrowed with concentration, his sister tugged quill after quill from the husky's tongue, lips, and muzzle. "She's pushed some of them so deep into the roof of her mouth, I can't get a grip on them."

"We'll take her over to the barns. Jake might be there by now." He released the dog's jaws and turned to Kimberley, meeting her eyes for the first time since the fiasco on Friday evening. He sensed her backing away, her gaze cool, cautious, and a hundred percent aware, like that of a prairie coyote ready to bolt into the bush. "The vet said he'd drop by around now to check on a sick cow. If we're lucky, we'll catch him and he can deal with the buried quills."

"Then let's go." She rose from her kneeling position and patted her husky's back. Already more compliant, the dog wagged its tail tentatively and poked its muzzle into Matt's hand. *Definitely a bond there.*

Lincoln wiped his hands on the wet grass and strode across the lawn with his son and sister at his side. He paused when Kimberley ran alongside Matt and handed him the leash.

"Take Lexi, would you, Matthew? My shoes and pack are in the house." She ran across the stone patio to the log house, her clothes damp from the drizzle and wrestling with her dog.

Lincoln's mother called after her, "You must be hungry. There's a fruit bowl on the dining table."

Seconds later, Kimberley dashed into the breezeway, her pack slung over her shoulder, sandals on her feet, and a banana and apple in hand.

Lincoln took the leash from Matt and nodded to where Terri already sat on the truck's rear seat. "Back seat, cowboy."

Kimberley took Lexi's leash from him, her hand as cool as her expression. "Thanks." She patted the floor mat in front of the passenger seat. "Up, Lexi." The husky sprang nimbly into the space. Kimberley took her seat, one leg on each side of her dog.

Lincoln reversed the truck, then shifted into forward. Beside him, the woman he'd held in his arms on Friday chewed bite after bite from the apple, her face pinched and wan.

Matt's hesitant voice broke the silence, "I'm sorry Lexi got quills."

"Did she pull the leash out of your hands?" Kimberley twisted in her seat to look at Matt.

"Yeah."

"Don't worry about it. She's almost pulled it out of mine lots of times. She's young and full of beans."

Terri leaned forward. "Mom told us about the nightmares. I'm sorry I bugged you about photographing predators."

Kimberley shook her head. "You were interested in my work. That's an incredible compliment. If you see the porcupine again, I'd like to get some shots of it."

"*Without* Lexi."

"Definitely without Lexi."

In the ranch yard, Lincoln nodded toward a white pickup beside the calving barn. "Good, Jake's here. Terri, tell him about Lexi. Take her with you and put her in the supply room. I don't want her scent in the barn. Matt, you go along. I'll get Kimberley something to eat." He turned to Kimberley, again meeting her wary gaze. "There's food in the office, and Jake might be a while yet."

She raised the banana like a dagger. "I should go with

Lexi."

Terri pushed open the truck door. "Matt and I promise to take good care of her, and Jake is an amazing vet. Go with Linc. You haven't eaten for a whole day."

"Dad brought muffins and yogurt," Matthew added, unclipping his seatbelt. "And Chinese food, if you're really hungry."

Indecision played over Kimberley's face before she finally lowered the banana. "I think I'm outnumbered."

Lincoln led her into a kitchenette tucked into an alcove at the back of the office. She looked bedraggled, her wet hair hanging in wavy black strings, her damp yellow top clinging to her breasts. He had a mental flashback of scars—white diagonal scars.

He removed his Blue Jays cap, ran a hand through his hair, and looked straight into her eyes. "Before we get interrupted, I owe you an apology. On Friday, I suspected you were upset about something, but I kept teasing you. I'm sorry."

Her expression changed to the measuring look. "I thought you were the biggest jerk in the world until I realized there was no way you could have known. Let's just forget it. Apology accepted."

"There's more I need to apologize for, Kimberley. You know that."

She looked away, shoving her damp hair over her shoulders with jerky movements.

"I was out of line," he told her. "I'm sorry. It won't happen again."

She threw him a look like a razor blade. "I'm sure it won't. For the record, I don't normally throw myself at men, but I was a little crazy that night. Why don't we leave it at that? Thanks for helping with Lexi. We're taking you away from your work."

No accusations. No guilt trips. She stood there with dignity wrapped around her and nothing but honesty in her eyes. Lincoln tossed his cap onto the kitchenette counter. Kimberley Colter was quite a woman. "It was no big deal for me to come. You're letting me off easy, like you did Matt and Terri."

Strings of hair slid from behind her shoulders and hung around her face. "Life is too short to hold grudges. People and dreams can die in an instant." Again, her face took on a pinched look. "I really could use a couple of muffins."

He pointed to a plastic box on the counter. "Cranberry and blueberry. Yogurt and Chinese food are in the fridge. Help yourself to whatever takes your fancy. Sorry, no herbal tea." He scooped up his cap, stepped toward the door, and then paused, drawing in a deep breath as he turned back to Kimberley. "Your scars—they don't mean anything to me."

She stiffened, ice swirling into her eyes. "How can you even *dare* to say that? When you saw them, your face *filled* with revulsion."

"Kimberley, that revulsion was never directed at you. It was directed at me."

"I don't believe you." She slashed the air with her hand. "You were so stunned, you couldn't even *speak*."

"Of course I was stunned. I'd just made a joke of teasing you about dealing with dangerous animals, and then I saw the scars. I couldn't believe what a jerk I'd been, how I'd hurt you. *That* was the revulsion you saw."

She went absolutely still, the measuring look returning to her eyes.

"Look," he said, "on Friday you asked me if I'd do anything for Matt."

"And you said maybe you would."

"That doesn't include telling lies. I've never lied to you." He donned his baseball cap and touched its brim. "Again, I'm sorry." Jaw clenched, he nodded and left the kitchenette. She'd looked at him as though he'd cut her heart out and thrown it away. *Can I ever mend things with her now?*

* * *

Kimberley entered the supply room where Lexi lay limp and tranquilized on a table. Lincoln, Terri, and Matthew stood near the husky, watching the man who'd removed Lexi's quills store his surgical tools in a green canvas bag that resembled a compartmentalized suitcase. When the veterinarian looked up, his grin encompassed them all, his gaze lingering on Kimberley. "Well, that porcupine provided your excitement for the day."

Terri laughed. "Definitely an adrenaline rush! Good thing Kimberley had pliers in her pocket."

As tall as Lincoln, but lanky rather than lithe, the veterinarian had an easy smile that lit his brown eyes. He offered Kimberley his hand. "I'm Jake Kruger. You must have been a Scout. You know, 'Be prepared.'"

"Kimberley Colter." She shook his hand. "And yes, I was."

"You don't happen to have a ball glove in there, too, do you?"

She frowned. "Sorry?"

"Our slow-pitch team is a woman short for our game tomorrow night." He tossed Lincoln a look. "Jane called this morning to say she twisted her ankle and can only hobble around, and Carol and Angie are still on vacation. That means we'll have to default unless we can find a woman to help us out. I made a few calls, but no takers so far. He grinned at Kimberley before nodding toward Lexi. "Thought I might as well ask. She'll sleep for another twenty minutes or so and then be groggy for an hour after that. Keep her confined until she comes out of it."

"I will." Kimberley watched Matthew gently caress her unconscious dog. After a split-second decision, she told Jake, "I'm really out of practice, but I did bring my glove. My brother mentioned that ball is big around here."

"Are you serious?" Delight spread over Jake's face. "Can you play second base?"

She recalled the summers of fastball she'd played in Calgary in her teens and early twenties before photography excursions to the Arctic and other destinations had taken precedence over the sport. She'd loved the intensity of competition and war of reflexes that playing infield had offered. "As long as you're not expecting miracles. I usually play third, and it's been a while."

"You're a miracle for volunteering."

"You might regret that statement." She ran a hand along Lexi's side. "When and where?"

He lifted his bag. "Six-thirty, at the Seton sports grounds."

"We could pick you up," Teri offered. "Couldn't we, Linc? Matt and I always watch."

Kimberley glanced across the table at Lincoln. He stood between his son and sister as though he was their guide and protector even when no danger loomed. She had to admit he'd impressed her with his cap-doffing, straight-up apologies. No playing games there. His sincerity had been unquestionable, his words those of a decent man showing accountability for his actions. For a fleeting moment, she imagined him standing rock solid beside her, but dismissed the idea. Despite his assertion that her scars meant nothing to him, she couldn't ignore his stark reaction.

And there were more scars.

Lincoln met her eyes briefly as he laid his hands on his son's shoulders. "Let's drive Kimberley and her dog home." Matthew looked up at him and stepped away from the inert husky. Before she could make a move, Lincoln lifted Lexi into his arms. "See you later, Jake. Terri, get the door. I'll drop you and Matt off after we take Kimberley home."

Minutes later, she and Terri hastily spread a blanket on the kitchen floor in the old Steele place, and Lincoln gently laid Lexi on it. Matthew knelt beside the husky and ran his small hands through the black-and-white fur, as though willing Lexi to wake up.

"She'll be okay, cowboy." Lincoln looked from his son to Kimberley, "What did you decide about the ride to the game?"

Perhaps she'd been foolish to say she'd play, but the unexpected invitation had been too tempting, too bright in the face of the past weekend's terror-infused nights. If Lincoln drove, she wouldn't have to worry about being behind the wheel when the exhaustion she always experienced from resorting to the anti-nightmare medication set in. "Okay, but I'd like to arrive early to warm up. I haven't played in years."

He nodded. "We'll pick you up at five. The kids and I usually grab a pizza after the game, so we'll be back around nine or nine-thirty."

"Sounds good."

The kids and I... Such a simple phrase—such a heartbreakingly simple phrase, yet the reality of a child of her own seemed further away than ever. Would any man truly want her, scarred as she was?

She changed into dry clothes and watched Lexi emerge from the caverns of unconsciousness. When her pet could walk, she led the husky outdoors to pee and then back inside. The drizzle had ceased, so she tugged on rain pants and hiking boots. She pulled her pack of camera gear onto her shoulders and then wandered beyond the shelterbelt north of the house. Hay stubble scraped her boots, and wet prairie grasses swished against her legs as she photographed prairie roses with raindrops lying like tears on their pink, upturned faces.

The nasal gabbling of ducks on a shrunken pond in the distance punctuated the air while graceful black terns skimmed over the remaining water. Like drought-stricken waterholes in Africa, the mud-edged wetland was a wildlife magnet. When Kimberley approached, ducks flushed from the water, their wings and feet beating silver splashes.

As she scanned the shoreline to choose a spot to erect a blind, a tractor's roar from across the ravine sent her thoughts to the Steele family. Lincoln was as much a father figure as a brother to Terri, who was as much a sister as an aunt to Matthew. Together, Lauren and Terri acted as a mother-substitute for Matthew. Lincoln had said the family had been scarred by death, yet he and his mother and sister seemed to have rebounded through the strength of incredibly close family bonds.

But what about Matthew? What were the "rough times" that had caused him to withdraw to the shelter of his family? From the moment she'd laid eyes on Lincoln's son in the park, she'd been struck by the intensity, sorrow, and anxiety she'd seen in the child's eyes. Now, as she walked over the rain-washed prairie, she recognized the reason she was so drawn to Matthew. Looking into his eyes was like looking in a mirror.

Chapter 9

Lincoln inhaled the earthy smell of freshly-graded ball diamond, a pang of loss lancing through him. He knew all about dreams dying in an instant. For a moment, he was back in the dugout in Florida, his dazed mind trying to process the devastating news that his stepfather was dead.

Gayle had hated leaving Florida. She'd loved the heat, palm trees, and action and had taken Matt out exploring somewhere new every day, although he'd only been a baby. That short stint in Florida had been one of the happiest intervals in their marriage. Lincoln shoved the memories aside. Why was he thinking about Gayle? For years, he'd done his best to purge her from his mind.

He watched Kimberley lace up a pair of cleats. The fact that she owned a pair of cleats revealed that she'd played more ball than she'd let on to him and Jake. Dressed for action, she wore a snug white top with sleeves to her elbows and stretchy blue pants that hugged her trim hips and legs. She'd confined her black mane to a ponytail that stuck out through the hole at the back of a plain red baseball cap. She rose from her seat on the team's bench, did a few stretches, and then picked up her glove and nodded to him.

He threw easy warm-up tosses, and she returned them smoothly, adjusting her stance and stepping into the throws, her throwing arm tracing a graceful follow-through curve. She had soft hands, her glove cradling the ball and feeding it precisely to her throwing hand. When he increased the distance, she eased into the longer throws and then fired a few hard ones at him. *The lady's full of surprises.*

He strode toward first base, feeling only the smallest twinge in his calf, the injury inflicted by the wayward Angus cow now almost completely healed. "Terri, hit Kimberley some balls. Matt, I'll need you to catch for me at home plate." The kids did as he asked, and Kimberley assumed her ready position. She fumbled several grounders and then settled into her space at second base and took control, fielding balls cleanly. Her throws to him were chest-high and hard. She knew what she was doing and looked good doing it.

"*Woo-hoo!*" Terri cheered when Kimberley snagged a line drive. "You've got yourself a star, Linc."

"That's enough." Kimberley tossed him the ball and jogged back to the bench. She sipped water from a bottle. "My batting will probably be a disaster."

"Like your fielding?" Terri teased.

Matt grinned. "That last catch was *awesome!*"

"But I've never played slow-pitch, only fastball. I really don't know how to hit in slow-pitch."

Lincoln noted the excitement in her eyes. This game

could be the perfect antidote to her traumatic weekend. "First, no bunting allowed. Second, be patient. The pitch will make a high arc. Wait for it and time your swing to meet the ball on its way down. Otherwise, you'll be way ahead of it."

Her first time at bat, she *was* way ahead of the ball. And her second. But her third time up, she connected and sent him a delighted grin from first base. An emotion kicked in his chest, taunting him with the promise he'd made to his mother to stay away from Kimberley.

* * *

Kimberley found herself blending in easily with the Seton team, a group of men and women out to have a good time but keen to play hard while doing it. At shortstop, Lincoln was phenomenally quick. Light on his feet, he seemed to know where the ball was headed before the bat connected with it. He covered a huge swath of ground as backup for pitcher, third base, and for her at second. The smooth grace she'd observed in his movements seemed magnified on the diamond. He was a team player, yet he was by far the most skilled athlete on the field. In fact, she had the distinct impression that he was holding back, particularly when batting and throwing.

"He doesn't belong on this team," she told Jake while they waited to bat.

"I've been telling him that for years." Warm interest lit Jake's eyes. "When he was twenty, he played in the minors for Toronto. Even got called up to spring training in

Florida."

Her eyebrows shot up. "That explains his skill. What happened?"

"His stepfather died, so he came home to run the ranch. Then he and his wife split up. He's had his hands full with the business and caring for Matthew ever since."

"But really, *slow-pitch*? He could probably play with any baseball team in the province."

"I imagine he has his reasons."

"He mentioned that Matthew's had a rough time."

Jake scuffed the ground with an aluminum bat. "He was abused by a babysitter his mother hired. He's never really gotten over it."

An icy sensation filled Kimberley's gut. "That beautiful child?"

Jake nodded. "He's doing better the last couple of years. I think it's been five since it happened. For the first year or so, he screamed to high heaven whenever Linc was out of sight."

"That must have made things difficult for both of them."

"It did. Matthew couldn't attend school, so Linc and Lauren homeschooled him for three years. Last year, they gave school a try and Matthew made it through, although with a lot of anxiety."

She studied Jake closely. "You've known Lincoln a long time, haven't you."

"Since we were kids in school. Linc and Jake, Jake and Linc. Sports and the outdoors were his passions, and I tagged along, basking in his reflected glory."

"Then went on to become a vet."

He shrugged. "Helping animals is what I've always wanted to do." He nodded to the batter's warm-up circle. "You're on deck."

She studied the playing field. The game was in its final inning. Seton had last bat, but the team was down by a run, with runners on first and second bases. The batter at the plate—was it Phil? —popped an infield fly, making it one out.

She stepped up to the plate. If she were playing fastball, she'd opt for a sacrifice bunt to advance the runners, but this was slow-pitch, so she angled her body toward first base, hoping for a hot grounder between first and second. She managed to time the high, arcing pitch correctly, slugged a hopper and sprinted for first. The second base player fumbled the ball, and Kimberley beat her throw to first by a fraction of a second. A roar of cheers erupted from the Seton bench.

Jake followed up with a hard grounder between second and third, sending Kimberley racing for second. She slid in as the second base player leapt into the air to catch a wild throw from left field. On landing, the woman stumbled over Kimberley's legs, trod on her arm, and fell on her, the sudden impact knocking the breath from Kimberley's lungs.

The player scrambled off her. "Hey, are you okay?"

She rolled onto her side, knees pulled to her chest in a fetal position, her arm on fire. Seconds later, Lincoln and

Jake were beside her, each with a hand on her shoulder as she sat up, gasping in air. "I'm okay. Goes…with the territory."

"Your arm's bleeding," Jake told her. "We'd better take a look at it."

She stared at a patch of blood spreading through the white fabric high on her right sleeve. The sight took her to different time, a different place. *So much blood. And Bryan…* Nausea coursed through her.

"Head down." Lincoln gently pressed her forward and down. "Breathe deeply."

She followed his instructions, focusing on the view between her knees—scuffed soil, dusty cleats, bright blue pants. As she rose shakily to her feet, both Lincoln and Jake reached out to steady her. "It's all right. I can walk."

"Forget that." Lincoln scooped her into his arms and strode toward the team's bench.

Kimberley stared up at him, his amber eyes accented by the green ball uniform. Since Friday, she'd involuntarily envisioned his face countless times—his teasing, his comforting, his passion, and then his final shocked expression that wouldn't leave her mind. She pushed her hands against his chest and tried to lift herself out of his grip. "I can get off the field on my own. She stepped on my *arm*, not my legs."

Beside them, Jake grinned. "Let him carry you. You're still shaken up. I'll get the first aid kit."

"Are those doctor's orders?" she snapped.

Jake laughed over his shoulder as he jogged to the

bench. "Vet's orders."

"I'm not a dog."

Lincoln probed her with a look. "Three mishaps in less than a week. Are you regretting your move to Manitoba?"

"Not because of this or the quills."

His mouth tightened.

"If you didn't want honesty, you shouldn't have asked."

Without a word, he set her on the team's bench. The rest of the Seton team and Terri and Matthew gathered around them.

Jake opened the team's first aid kit. "Pull up your sleeve so I can have a look."

Preparing herself for the inevitable reaction, she tugged her sleeve up onto her shoulder, revealing her arm. Amid a web of white scars, three cleat marks marred her skin. Blood streamed from the highest one, the skin split wide open. She heard startled intakes of breath and caught the look of shock on Matthew's face.

Jake's questioning eyes met hers as he placed a bandage over the wound. "That needs stitches. Game over." A faint smile touched his mouth. "Your hit helped bring in the winning run."

In the hospital waiting room, she sat with the Steeles and Jake and laughed as Terri and Jake sparred with quirky banter. After the on-call doctor had glued the split, she winced as she climbed into Lincoln's truck, wondering if she'd be covered with bruises in the morning.

"Would you like me to walk Lexi, so you don't have to?" Matthew's shy voice came from the back seat.

"That would be wonderful, Matthew. I feel like I've been hit by a truck."

"Pizza will revive you," Terri said cheerfully.

Surprisingly, the thick-crusted pizza topped with the works did take the edge off her fatigue and discomfort. Back at the old Steele place, she unlocked the back porch door, allowing Lexi to bound out. "Now, you behave for Matthew." She clipped the leash onto her dog's collar. "No pulling the leash out of his hands, do you hear?"

"I'll go with them, just in case." Terri glanced at her nephew. "Is that okay, Matt?"

"I guess."

Exhaustion rolled over Kimberley as she dumped her sports bag in the porch and removed her sneakers before entering the kitchen.

Lincoln followed her inside and nodded toward the sofa in the living room. "Why don't you put your feet up? I'll make you a cup of tea. What would you like?"

"Thank you. Chamomile, please." She positioned a cushion to support her head and sank onto the sofa. "You've done a good job of teaching Matthew to be considerate of others."

Out of sight in the kitchen, he replied, "That would be my mother's influence."

"It's not your mother making me a cup of tea."

"I guess she trained me, too."

A mug clinked against the counter, and a cupboard door squeaked open and closed. Kimberley closed her eyes, the events of the past several days racing through her mind. She nearly missed Lincoln's quiet steps when he entered the living room, a mug of tea in one hand and a saucer and spoon in the other.

"I don't know how strong you want it so I left the bag in. You don't put anything in it, do you?"

She pushed herself up into a sitting position. "You remembered."

He handed her the mug and saucer. "I remember everything about that evening."

Now that was a loaded statement. "It was something of a revelation, wasn't it?"

His gaze held hers steadily. "Will you be able to sleep?"

"I'll take more meds to break the nightmare cycle."

The kitchen door opened, and Lexi romped into the house, followed by Matthew and Terri. "I could come again tomorrow," Matthew offered, his eyes shining.

Kimberley lifted her mug away from the playful husky. "I'd like that, if it's okay with your dad. I'm not sure how my arm will feel. I was planning to set up a blind by the pond, but I think that will have to wait."

Matthew looked up at his father. "We could do it, couldn't we, Dad?"

Instantly, she regretted her words. "Oh, no. You don't have to do that. I wasn't asking for help—I was just saying."

Lincoln looked from his son to her. "If you want a hand, I could help out before supper, say five-thirty? And Matt could walk your dog. Would that work for you?"

She scanned Matthew's excited face and knew she

couldn't say no. "Five-thirty, it is."

* * *

Late afternoon came on a sultry, whispering breeze thick with impending rain and charged with electricity that promised a whopper of a thunderstorm. Standing on his cedar deck, Lincoln drained his coffee cup. Inside the bungalow, Matt waited impatiently, drawn to Kimberley like an abandoned kitten drawn to a dish of milk. A sardonic smile tugged at Lincoln's mouth. His son wasn't the only one drawn to Kimberley. "Okay, cowboy, we can go now," he called through the screen door.

She was waiting for them on a bench outside the back door of the old Steele place. A circular mound of folded brown camouflage canvas and a lumpy bag lay on the broad cement doorstep beside her. Lincoln searched her face for signs of sleeplessness, but noticed nothing obvious. Purple bruises marred her right arm below her T-shirt sleeve. "That looks sore."

"It is."

"We'll have to hurry." He glanced up at towering thunderheads in the western sky. "There's something ugly in that."

She rose from the bench. "I usually have the blind up in a few minutes."

"Matt, take the bag." Lincoln hoisted the canvas and discovered that the fabric hid supports of some kind.

"It has a spring steel frame that pops up and locks," she told him.

They dumped the gear into his pickup's box and climbed into the cab, Kimberley wincing as she closed the passenger door. She said, "I want the blind on the east side of the pond so I can have the morning sun behind me."

He sped toward the wetland, the truck's tires kicking up dust from the dirt track through the hayfield. Turning off the track, he jounced over native prairie to within thirty yards of the pond's edge. "Pick your spot."

"Over there." She pointed to a small clump of wolf willow shrubs. "The willows will help disguise the blind."

He stopped the truck near the silver-leaved shrubs, switched off the ignition, and unloaded the blind and bag from the truck. As she'd said, the blind's frame popped up, forming a domed hexagon of camouflage canvas.

A gust of wind whipped hair around her face as she removed a mallet and pegs from the bag and handed them to him. "Peg down the metal struts inside. They've got holes in them. I'll attach the guy ropes, and then you can peg them down." She pulled four nylon ropes from the bag and turned to his son. "Can you reach to clip on a rope, Matthew? I don't want the blind to blow away."

Lincoln tapped pegs through holes in a wheel-like metal frame on the ground inside the blind. Then he secured the rope ties to tether the blind against a sudden, fierce wind that lashed prairie grasses and cattails. Their workmanship was about to be tested.

Crooked shafts of lightning ripped open the darkened sky, and wind spat rain onto them. Seconds later, ice pelted down. Matt winced against the frozen pebbles. "Dad, there's hail!"

The three of them ran for the truck, the air around them white with ice and water as hail pounded down in slanted sheets, beating down grasses and tearing off willow leaves. Afternoon turned dim as dusk, with eerie blue light infusing the lightning-shot air. Inside the pickup, Lincoln wrapped a reassuring arm around his son and met Kimberley's exhilarated gaze.

"It's wild!" she shouted over the hail's drum roll on the truck roof.

Moisture spotted her T-shirt, and raindrops glistened on her hair. *She* was wild and beautiful—he couldn't tear his gaze from her.

"Dad?"

He looked blankly at his son.

"The hail stopped."

So had the gale-force wind. The storm had swept on to the east.

Matt pointed. "The blind's still standing."

It was, but the willows beside it were missing half their leaves. All around the truck, broken grass stems protruded through a slushy blanket of pea-sized hailstones.

"So much for a second cut of hay," he muttered, his spirit plummeting as he envisioned the other crops—oats, wheat, barley. He started the pickup and met Kimberley's gaze. "I need to check our crops. Will you come with me?" Right now—promise or no promise to his mother—he wanted Kimberley beside him.

Chapter 10

Kimberley stared at the devastation surrounding her. She was a city girl, but the damage to the Steele Cattle Company's wheat field was obvious. Green-gold stalks bearing heads of kernels lay broken and flattened into tangled heaps that would be impossible to harvest. Lincoln and his son walked ahead of her, the dark eastern sky brooding beyond them. Matthew kicked at a drift of hailstones while Lincoln bent to pluck a handful of battered wheat stalks from the ground. She shielded her small digital camera from errant raindrops and unobtrusively snapped photos to capture the storm-washed colors and poignancy of human gestures so small against the destructive storm's aftermath.

"What does this mean?" she asked, returning the camera to her pocket.

Lincoln tossed the stalks to the ground, his face grim. "It means no harvest and no more hay. We're a hundred percent hailed out."

"You've lost *everything*?"

He shook his head. "We've got crop insurance. That'll cover part of the loss. Some farmers on the mountain won't even have that."

"What will they do?"

"Sell what they can. Do contract harvesting or whatever they can to make ends meet."

Her mind reeled. Poor weather had occasionally caused the cancellation or rescheduling of photo shoots, but her year's livelihood had never been threatened—let alone destroyed—by a single storm. She'd come to Turtle Mountain to experience rural life. The past thirty minutes had taught her that prairie farmers and ranchers paid a high price for the intimate freedom of working the land.

A green pickup pulled in behind Lincoln's, and she recognized one of the Seton slow-pitch players behind the wheel. Red-haired and paunchy, he'd batted ahead of her and played left field. *Phil.* The man strode to where they stood at the wheat field's edge. "Sure is a mess, boss. And there's more back in the yard. Broken windows and branches down off the big elm."

"The stock?" Lincoln asked.

"Spooked, but they've quieted down. No injuries."

The red-haired man's eyes slid to her and scanned her damp clothes. "Hullo, Kimberley. Quite the storm, eh? How's your arm?"

Nothing was amiss in his words, but she had the impression he was mentally undressing her. She injected frost into her voice, "Sore, but thanks for asking."

Lincoln dismissed the man with a curt nod. "I'll be back in a few minutes."

Phil slid another look over Kimberley before returning

to his truck.

"He works for you?" She was unable to disguise the distaste in her voice.

Lincoln sent her a keen look. "I noticed you doused him with some of that ice you threw at me in the park."

"And there's plenty more where that came from."

He grinned and glanced at his son. "Your grandmother has the sometimes annoying habit of saying that we should be thankful in all circumstances, doesn't she?"

Matthew looked up from squeezing hailstones into a ball and dipped his head emphatically. "She says that all the time."

Lincoln looked out over the flattened crop. "It's not easy, is it?"

Matthew threw the ice ball out into the field. "Sometimes I just can't do it."

"Well, this time I can. So...thanks, Kimberley."

Her jaw dropped. "For what?"

"For not packing your truck and heading back to Calgary."

Of course he would say that because of Matthew. "My parents taught me that life isn't a bed of roses. I'm pretty good at facing up to things." *Liar*, taunted the voice inside her head. *Never set foot west of Calgary. Never returned to the Rockies. Still wedged in a rocky crevice, screaming in terror.*

"I'm *really* glad you and Lexi came," Matthew said.

"Oh, my gosh! I completely forgot about Lexi. She's never been in a storm like that. She was probably terrified. Good thing I left her in the house."

Lincoln strode toward his pickup. "Let's go. I'll check the house for broken windows."

When she opened the back porch door, Lexi bounded out, whining and rubbing against her legs and then nearly bowling Matthew over. Boy and dog raced across the yard, Matthew's laughter floating in their wake.

Lincoln watched his son. "That dog is like therapy for him."

"For me, too." At his questioning look, she explained, "My father gave me Lexi after I was released from hospital. She was eight weeks old and the cutest puppy that ever lived, but she needed someone to look after her. That meant I had to drag myself out of the post-traumatic stress pit I was in. I bawled into her fur more times than I can remember."

"And the nightmares?"

"Every night until medication finally broke the cycle. Before last weekend, I hadn't had any for six months, so I thought I was over them and didn't renew my prescription." She watched Lexi crouch playfully and race past Matthew. "I still have flashbacks, but more often it's mood swings and uncontrollable urges to cry." She slanted a wry look at him. "Hence my bitchiness after I got hurt at the ball game."

Understanding lit his eyes. "And your crying in the park. Did the kids and I trigger it?"

Lexi pranced around Matthew, her tail waving like a plumed flag.

"No. It was a toddler running on the beach. One

moment I was laughing, and the next—" Her voice caught in her throat. *Talk about it*, the therapist had pounded into her head. "Bryan—my fiancé—and I were going to be married the weekend after the shoot in the Rockies. We'd both wanted children."

Lincoln nodded, empathy in his face. "That's hard. If you want to talk about it, I'll listen."

Her eyebrows lifted. During that tumultuous evening at the old Steele place, he'd also asked if she'd wanted to talk. He had more sensitivity than she'd credited him. "Thanks for the offer. I'll keep it in mind."

He reached into his shirt pocket and retrieved a scrap of paper. "Burrowing owls. Here's the CO's number. His name is Jack Bos. I went to school with him."

"Wonderful! Thanks, Lincoln. I really appreciate the contact."

"No problem." He teased her with a grin. "Unlike the moose, the owls probably won't chase you."

"Good. It's hard to photograph an animal when you're running away from it."

They checked the windows and found none broken. The big elms that shaded the house had taken the brunt of the storm. Broken branches littered the lawn, and torn leaves lay strewn over the grass like green confetti. After Lincoln called to Matthew, Kimberley snapped a series of images as the laughing boy and romping husky bounded toward her.

* * *

The next morning, Lincoln turned into the ranch yard after driving every road bordering Steele land in order to more closely assess the extent of the hail damage. His inspection had confirmed his initial impression that the cattle company's pastures, hay fields, and grain fields had taken the brunt of the storm. In a sour mood, he parked in front of the office. *God's testing us again, slamming us to the floor.* Then he recalled Matt's joy when his son had raced across Kimberley's yard with Lexi and knew he'd trade every crop from now to eternity to have that joy remain on Matt's face.

"The Lord gives, and the Lord takes away. Blessed be the name of the Lord." How many times had his mother said those verses? And every time, he'd railed against them, torn by the injustice of death and abuse, grasshopper plagues and drought. He'd wanted to shake her and ask how she could say *blessed.* But not now. Now the giving outweighed the taking, all because of Kimberley.

As though his mother had read his thoughts, she stepped from the office and searched his face.

He leaned against his pickup and crossed his arms. "God used a big black marker to draw a line around Steele land and dumped all that hail inside it."

She spread her hands. "The earth is his to do with as he wishes. We've been blessed with abundance in past years. This is one of the lean ones. We'll sell more cattle, batten down the hatches, pull up our socks, and face the winter."

"You're mixing your metaphors."

"And you're not angry." Her mischievous smile surfaced. "Who knows what might happen next?"

What had his mother been like as a girl, a young bride? He knew she kept an old wedding photo in a cedar chest. It showed her standing radiant at the side of his biological father, Andy Janes, who smiled gently, his hand curved lovingly round his bride's shoulder. Lincoln couldn't recall the last time he'd seen that photo. "I knew what you'd say."

His mother nodded, dimples appearing in her cheeks. "Sandra's arrived. Matt's up first for his lesson. You know, it's hard to believe how much he's changed during the past month. That shrinking anxiety has almost disappeared." A pensive expression settled over her face. "I hope Kimberley stays long enough for him to stabilize and grow confident."

Lincoln straightened. "You think she won't stay?"

"She's seeking, Lincoln, and running."

"*Running?*"

His mother extended her hands, palms up. "Why else would a world-class photographer rent a farmhouse here? This is farming and ranching country, not a wildlife mecca. And there's the portrait photography."

He stepped away from the pickup. "You think she's lost her nerve."

"I do. Understandable, given what's she's been through, but I'm wondering what will happen when she finds it again."

"Maybe she'll give up the wildlife part. She wants children."

His mother scrutinized his face. "Be careful, Lincoln. Don't use Matt to try to hold onto her."

"We're getting way ahead of ourselves." He gave a brisk nod. "I'm going to watch Matt." As he strode toward the riding ring, he quashed his unease. Kimberley was here, and Matt was happy. He'd do whatever he could to keep things that way.

* * *

At dawn, Kimberley crept into her blind by the pond. She erected a folding stool and removed her Nikon camera fitted with the telephoto lens from her pack. She mounted the camera on a tripod and guided it into one of the blind's two projecting fabric snouts intended to camouflage long lenses. While she waited for the sun, she quizzed herself on bird calls. A male clay-colored sparrow's insect-like buzz was easy to identify, and she instantly recognized the ricocheting vibratos of sandhill cranes in flight. A faint breeze brushed her face. *Good.* She was downwind from the pond.

After twenty minutes, shadowy movement caught her attention. She trained her camera lens on the spot and picked out the shape of a red fox stalking through hail-broken grasses. Her heart kicked into high gear as she adjusted shutter speed and fine-tuned the lens's focus. The rising sun cast gold over the scene, gilding the fox's fur and turning it to burnished flame. She popped off ten shots per second as the fox pricked its ears, leapt into the air, and pounced. Moments later, it trotted away from the pond with its head held high, the limp body of a hen mallard dangling from its jaws in a graceful curve. *Beauty even in death.* Kimberley zoomed in for several close-ups, the fox's tawny eyes lit by the sun into bright amber that reminded her of Lincoln's eyes.

He was a mystery—a handsome, charming mystery with a failed marriage and chosen career, a hurting son, and a loyal friend who thought the world of him. He'd said he wanted her here for Matthew and had admitted he might do anything for his son. *What exactly might that anything be?*

She remained in the blind for another hour, capturing images of ducks, shorebirds, and a muskrat that swam across the pond's still water, leaving a rippling V-wake behind it. Then she washed away the early morning chill in a hot shower and drove to Seton for supplies. After buying groceries, she found the veterinary clinic and introduced herself to the receptionist. "I'd like to pay the bill for my dog's emergency surgery at the Steele Cattle Company on Tuesday."

The young blonde woman looked Kimberley over before keying information into a computer. A faint frown creased her brow. "I don't see your name in our accounts. The dog's name and breed?"

"Lexi. L-E-X-I. Siberian husky." Kimberley removed her wallet from her cargo pants pocket and extracted her Visa card.

"Found it, but the fee's already been paid."

"By whom?"

The receptionist raised her eyebrows before schooling her expression into customer service discretion. "Lincoln Steele."

Kimberley tapped her credit card against the counter. "Thank you."

Off to the side of the receptionist's desk, an examining room door opened, and a petite woman with a white miniature poodle in her arms preceded Jake through it. Crowned with tumbling dark curls, the woman looked familiar. As Kimberley walked toward the exit, she realized that she'd seen her in the Steeles' riding ring, where she'd called out instructions to Matthew in an arrestingly deep voice.

"Good day, Kimberley." Jake gestured toward the petite woman. "Have you met Sandra Aguilera, Terri's and Matthew's riding coach? Sandra lives west of Winnipeg and instructs show jumping and dressage in half a dozen communities spread over southern Manitoba." He patted the poodle's back. "This little fellow goes everywhere with her. Sandra, this is Kimberley Colter, a nature photographer living at the old Steele place."

Kimberley's photographic eye appreciated the way the other woman's wild curls teased an onlooker to look closer, to observe her olive skin, dark eyes, and ravishing Latin smile. "Nice to meet you. I saw you briefly at the Steeles' riding ring last week."

Sandra raised a speculative eyebrow. "So, you're the

one who's brought out Matthew's smiles. Good to meet you." She glanced up at Jake. "I have to rush. Lessons."

"Kimberley, would you have a minute?" Jake nodded toward the examining room.

Frowning, Kimberley followed him into the room. "Is it something to do with Lexi?"

He smiled sheepishly, his eyes dancing. "It's a ploy to get you away from the sharpest ears in town—my receptionist. The ball team is putting on a dinner and dance a week from Saturday. Would you like to go with me? I tried to get your number from directory assistance, but they didn't have it."

A dance... Her last dance had been with Bryan the day before they'd left for their pre-wedding shoot in the Rockies. Bryan had been the only man she'd ever dated, the only man she'd ever loved. Six years her senior, he'd hired her as his assistant in the nature photography tour business he'd operated and had promoted her to his partner four years later. They'd scoured the Rockies and Arctic and had jetted to Africa and Australia to put together tour packages, building both their reputations and their relationship. Then he'd died giving her a chance to live.

A thought reared up, a thought she'd suppressed for a year. *Am I to blame for Bryan's death?* She'd insisted on the shoot before the wedding because she'd wanted more images of grizzly cubs for the book she'd been commissioned to illustrate. She'd chosen their backpacking route specifically because a grizzly sow and cub had been sighted on open alpine tundra high above Skyline Trail the previous day. She hadn't expected that another sow would charge from an aspen grove beside the trail in a completely different location.

Jake moved a step closer. "Are you all right? You've gone pale."

Kimberley forced a smile. *Life moves on.* "I don't have a land line, just a cell." Did she want to attend a dance with Jake? She barely knew him, but he was an easy companion and seemed like a good man. Maybe it was time to go on a date. "I haven't been to a dance in ages, so why not? What should I wear?"

A grin spread over his face. "Excellent. We're abandoning sweaty uniforms and going semi-formal. Pick you up at six? Earlier if you'd like a drink before dinner. I'm a teetotaler."

"Six is fine. I'm looking forward to it." As she left the clinic, Kimberley mentally perused her wardrobe: camo, cargo, casual. A shopping trip was definitely in order, but not today; the burrowing owls had priority.

En route to the old Steele place, she stopped in at the ranch yard and found Lincoln and his mother in the office. "Hello. Excuse me." She swept a hand toward the door. "If you don't mind, Lincoln, I'd like to speak with you outside."

"All right." He stood from a desk and followed her outside. "What's up?"

She lifted her chin. "You paid my vet bill."

He braced his hands on his hips. "I did."

"Why?"

"Because my son let your dog get away. It was an accident, but it happened."

"Lexi is my dog and my responsibility."

"And you couldn't look after her because of me."

She stiffened. "I told you we should forget that incident."

"I'll never forget it."

She slashed the air with her hand. "Lincoln, stop trying to make up for it!"

He stepped back, dropping his hands to his sides. "What's that supposed to mean?"

"I'm a grown woman. I can deal with your reaction. You don't have to be constantly *doing* things for me."

His expression tightened. "Look, if my son had hit a baseball through your window, I'd pay for a new window. The same goes for the vet bill. If you've got an issue with that, it's your problem. As for constantly doing things for you, in case you've forgotten, the offer of a ride came from *Terri*, and it was *Matt* who wanted to help you with the blind. If you didn't want me around, you could have said no to both of those. This isn't the city, Kimberley. Here, people lend a hand."

Heat poured into her face. Before she could open her mouth, Lincoln turned on his heel and shoved open the office door, slamming it closed behind him.

Chapter 11

Evening sunlight painted shades of gold over the prairie landscape as Lincoln drove north from his house with Matt beside him. *Will this drought never end?* The moisture from the hail storm had barely wet the dust, and no rain had fallen since. It was mid-July, which meant at least two more months of warm weather ahead. He shook his head. He'd drop Matt off with Terri and then pick up where he'd left off, filling out hail insurance claims.

Ahead, Kimberley's red truck ascended the rise at the end of the access road to the old Steele place. Lincoln quashed the irritation that spiked through him. She sure got under his skin. In the space of ten seconds, she could warm his heart or set his teeth grinding. That morning, she'd made it sound like he'd been falling over himself to help her when instead they'd been thrown together by situations that had cropped up out of the blue—the dog's quills, the ball game, setting up the blind. He hadn't planned any of that. God was turning his stay-away promise into an ironic impossibility.

Dust swirled around his pickup as he braked opposite the end of the access lane. He stepped out, and Matt scrambled out after him, following him across the gravel.

Kimberley pulled to a stop at the end of the lane and rolled down her window, the measuring look in her eyes. "Hello Lincoln, Matthew. What's up?"

He touched his cap brim. "Apologizing to you could become a habit. I'm sorry I was so abrupt this morning."

She held up her hand like a stop sign. "No, I'm the one who should apologize. I completely overreacted and lashed out at you. Sorry for that, and I don't believe I ever thanked you for helping when Lexi had quills. Thank you."

"No problem. How's your arm?"

"Much better. I'm on my way to set up a blind at the burrowing owl site. I got the go-ahead, as long as I stay back from the burrows the owls are using." She tilted her head. "Actually, I'd like to ask a favor, if you have time."

"At the risk of being accused of constantly doing things for you, name it. We're in no hurry."

She laughed, wry amusement filling her gaze. "Good one. Here's the favor. Crows are the only birds I know that can count, at least around here, so if three of us set up the blind and you and Matthew walk away from it..." She winked at Matt.

"The owls will think we're all gone."

"Exactly."

Lincoln nodded. "We can do that." He led the way to a close-cropped pasture two miles east of Seton and parked on the highway's verge. While Kimberley shrugged on her pack of camera gear and slipped her binoculars' strap over her neck, he hauled the blind and bag of rope and tools out of her truck box. He handed the bag to Matt and hoisted the collapsed blind onto his shoulder. "Jack probably told you the owls are in the northeast corner." He pointed to a far corner of the pasture. "Matt and I helped him band the juveniles last week."

"There were six," Matt chipped in. "They snapped their beaks at us. When we let them go, the babies ran and dived into gopher holes."

They strode through sweet clover in the roadside ditch, crossed a barbed-wire fence, and dodged dried cow patties in the empty pasture. Lincoln scanned the pasture's northeast corner and spotted a distinctive oval shape atop a fence post. "There's one of them. They hunt from perches."

The woman at his side nodded. "I did a little research and discovered that they're active day or night and are fairly tolerant of humans." Thirty yards from the fence, she stopped. "This is close enough."

Working together, they had the blind up and tethered within minutes.

"Can I watch them with you sometime?" Matt asked Kimberley. "I have binoculars."

Lincoln's heart jolted. Matt was reaching out, reaching for freedom from the past.

Kimberley unzipped the blind's door. "That's fine with me if it's okay with your dad. How about next Saturday morning? I'm not coming back for a week because I want the owls to have a chance to get used to the blind."

"Dad?"

He looked into his son's imploring eyes and then met Kimberley's steady gaze, his own words coming back to him: *Something tells me she's the person to help Matt.*

"I'll take good care of him, Lincoln."

"Okay," he finally replied, squeezing Matt's shoulder. "Will you need me to act as a decoy?"

She shook her head. "We'll take our chances."

"What time should I bring Matt to your place?"

"Early. Five-thirty." She smiled at Matt. "Bring warm clothes, a snack, and something to drink. Maybe a book in case you get bored."

Matt nodded, his eyes lit with anticipation. "Thanks, Kimberley. Thanks, Dad."

She stepped inside the blind, and Lincoln walked away from it with his son skipping across the prairie beside him.

* * *

For the next week, heat gripped Turtle Mountain, the sun relentless in the clear blue sky. It seemed to Kimberley as though she could see the sloughs shrinking. Dust coated roadside shrubs. Sweat trickled down her face and body as she hiked across sun-bleached pastures and through woodlands caught in the grip of hot, still air. She found an oasis of coolness in shade under tall aspens growing in the ravine, to the south of the old Steele place, where she photographed a beaver reinforcing its dam at the downstream edge of a shrunken pool.

Local residents acknowledged her with a lifted hand as they drove dusty gravel roads, and she responded in kind as she continued to explore. Three mornings in a row, she met Lincoln and Matthew on Sanderson Road and braked to a stop to exchange greetings. Each time, Lincoln asked where she was headed.

"Keeping tabs on me?" she asked on the third morning.

"No harm in letting someone know your whereabouts. You spend a lot of time alone in the bush. You could fall and break a leg."

The thought hadn't even occurred to her. She and Bryan had always relied on each other, although they'd logged plans with national parks staff and with their transport on occasions when they'd been dropped off in remote locations. "I do have a cell phone, but thanks for looking out for me."

"Cell phone reception isn't always reliable around here." Lincoln glanced at his son before returning his gaze to her. "Are you still up for taking Matt with you to the blind on Saturday morning?"

"Absolutely. I'm keen to see what those owls are doing."

A huge smile spread across Matthew's face. "Me, too. It's been so hard to wait!"

Lincoln's eyes held indulgence. "Well, you'll have to wait one more day. We'd better get moving." He nodded to her. "See you tomorrow morning."

That evening, Jake phoned to confirm their dinner-and-dance date, his voice a welcome sound in the quiet of the old Steele place.

"Hot enough for you?" he asked, a smile in his voice.

"Too hot. Lexi and I spend afternoons in the living room, with a fan blowing air over us, or we go down in the cellar for a while. She seems to like it down there."

"No air conditioning at the old Steele place?"

"Not a whisper."

"Well, there is at the banquet hall."

"Thank goodness!"

"So, I'll see you tomorrow at six?"

"Yes, at six." As she pressed the end call button, she remembered that she needed to buy a dress.

* * *

On Saturday morning, Matt scrambled out of bed, dressed in record time, and ate every morsel of the bacon, egg, and toast Lincoln had prepared for him. Then he tugged on a hoodie and jacket.

Lincoln handed him a thermos and paper bag. "Here's your hot chocolate and sandwich. I threw in a few cookies, too."

His son added the food to his daypack, which already contained several Spiderman comics, a water bottle, and binoculars. "Thanks, Dad. We should go."

No anxiety. No hesitation. For five years, Lincoln had waited for Matt to be released from fear, even prayed for it, although he never described his thoughts as prayer—just a silent, gut-ripping plea for help for his son. That help had come in the form of a beautiful black-haired photographer named Kimberley.

Fresh and clear, the dawn held a promise of heat in its breath as he drove his son to the old Steele place and handed him over to the woman his mother had said was running. Dressed in brown camouflage pants, anorak, and cap, Kimberley didn't look like she was running. She looked every inch the professional wildlife photographer as she carried a tripod and her pack to her truck. The same adrenaline-light he'd seen in players' eyes on the diamond at spring training shone in hers. So much for the idea of her giving up wildlife photography.

"When will you be back?" he asked.

"Ten at the latest. Should I drop Matthew off at your house?"

"The office would be better. Thanks, Kimberley. Have fun, Matt." Lincoln hugged his son and then strode to his truck, stepping lightly, the rising sun beckoning him into a new day.

Chapter 12

In the blind, Kimberley showed Matthew how to erect a sturdy folding chair she'd brought for him to sit on. Then she showed him how to open the viewing portals spaced around the hide. "There's even one here at the bottom, in case you want to see at ground level." She lifted the flap. "To see out some of them, you might need to stand on the chair."

"Cool." Lincoln's son stepped onto his chair and peered out a high portal, his face radiating excitement. By six-thirty, they'd settled into quiet observation.

Within minutes, the owls seemed to appear out of nowhere. One moment, the pasture's northeast corner was empty, and the next, five leggy owls stood on a mound of soil pocked with gopher holes. Morning sun accented the birds' bright yellow eyes. Two of the ground-dwelling owls were adults, their brown plumage streaked and barred with white. The other three were juveniles with buff breasts.

Kimberley glanced at Matthew, his binoculars raised to his eyes. "Do you see them?" she whispered.

He strained toward the portal. "Yes."

For two hours, she pursued the owls with her long lens,

snapping images of the adults feeding their offspring grasshoppers and field mice. When a goshawk flew over the pasture, she switched to continuous mode and caught the fledglings sprinting for the burrow. A few minutes later, the juvenile birds cautiously re-emerged from the ground, and she and Matthew shared a grin. She showed him how to focus her telephoto lens and allowed him to take several photographs of the young owls. The rest of the time, she left him to his own devices. He watched the owls through his binoculars, quietly looked out various portals, and read comic books.

As the morning warmed up, Kimberley and her young charge removed their jackets. Matthew also stripped off his hoodie before sitting on the folding chair and tucking into his snacks. Kimberley rolled her T-shirt sleeves high onto her shoulders and ate a granola bar, all the while keeping an eye on the owls through the camera lens.

"I have scars, too."

The quiet words startled her. Matthew was staring at her right arm. "A bear gave me these," she told him.

His blue gaze met hers. "The one that killed that photographer guy you were going to marry?"

"Yes."

"I'm glad it didn't kill you."

"So am I. Otherwise, I wouldn't be here with you, watching long-legged, snappy-beaked owls."

A fleeting smile touched his lips and faded. His mouth opened and closed as though he was searching for words.

"What is it, Matthew?"

He swallowed hard. "A babysitter hit me with a belt. It had a hard buckle, and she kept hitting me—*over and over.* She wouldn't stop." His voice broke as he looked away. "My mom never came."

Hot, still air pressed against Kimberley. Beyond the blind's walls, a grasshopper droned its soaring buzz. "Your dad came?"

Matthew nodded, tears in his eyes. "Once I heard him tell my grandma that it was my mom's fault I got hurt. I think he hates her even when she's dead!"

Kimberley sat on her folding chair and took Matthew's hands in hers. They were small, soft, fragile. "Matthew, how old were you when your mother died?"

"Five."

"You must miss her. My mom died when I was seventeen, and I still miss her."

His head bobbed.

"What was she like?"

Tears slid down his cheeks. "She played lots of games with me and sang songs. Her hair was long and wavy like yours, but it was red."

"Do you have a favorite picture of you and your mom? When I'm missing my mother, I look at pictures of us together. Then she feels closer."

He shook his head and pulled a hand free to wipe it across his face. "Grandma and Nana and Papa have pictures, but I don't." He slid his hand back into Kimberley's.

No pictures of his mother? Kimberley recalled

Lincoln's bitterness when he'd mentioned his marriage, but to ban his former wife's image from his home? That was extreme. "Ask your dad about pictures. Tell him you miss your mother."

Matthew began to pull away. "But he'll get mad at me. He *never* talks about her."

She leaned toward the boy. After her mother's death, her soul had cried out in anguish, healing only through time's softening years. Matthew's eyes held the same anguish. "Matthew, your father loves you more than anything in the world. I know that. Talk to him. He'll listen."

"Okay."

She released his hands and sat back. "Whew! It's really hot in here, isn't it? We should go."

Late July sun shone on their bare arms as they walked through the pasture. A prairie wind carried the sweet scent of dry grass and clover. Out of nowhere, like the burrowing owls appearing in the dawn light, Matthew said, "You can call me Matt, if you want."

She smiled down at him. "And you can call me Kimmie, if you want." For an instant, Bryan screamed that name in her memory; then his voice floated away on the wind.

* * *

Tires crunched on the gravel outside the ranch office. Lincoln blew out a relieved breath and pushed out of his desk chair.

Matt swung the office door open, his eyes shining. "Hi, Dad."

"Hey, how'd it go?" He lifted his gaze to the black-haired woman who'd followed his son into the office. She'd rolled her T-shirt sleeves up onto her shoulders, revealing the scars on her right arm. Wisps of black hair had escaped her ponytail and dangled around her face, yet her eyes were calm. Apparently, entertaining an eight-year-old for four hours had been no big deal.

Matt shrugged out of his daypack. "Kimmie showed me how to use her camera. The telephoto lens made it seem like the owls were right in front of me. There were only three babies left."

"A goshawk flew over." She lifted a hand to push the dangling hair behind her ears. "It might have made earlier raids. I'll e-mail Matt's pics to Terri so he can have them."

Kimmie. Matt. Put two people in a blind for a few hours and look what happens. He nodded to her arm. "Your bruises are fading."

Her eyes played blue mystery with him. "And I have a new scar to add to my collection."

"We all have scars, Kimberley."

Matt piped up, "Dad has one where a cow kicked him."

"That's right." He scanned his son's flushed features. "Want something cold, Matt? Water? Lemonade? Ice cream?"

"Can I have lemonade *and* ice cream?"

"'May I,' remember? Or your grandmother will get on my case again. Go for it. Then get ready for your riding lesson. Clothes are in the bathroom. Darby's ready to go."

His son skipped into the kitchenette.

Lincoln turned to Kimberley. "Can I get you something cold?"

"No, thanks. I'm off to Brandon." She frowned as she looked down at her camo pants. "I need to buy a dress."

Her expression made him smile. "You make that sound like fun."

When she looked up, sadness tinged her features. "When I was a kid, my mother designed and sewed dresses for me, but I was such a tomboy, it was like pulling teeth to get me into them. Then she was diagnosed with pancreatic cancer and I wished I'd worn them more often."

Like he wished he'd made peace with Terrence before the accident. "Must be something big happening now, if you need a dress."

She shrugged. "I'm going to the ball team's dinner and dance with Jake. I'll probably see you there."

Lincoln fought a kick of surprise and forced himself to nod casually. "Save me a dance."

She pointed to the door, her eyes taking on that measuring look he'd come to know. "I'd like to speak with you outside. Bye, Matt," she called.

Matt appeared in the kitchenette doorway, a bowl of strawberry ice cream in his hands. "Bye, Kimmie."

"Back in a minute," Lincoln told his son. He followed Kimberley outdoors, where hot sun beat down into the ranch yard. In its harsh light, he noticed a scar that traced her hairline above her forehead and right temple and disappeared behind her ear. He braced his hands on his hips. "What's up today?"

She lifted her eyebrows, her expression cooling several degrees. "You're making it sound like I always have some kind of issue."

He dropped his hands. "Okay, that was a poor choice of words. What would you like to discuss?"

"Scars."

"We've been through this, Kimberley. I told you they mean nothing to me. I just noticed the one along your hairline. Did I express revulsion?"

"No, but that's not—"

"Look, this might be hard for you to swallow, but have you considered that maybe your obsession with your scars is more about vanity than anything else?"

Her mouth dropped open. "*Vanity?*"

"Let me put it this way: If you want to go through life hiding your scars because you think they make you less of a woman, that's your choice, but the whole world is out there waiting for you."

The blue ice in her eyes changed to blue fire. "So says the man who can't look at a picture of his former wife. Tell me, Lincoln, just which one of us is it that's hiding?"

He lifted his chin. "You know nothing about my relationship with Matt's mother."

"And you know nothing about *me*." She turned on her heel and strode to her truck, hands clenched at her side.

Lincoln watched her drive away, bitterness like a bad

taste in his mouth. Who had talked to her about Gayle and him? He was still riled up when he walked beside Matt and Darby to the riding ring to watch his son's lesson. After five minutes, Sandra Aguilera marched to the fence and told him, "I don't know who or what put the burr under your saddle, but if you don't stop glaring, I'm going to ask you to leave."

His eyes warred with the riding instructor's, but he reined in his temper and nodded. By the lesson's end, he knew she'd been right. As soon as he'd relaxed and sent Matt an encouraging smile, his son's tension had eased and he'd melded with Darby, repeatedly clearing the series of low jumps with only a single clip to a rail. Now the pony trotted from the ring, with sunlight gilding its sorrel coat and Matt grinning, his young, gloved hands steady on the reins.

When Sandra took a late lunch break and microwaved a mini-pizza in the office kitchenette, Lincoln told her, "You made the right call, Sandra."

She reached down to hand a doggie treat to her poodle. The fluff ball danced up onto its hind legs to receive it. "The students are always my top priority."

He pulled a coffee mug from the cupboard and a glass for the milk Matt had requested. "How many days on the road this week?"

"Five. It's been a heavy week. I'm heading home when I'm finished here."

"Two more lessons?" He removed a carton of milk from the refrigerator and filled the glass.

"Three." The microwave beeped. She removed the pizza and looked at it with distaste. "After which, I'm going to splurge on a decent meal. Preferably with a salad bar." Her eyes narrowed in consideration. "Barbecue would be good. Maybe even a decadent dessert. Any recommendations?"

He set the glass aside on the counter and measured ground coffee into a French press. "How about a steak and chicken barbecue at the Seton Community Center? It comes with salads and homemade desserts—pies and cheesecakes. The ball club's putting it on. I've got two tickets, but I only need one. You're welcome to the other. There's even dancing after, if you're into that."

Her look warned him off. "I don't consort with parents of my students."

"Who said anything about consorting? The ticket's yours if you want it. I'll be there, but you can ignore me, if you want."

Sudden amusement glinted in her dark eyes, but all she said was, "I'll take it. I love a free meal."

* * *

"Turn around," Wendy said. "I need to see the back again."

Kimberley stared at the sea of yellow covering her body. "I look like a daffodil."

"Turn."

Obediently, she turned in a circle, entrusting herself to her sister-in-law's artistic eye.

"It's perfect."

"Not too tight?"

"Definitely not too tight." Wendy arched her back and pressed a hand against it. "The vet will like it. By the way, what happened to the handsome rancher?" She slid her hand to her belly and rubbed it.

Kimberley eyed her sister-in-law. "Are you sure you're all right? Maybe this is too much for you. You're thirty-nine weeks pregnant."

"It's just Braxton-Hicks contractions. They'll pass. I've been having them all week. You should wear your hair up, and we need to find shoes and a little purse to go with the dress."

"A *purse?*"

"I know you're the backpack type, but we're doing this right. Now, what about the rancher?"

She envisioned the anger on Lincoln's face after her barbed comment to him outside the ranch office that morning. "He saw my scars. End of interest. He told me they don't matter, but he definitely backed off after seeing them."

Wendy frowned. "After that look he gave you in the park? It was the kind that transcends anything. The only other time I've seen one like it was when I told Gary I'm a feminist, quasi-vegetarian who likes to paint nude men, and he still asked me to marry him."

Kimberley made a move toward the fitting room. "Gary used to be such a stiff shirt. You're good for him."

"Not so fast. How did you react when the rancher saw

your scars?"

If ever an expression was a dead giveaway, Kimberley knew hers was that expression.

"You fell apart."

"Into a million pieces."

"So, maybe he's waiting for you to put them back together again."

As far as Lincoln was concerned, she doubted she could put anything together. The closer she drew to Matt, the farther Lincoln backed away. "I don't think so."

"Then I think less of him."

"Wendy, is hiding my scars a form of vanity?"

Her sister-in-law's eyebrows shot up. "Well, going to great lengths to hide them would show…self-absorption."

"Do I go to great lengths?"

"You tell me."

Kimberley looked down at the daffodil. "I chose this dress because it hides them."

A kind smile curved her sister-in-law's mouth. "It's a beautiful dress, and you look like a million dollars in it. Forget you chose it because of the scars."

As Kimberley removed the yellow dress, her mind replayed her conversation with Lincoln outside the ranch office and the talk she'd shared with Matt in the blind. Two weeks ago, during that turbulent evening at the old Steele place, Lincoln had told her he wanted her on Turtle Mountain for his son. Well, as long as she stayed, Lincoln would have his wish—even if it meant going to bat for Matt against him.

Chapter 13

Lincoln pressed his electric shaver hard along his jaw line as though he could shave away the lingering irritation. His mind refused to drop his conversation with Kimberley outside the ranch office that morning. He glanced at Matt's reflection in the mirror. His son sat on the bathtub rim, swinging one leg back and forth. The kid's face was pensive, brooding. Lincoln turned off his shaver. "What's up, cowboy?"

"Did you hate my mom?"

He stared at his son. "Where did that come from?"

"You never talk about her. We don't even have any pictures of her."

He recalled the rage with which he'd crammed every photograph of Gayle he could find in the house into a box. He would have burned them except for his mother's plea to save them. She'd said that someday Matt would want them. It looked like that someday was now. He set the shaver on the sink counter and sat beside his son. "Your mother and I couldn't live together anymore, but I didn't hate her. There's a box of pictures at Grandma's house."

"I want to look at them—tonight." Belligerence tinged

Matt's voice.

He ignored it. "Okay."

"Kimmie said I should ask."

"Did she?" So that's where her comment about him not being able to look at a picture of Gayle had originated. "How did you and Kimberley get to be talking about your mother?"

"I told her about my scars."

The world shrank to the two of them seated on a bathtub edge. At last, Matt had splintered the darkness that had held him in its grip for five years. Since the beating, he'd seemed so much younger than his age—clingy and anxious. Now, suddenly, he was brave—challenging—and his eyes held a strength Lincoln had never seen before. *Maybe they can heal each other*, his mother had said. Now, it was happening. He'd remember Matt's matter-of-fact words for the rest of his life.

"Good job." He hugged his son to his side and sent silent, fervent thanks to Kimberley, every wisp of his irritation vanishing. Maybe the scars she'd wanted to talk about that morning were Matt's, not hers. And he'd jumped to the wrong conclusion, putting his big, clumsy foot into it again. "I'd better get a move on so I can fire up those barbecues."

"How many chickens and steaks this year, Dad?"

Lincoln rubbed a hand over his son's hair. "Enough to keep me busy." His mind flashed him an image of Matt in a Snugli baby carrier on Gayle's chest, his fine baby hair sticking straight up. People in the supermarket had stopped and asked to touch the softness of that red halo above Matt's sleeping face. And Gayle... Lincoln barricaded the image from his mind.

Matt hummed all the way to his grandmother's house. As he listened to the happy sound, Lincoln wished the distance was longer than three miles. He followed his son inside and breathed in the aroma of fresh-baked bread. He kissed his mother on the cheek. "If you ever want to sell this place, bake bread before the real estate agent shows prospective buyers around."

His mother slanted him one of her droll looks as she rubbed the hot loaves with buttered waxed paper. "I'll never sell. When I'm dead, just throw my ashes in the garden to add a little fertilizer."

"Hey, Matt." Terri rolled pastry dough on the kitchen's marble-topped island, a bowl of cinnamon-dusted apple wedges at her elbow. "Kimberley e-mailed me the owl pictures you took. I'll show them to you after I put this pie in the oven." She draped pastry over a ceramic pie plate and then began rolling out a second crust. "Want to go for a bike ride after supper? Maybe we can visit Kimberley."

Matt reached for an apple wedge from the bowl. "She won't be there. She's going to the barbecue, right, Dad?"

Lincoln met his mother's inquiring look. "That's right. She's going with Jake."

Terri's rolling pin clanked against the bowl, and he caught a stricken look in his sister's eyes before she batted Matt's fingers away. "Wash your hands." She coughed to clear her choked voice. "Then you can make the nibblies."

So that's how things stand. Snippets of Terri's spirited banter with Jake flitted through Lincoln's mind, as did memories of her attendance at every ball game. Obviously, his sister hadn't merely been keeping Matt company. But she was too young. What she felt for Jake had to be no more than a crush, although, come to think of it, she'd never had a boyfriend, never dated except for her prom, never expressed an interest in any of the boys at school or any of the male riders she'd met at competitions.

He watched Matt sprinkle sugar and cinnamon onto leftover bits of pastry on a cookie sheet, creating the family treat they called nibblies, and then turned to his mother. "Do you still have the box of pictures I packed up years ago?"

Her eyebrows lifted. "I do."

"Matt wants to see them."

There were times when his mother, calm and measured in so many ways, flamed with joy as though she'd caught a glimpse of eternity. She had that look about her as she smiled at Matt. "Of course. I'll find them after supper."

Lincoln wrapped an arm around his son. "See you later. I'll be back as soon as I can get away." He glanced at Terri. His sister's face was frozen into a strained smile.

* * *

In the old Steele place, Kimberley smoothed the yellow dress over her hips for the tenth time and touched her hair. Wendy had taught her how to coil its thickness into an elegant knot atop her head. She barely recognized herself in the mirror. *What am I playing at? I'm no fashionista.*

At six o'clock, she opened the back porch door at Jake's knock. His mouth dropped open, and he stood stock-still on the step, dressed in neat charcoal dress pants and a short-sleeved green shirt. "You look stunning!" he finally said, his brown eyes warm with appreciation.

"Hi. Thanks." She stepped to the side as Lexi pushed past, tail wagging.

Slanting her a smile, Jake ran a hand over Lexi's back. "She's forgiven me for jabbing a needle into her."

Kimberley guided Lexi into the porch and locked the house. "That was the least of her worries. When we pulled out the quills, anyone within hearing distance probably thought she was being tortured. I'm glad you were at the ranch."

Jake touched her elbow lightly as he walked with her to a silver BMW convertible he'd parked behind her truck. "So am I. Meeting you made my day." In the car, he flipped a switch to close the roof. "Save your hairdo."

Bemused, she relaxed into the convertible's rich burgundy upholstery. Two years ago, she and Bryan had jolted over desert tracks in the Australian Outback in a Land Rover, the vehicle coated with red dust and filled with camping and photography gear, extra vehicle parts, tools, and five-gallon jugs of life-sustaining water. They'd strapped jerry cans of gasoline to the roof and sweated their way through shoots across the continent. Saving her hairdo had never entered their minds. It had all been about the subject material, the adventure, the challenge, their passion for the outdoors. She reined in her reminiscences. Those days with Bryan were gone. Was she even the same person she'd been then? "It's a beautiful car," she told Jake. "Do you get called out at all hours, like the vets in the James Herriot books?"

"Two or three times a week." He reversed the car and turned it smoothly onto the driveway. "The woman I marry will have to be the understanding type. So will my kids."

"Maybe you can take them with you sometimes, like James did."

He threw her a grin. "Maybe. How's the photography going?"

"Excellent. I got some good shots of a fox hunting a mallard, and even better, Matt and I shot burrowing owls this morning."

Surprise swept across Jake's face. "Matthew went with you?"

"Yes, he asked if he could, and Lincoln gave me permission to take him."

"Then you've made a big impression on them both." He turned the car onto Sanderson Road. "Have you been to the park yet—Turtle Mountain Provincial Park?"

"Briefly, about two months ago. It's on my list for Monday."

"Keep an eye out for wild boars. A local couple out hiking last weekend got chased by one. I've also heard of people being bitten."

A tingle of unease lifted hairs on the back of her neck.

Bryan's face flashed into her mind. *Ready, Kimmie?* Working with Bryan, she hadn't been afraid of anything. Without him, would she ever be ready again? "I didn't know the park had wild boars."

"A few farmers to the north got permission to farm them in the eighties. Some escaped and hightailed it into the woods."

"I'm surprised they can survive the winters here."

"They're incredibly hardy, and they're major pests. They root up crops and gardens. People are allowed to shoot them almost anytime and anywhere."

"Thanks for the tip. I'll keep a lookout. Have you done much hiking in the park?"

"Nope, I'm not a hiker. Years ago, Linc used to drag me out once in a while, but it never stuck. He, on the other hand, was always out in the bush when he wasn't playing ball or doing ranch chores. He used to wear moccasins and trail animals and the whole bit. I was more of a bookworm. I'd tell him about something I'd read—*The Count of Monte Cristo* or something like that—and the next thing I knew, he'd read it, too." Jake shook his head. "He's a hard man to stay ahead of. Maybe that's why I've always liked him."

"Friendly competition?"

"Sometimes. Mostly, I think we've inspired each other."

In Seton, Jake parked outside a chunky, two-story building adjacent to a sun-scorched golf course. "It's a multipurpose building that houses the golf pro shop and curling rink downstairs and a banquet hall upstairs." He guided her inside and up a set of stairs. "Just in time," he added as they stepped into the hall.

She scanned the large rectangular room crowded with men and women seated at cloth-covered tables, with drinks in front of them. Other guests drifted toward a row of tables laden with bowls of salads and buns and with chafing dishes piled with grilled meats. "I thought this was a supper for the ball club."

"It's a supper put on *by* the ball club. We do it as a fundraiser for local charities. Linc came up with the idea. The Steele Cattle Company donates the meat, and other businesses make cash or food donations." Jake pointed to the hall's kitchen. "We cook it up, feast on it, and work it off on the dance floor. A few volunteers from outside the club come in to serve up the food so we can relax and enjoy it."

Here, people lend a hand. As Kimberley recalled Lincoln's comment, he stepped through double doors between the hall and a railed deck at the far end of the building, several shiny propane barbecues visible behind him. He carried a foil-covered tray to the kitchen, his movements laced with the feline grace so evident on the ball field.

"There's Linc. He's head barbecuer." Jake ushered her toward his friend. "Let's say hello."

She tensed. A snapshot of Matt's tear-streaked face appeared in her mind. The bases were loaded with a thousand conflicting emotions as she stepped forward to pinch hit for Lincoln's son.

* * *

After Lincoln washed his hands at the kitchen sink, he stepped into the hall and almost collided with his best friend and a vision in yellow. "Jake." He shook his buddy's hand and turned to Kimberley. She could have stepped out of a fashion magazine. A bright yellow dress hugged her curves and revealed an inch of tanned thigh above her knees. Flowery lace covered the dress's opaque fabric and ran sheer over her shoulders and down to her elbows. Light makeup disguised the hairline scar, and she'd twisted her hair up onto her head. So far as he could tell, not a single tendril hung loose. He'd like to pull out the hairpins and let that black mane fall over his hands—hardly the thing to do with his best friend's date. "Hello, Kimberley. You look—"

"Like a vain city girl?" Her eyes threw blue light into his.

So, his comments had stung. "Beautiful is the word I had in mind. I think your mother would have approved."

She lifted her chin, her gaze cool. "Speaking of mothers, Matt told me about his mother this morning. He really misses her."

Old anger sliced through him. "Matt's mother neglected him."

"Once." Jake's voice was calm. "Gayle didn't pick him up on time from the babysitter *once*."

"That I know of."

"It just happened to be the day the abuse occurred.

Come on, Linc, the babysitter was new, and Gayle couldn't have known it would happen. If you'd let yourself admit it, you'd know that from the day Matthew was born, Gayle adored him."

Kimberley frowned. "Matt said you blamed his mother for the abuse."

"I never told him that."

"He overheard you telling your mother—perhaps years ago. I don't know."

"There's a lot you don't know."

Jake's gaze warned him. "Ease off, Linc. Kimberley's not attacking you. She's just relating a conversation she had with Matthew."

Storm clouds roiled in Kimberley's eyes. She looked as though she intended to pursue the subject, but instead drew in a breath and said, "I hear you're head barbecuer."

Taking her cue, he wrestled his irritation under control. Despite the sparks that had flown between them, he owed her a huge debt of gratitude for the way she'd helped his son that morning. "It's my one cooking skill. Matt and I live on burgers and steaks."

"Hardly." Jake's face relaxed. "For Matthew's birthday last summer, Linc barbecued a salmon and even grilled bananas and peaches to go with our cake and ice cream. Terri dragged me to the feast after I'd stitched up a cow's shoulder."

That scenario took on a different light now. A pang for his sister darted through Lincoln. "You were so hungry, you looked like you could've eaten the whole salmon."

"After the meal, I felt like I had."

A flash of red caught Lincoln's eye. He flicked a glance past Kimberley to where a tiny woman in a shimmery scarlet halter dress stood near the hall door. Her dark curls tumbled onto her shoulders, one wing of hair swept behind an ear and secured with a sparkling comb. "Well, what do you know."

Jake's eyebrows shot up. "Sandra." He lifted a hand in acknowledgement, and Sandra Aguilera responded in kind. "I didn't expect to see her here. We should say hello."

"Go ahead. I'll catch up with you later." Lincoln nodded and stepped away. Memories he'd banished to a dark corner of his mind clambered up the walls of his self-control, their chains loosed by the conversation with Kimberley. He greeted team members and guests and exchanged comments about the drought and the severe thunderstorm warning in effect for the night, all the while sensing that he was tail-spinning into a collision with his past. He joined the food line and piled his plate with meat and salads and then looked around for an empty seat. Jake waved him over to a table cluttered with ball players, Sandra and Kimberley a couple of exotic flowers among the men. The only empty seat was beside Kimberley. "Mind if I sit here?" he asked.

Her eyes met his, a storm watch in their depths. "Not at all."

As he seated himself, he ran his gaze down her tanned legs to open-toed pumps the exact shade of her dress. "The shoes are a nice touch."

"My sister-in-law painted them." She gave a slight grimace. "They look great, but my feet are already balking at wearing them. I'm more the hiking boot type."

"Boots might be a bit awkward on the dance floor."

Her teeth gleamed in her tanned face. "They might at that."

He was close enough to catch her hair's faint lemony fragrance, to get lost in the blue of her eyes. Kimberley Colter was turning his world upside down.

From across the table, Sandra commented, "This is the best coleslaw I've ever eaten."

Jake leaned back in his chair. "It's a secret family recipe."

"Passed down through generations, no doubt."

"Of course."

"You made it?"

"I did."

Sandra raised her eyebrows. "A vet who cooks great food. At the risk of sounding sexist, I'm surprised you're not married."

Jake laughed, and so did the other ball players seated near him. "I'm hoping to rectify that situation soon," he said.

"Good luck."

Surprise skimmed across Kimberley's face.

Lincoln encircled her wrist with his fingers, his action hidden below table level. The same electric awareness from the park; from the meadow; from the old Steele place flashed between them. Her eyes widened. He asked softly,

"And you? Are you hoping to marry soon?"

"You know I was nearly married and wanted children," she whispered.

"And now?"

Her pulse throbbed beneath his fingers. "More than ever."

Releasing her wrist, Lincoln reached for his fork and knife and spoke up. "Then it looks like you've come to the right place."

"The right place for what?" Jake asked, looking at him over Kimberley's head.

"Prairie wildlife."

"Kimberley mentioned that she photographed burrowing owls this morning."

The team's catcher, a short, burly farmer named Mike, addressed Kimberley, "We've got a badger den on our land. I saw the old one and two young 'uns a few times last week. You'd be welcome to take pictures of them."

Mike's comment set off a flurry of invitations for Kimberley to photograph local fauna.

As he listened to her keen responses, Lincoln ate his meal in silence. Life had thrown him plenty of curve balls in his twenty-eight years, but Jake's pronouncement about hoping to marry soon left him swinging at thin air. There was little doubt that his friend was referring to Kimberley, even though he'd met her less than two weeks ago. But that was Jake. All his life, he'd cheerfully worked his way from one accomplishment to the next, his focus absolute on the task at hand. Now that focus was on Kimberley.

After Lincoln had emptied his plate, he had no recollection of tasting any of the food. He pushed his chair back and rose to his feet.

"Where are you headed?" Jake asked.

"My shift at the bar."

Hip-to-hip or hands entwined, couples abandoned tables for the dance floor. A DJ's mix of pop and country music led them into waltzes and polkas, foxtrots and jives, even the twist and chicken dance. From behind the counter at the bar, Lincoln watched Jake take Kimberley in his arms and considered the price of his son's happiness.

* * *

After several dances with Jake, Kimberley reclaimed her chair and eased off her pumps. A sweet-scented breeze wafted in through open doors and brushed her face, making her want to pull herself hand over hand along its whispered length to the prairie beyond the town—to the dried grass and burrowing owls.

Jake leaned toward her and spoke over the loud music, "I'm going to grab another coke. Would you like something?"

"Orange juice and soda, please."

She watched him wind his way along the edge of the dance floor to the bar, where Lincoln stood dispensing drinks behind a counter. She'd pushed a red-hot button when she'd mentioned Matt's mother. Lincoln's reaction had been instantaneous and totally unforgiving of his former wife. Would one instance of forgetfulness on his ex's part—although it had resulted in traumatic consequences for Matt—have been enough to trigger such a vehement response? And what had he meant by ensnaring her wrist and questioning her?

"Would you like to dance, Kimberley?"

She jerked her attention to the red-haired man who had slipped into Jake's seat. Instantly, her internal warning system kicked into gear. *Phil.* The last thing she wanted was to insert her feet into her pumps again and dance with anyone, let alone the Steele Cattle Company's stockman. Yet his eyes stayed on her face—no body scan this time. Perhaps she'd misjudged him in the wheat field. "All right. Just give me a sec to put my shoes on." She was new in the area, and Seton was a small town. No point in stepping on anyone's toes. Phil guided her onto the dance floor and into a jive. Surprisingly light on his feet, he was a much better dancer than ball player. Her shoulders relaxed, and she actually enjoyed the dance.

When the music changed to a waltz, she expected Phil to accompany her back to the table. Instead, he drew her into a tight embrace. She tensed into withdrawal and tried to ease back, but his grip locked her within an inch of him. His thighs brushed hers, and his exhalations smelled of whiskey. This was a close encounter she could have avoided had she listened to her intuition.

Phil grinned at her, lust smoldering in his eyes. "You look so good tonight, a man could forget about those scars on your arm."

"Really?" If only he knew. "What a gentlemanly thing

to say."

"I aim to please."

"Then loosen up. I'm feeling squashed."

"I'd rather get a whole lot closer." He tugged her against him, his chest thrusting against her breasts, his paunch pressing into her navel.

Outraged, she pushed her palms against his shoulders. "Let me go!"

He barked out a laugh. "I like a woman with a little fight in her."

Stumbling over his foot, she caught her balance and raised her right pump high, ready to slam it down onto his instep.

* * *

Lincoln saw Kimberley stiffen when Phil Johnson asked her to dance. His gaze followed the couple onto the dance floor.

Across the counter from him, Jake asked, "What's up?"

Lincoln nodded toward the dancers, and Jake turned to follow his gaze.

Sandra strolled up to the bar. "The two of you look ready to tear him apart."

As if on cue, Jake's cell phone rang. He grimaced. "It's a work call. Excuse me."

Tom McCorquodale, the team's pitcher and a school buddy, thumbed Lincoln away from the bar. "My turn. Go have some fun."

Lincoln smiled wryly. God was playing games again.

Why not just tap him on the shoulder and point? He turned to Sandra, "Is a dance considered consorting?"

She raised an eyebrow. "Not one dance, no."

"How good are you at handling belligerent men?"

"Not you, I take it."

He grinned. "Not this time." He nodded to where Phil pulled Kimberley into a tight embrace, tension written all over her. Right now he wanted to rip Phil's arms from their sockets. "Phil has a hard time keeping his hands to himself."

Sandra's eyes narrowed. "He won't know what hit him."

"Then let's dance."

Her olive skin bared by the halter dress was warm and smooth under his hands as he took her in his arms. "Do you stash a dress like this in your car every week when you're on the road?"

Her lips curved into a bewitching smile Lincoln had never seen in the ring or arena. "I could say that a woman never knows when she might need a red dress, but the truth is that I bought it and the shoes in Winnipeg on Tuesday and haven't been home since. Time to cut in, wouldn't you say?"

He twirled her under his arm, the flashy dress flaring. "You're a good sport, Sandra."

"Like I said, I love a free meal."

They glided up to Phil and Kimberley, and he tapped Phil on the shoulder. "Trade partners, Phil? Kimberley promised me a dance."

The other man threw him a hard look. "You're not the boss here. I—" On catching sight of Sandra, his expression switched to a surprised smirk. "Well, well. Things are looking better by the minute." He released Kimberley. "She's all yours. She was getting ugly anyway."

* * *

"I could have dealt with him," Kimberley snapped when Lincoln took her right hand in his left and placed his other hand on her back. A tremor ran through her as she raised her free hand to his shoulder. No man had the right to look as good as he did and be so mercurial. Yet he was always near, always helping her.

He ran his amber gaze over her face. "I asked you to save me a dance. This is it."

Why couldn't she rest as easy with him as she did with Jake? All evening, her escort had been attentive, sharing humorous comments about Turtle Mountain life and drawing her into conversations with his friends and acquaintances. Even so, it had been impossible to get Lincoln off her radar. "Are you saying it's a coincidence that you asked for this particular dance?"

"No, I'm not, and I know what you're going to say."

"I doubt it. In another second, I would have ground my heel into his instep."

Dimples appeared in his cheeks. "Sorry to have deprived you of that satisfaction."

She tilted her head to study him as she followed the smooth, one-two-three pattern of his steps. "Why do you talk like that?"

He frowned. "What do you mean?"

"Some of the time you're a normal guy, and some of the time you talk about magic in a meadow or say 'Sorry to have deprived you of that satisfaction.' I didn't think ranchers carried English books in their saddlebags."

"Does it bother you?"

She found herself rising onto her toes on each of the waltz's downbeats, guided by his hand's firm pressure on her back. "No, it doesn't bother me, I just wondered. And I feel like I'm on a boat."

The heart-throb grin appeared. "You'll get used to it. The rise and fall makes a waltz smoother and more elegant." He drew her closer when a couple swept past her shoulder, then eased his grip. "My mother was working on a masters in English when my biological father died. She switched to accounting as a more practical career for a single parent. Terri and I grew up hearing the classics read to us. I guess some of it rubbed off."

His touch burned through the bright dress. "Why are you so protective of me when you've never—"

A different couple bumped her arm. The man immediately apologized, and Kimberley assured him she was fine, then flashed a look up at Lincoln. "I've never thought of dancing as a contact sport."

"It's like sardines in here," he muttered, drawing her close and not easing his grip this time.

Her breath left her body. Two more inches and she'd be right back where she'd been that night at the old Steele place.

"You were saying? When I've never…?"

She swallowed hard. "Forgiven your wife."

"I don't have a wife."

"Your ex-wife."

"We never divorced."

Her temper flared. "Now you're being obtuse."

"And you're spoiling for a fight."

She flashed a challenge up at him. "Maybe I am. What did Gayle do that was so horrible that you won't let Matt have a picture of her?"

His eyes held a warning. "Kimberley, you don't know anything about it."

"I know she wasn't the one who abused him."

"Let's drop it."

"Matt *cried* this morning. He told me he thinks you hate his mother even when she's dead."

"I said let's drop it."

"Obviously, she made a big mistake in her choice of babysitter, but is that enough to ban her image from your home?"

His grip slackened. "Why this sudden interest in Gayle?"

She didn't step away. "I'm not interested in Gayle. I'm interested in Matt. He doesn't understand why you act like his mother never existed, why you never talk about her. Maybe you didn't trust her, but—"

"You got that right," he bit out harshly.

Loud music filled the air, and dancers pressed against

them, yet everything faded except for his expression. Agony slammed across his features before bitterness replaced it, and in that instant, she knew. "It wasn't just what happened to Matt, was it? It was what she did to *you*."

Chapter 14

The waltz ended as Kimberley uttered her catalytic words. Lincoln held himself together long enough to escort her back to Jake and then escaped onto the deck. He gripped the railing. His life was imploding. A vision tore at his mind: the bedroom door open, Gayle's long red hair spilling down her back, her naked body arching into Lane Brake's. In one prolonged afternoon indiscretion, Gayle Steele had destroyed both her marriage and her son's innocent joy. Lincoln sucked in the prairie wind as though its freshness could erase the image scorching his mind.

"You all right?" Jake leaned against the railing, his brow creased. "You didn't look so good in there."

"I just needed some air."

"Kimberley hit another sore spot?"

He didn't answer.

"You know, it might be a good thing if, one of these days, you talk to someone about what happened that day."

"You mean a shrink?"

His friend eyed him calmly. "Maybe. Or someone you trust. Whatever Gayle did or didn't do, you need to let it go. It's been eating at you for five years and the bite-marks aren't pretty. You were downright rude to Kimberley earlier. She has Matthew's best interests at heart, you know."

"She packs quite a punch."

A faint smile touched Jake's mouth. "So far, I haven't been in her line of fire. I came to ask you a favor, but now I'm not sure it's a good idea."

"What is it?"

"I've got an urgent case thirty minutes west of town. I could be there for hours. I was going to ask if you'd drive Kimberley home."

"She'd probably prefer to walk barefoot over hot coals."

Jake searched his face. "She told me to tell you that she'll behave. If you don't mind me asking, is there something going on between the two of you?"

"Yeah, a whole lot of aggravation."

"That's it?"

"You think there's more?"

"You trusted her with Matthew this morning. That says a lot."

"There's a bond between the two of them, ever since they met in the park two months ago."

Jake stiffened. "I didn't realize you'd known her before she moved here."

"I didn't know her."

"So, how did she end up here?"

"God only knows." Almost to himself, he added, "Maybe he thought it was time to set Matt free."

Jake pushed away from the railing. "Maybe he thought it was time to set you free, too."

Thunderheads towered over the western horizon. Lightning flashed silver against the dark mass. Lincoln stared at the approaching storm. If this emotional turmoil was God setting him free, then the Man Upstairs had left spikes in the gateway.

"Will you take her?" Jake asked.

"I'll take her."

* * *

Kimberley eyed Lincoln's truck. Jake's BMW had been easy to step into, but the pickup was a different story. How was she supposed to climb into it without hiking up her dress? She grimaced at the yellow sheath and stepped out of her pumps. The parking lot's gravel gouged her bare feet.

Lincoln scowled as he opened the passenger door. "What are you doing?"

She sighed. It was going to be a long ride home. She picked up her shoes and tossed them into the immaculate truck. "There's a reason why climbers don't wear pumps and tight dresses." She tugged the dress high onto her legs. The action exposed a dozen white bite scars on her right thigh, the skin faintly puckered around each mark. What did it matter? He'd already seen more of her scars than any man who wasn't a doctor or family member. She placed her left foot on the door frame and, as she hopped up, prayed the dress wouldn't rip. When she was seated, she pulled the bright fabric down over her thighs and met his gaze defiantly. "Another part of the collection."

"So I see. You said there were more." He nodded toward the daffodil. "That dress was made for you. You should wear it often."

She stared at him. Where had his annoyance gone?

In the truck he nodded at the thunderheads stacked over the prairie. "Good thing you're not afraid of storms."

They drove straight into it. Evening vanished in blue-black air denser than night. Lightning bolts blasted searing light over the prairie, their strobe-light flashes revealing farmhouses surrounded by towering shelterbelts and grain fields heaving in the wind. Sky-shuddering claps of thunder chased the lightning, and rain spattered the windshield and then pounded down in liquid fury that reduced visibility to next to nothing. A transport truck roared past, the lights on its phantom bulk smeared by sheets of rain.

"My stepfather died in a collision with one of those in a storm." Lincoln steered the pickup onto the highway's shoulder and inched forward into a barely-seen access track to a farm field. "We'll wait out the worst of it."

She groaned silently, pressing her fingertips along her hairline. *How long?*

"What's wrong?"

"I don't mind waiting, but my scalp is screaming from this hairdo."

"So, undo it."

In the muted light of the truck's interior, she removed

every pin, allowing her thick, heavy hair to uncoil and spill down over her upraised arms. She shook her head and ran her fingers through the tresses. "That's better. I've felt like an imposter all evening. Now all I need to do is get out of this dress." Her gaze locked with his. Why not just issue him another invitation? "I didn't mean that the way it sounded."

A muscle twitched in his jaw. "How did you escape?"

The question wasn't at all what she'd expected. "I beg your pardon?"

"The grizzly killed your fiancé. How did you escape?"

Brown blur charging with unbelievable speed. Mountain of fury. Jaws wide. Bryan's shout, "Get into the rocks, Kimmie!" Her body thrown across the trail. And then, Bryan's screams. She clenched her hands as the memories flooded her mind. "Bryan stepped between the sow and me. She sent both of us flying, but I was able to roll into a rocky crevice while she...killed him."

"I'm sorry. I shouldn't have asked."

"No, the therapist hammered into me that it's important to talk about it." She drew in a shaky breath. "The bear pulled me out of the rocks. My pack gave me some protection, but she had me by the shoulder, then the leg, and was clawing at my chest and scalp. I felt like I was being torn apart."

"But you got away."

"No. She left. The seconds Bryan had given me were just enough for me to get my pepper spray off my belt, and I managed to blast her in the eyes while she was biting my leg. She let go and ran off. Some hikers found me—they'd heard screams. One happened to be a doctor. I was told later that I would have bled to death except for her. I was airlifted out, and then the plastic people sewed me back together."

They sat silent in the truck. Scattered raindrops speckled the windshield, and thunder rumbled in the distance to the east. In the west, late evening sunshine cast golden light over the prairie and painted a rainbow on the dark eastern sky.

So much beauty, so much promise when the storm is over. Exhaustion swept through Kimberley, yet it was exhaustion infused with peace and the knowledge that she'd crossed a threshold. "Do you know something, Lincoln? For a year, I've wondered why—when Bryan died—God allowed me to live. Now I know why. It was so I could help Matt. I really haven't done that much yet, but we seem to have a connection."

"That you do. Matt definitely broke through a barrier when he told you about his scars. I intended to thank you at the banquet, but we got off on the wrong foot."

"You mean *I* got off on the wrong foot. I had no right to pry into your personal life. I'm sorry. My brother calls me a tank."

His eyes teased her. "Prepare to be crushed."

"Ouch! I deserved that. Take me home, Lincoln. It's been a long day."

The rest of the drive passed in silence. She rested her head against the headrest, her eyes closed. He escorted her to the farmhouse door, where she turned to him, her shoes in one hand, her small white purse in the other. "Truce?" she asked quietly.

"Truce."

"By the way, I'd like to enter a pic of you and Matt in this year's Nat Geo photography contest. It's a shot I took of the two of you in the wheat field after the hail storm. Would that be okay?"

"Go for it. Show it to me sometime."

"I will. Goodnight, and thanks for the ride."

As he drove away, she walked with Lexi through the darkness beneath the elms, her husky a white-edged ghost beside her.

* * *

In the log house, Terri put a finger to her lips and motioned for Lincoln to follow her into the living room, where Matt lay asleep on the sofa, a framed photograph clutched in his small hand. Other framed pictures lay beside an empty box on the floor.

Terri's eyes glistened. "We told him every good thing we could remember about Gayle."

"Something you should have done years ago," his mother added, her face weary. "Darling, Gayle truly loved Matt. I've always believed that. She would never have knowingly put him in danger."

"Thanks, both of you." If Kimberley's questions earlier in the evening had set him on a collision course with his past, the fallout from that collision was landing all around him. As he walked toward the sofa, Lincoln knew he was walking toward heartbreak. He knelt on the carpet and looked down. Gayle smiled boldly up at him from their wedding photograph. Gayle looked enchantingly sweet in a maternity dress. Gayle's face radiated love as she looked down at Matt in a Snugli on her chest, his fine baby hair sticking straight up like a red downy halo.

With trembling hands, he gathered the photographs, placed them in the box, and then tugged at the frame in Matt's hand.

His son roused from sleep. "No! I want to take it home."

Lincoln scooped him into his arms. "*Shh*. It's all right. We'll take it home. We'll take them all home."

At the cedar house, he tucked Matt into bed and then carried the box of photographs out onto the deck. Bats swooped to capture insects fluttering around two deck lamps as he carefully placed each picture face-up on a picnic table. He pored over the images in turn, studying the fiery girl who had captured his heart, the restless young woman who had given him his son. His wife. His family.

A Christmas photo taken the year before his and Gayle's marriage breakup drew his gaze again and again. In it, he and Matt, both dusted with snow, grinned at the camera, but Gayle...He frowned and looked more closely. Gayle's lips curved, but her eyes held sadness, as though behind the smile her heart was broken.

His chest tightened. How could it be that he only noticed the sadness now? That he'd never seen it when she was alive and beautiful and in his arms? Remorse slashed through him. When had he stopped seeing his wife? How much of what had happened that fateful day had been his fault? If he'd been less absorbed in the ranch, would Gayle have remained faithful instead of turning to another man? Would Matt have never suffered the abuse? Would Gayle still be alive?

Pain ripped through his heart as he stared at the picture of Gayle holding Matt in the Snugli. His wife had loved their son, had absolutely, undeniably loved Matt. *I'm sorry. Forgive me.* As a three-quarter moon rose in the storm-washed sky, Lincoln cradled his head in his hands and wept.

Chapter 15

Morning mist hung over the wetland north of the old Steele place. In her blind, Kimberley peered into the whiteness. She wanted a moody shot of vapor-screened water birds or the juxtaposition of black silhouettes and sun-shot mist. When her cell phone vibrated in her pocket, she glanced at the number and paused to take the call. "I'm shooting, Gary. What's up?"

"We're at the hospital. Wendy's in labor. It's going fast." Anxiety laced her brother's voice.

"I'm on my way." She slipped out of the blind and hurried through the dew-drenched prairie and hay field. In the yard, Lexi strained against the leash clipped to the clothesline strung between two elms.

"What am I going to do with you?" She unclipped the leash. "I don't know how long I'll be gone." Her husky bounded away and pounced on a fallen branch, dragging it back to her to play tug-o-war.

Matt. She called Lexi to heel, hurried into the yellow house, and paged through the worn telephone book, punching Lincoln's number into her phone. After four rings, she glanced at her watch and could have kicked herself—it was seven-thirty on a Sunday morning. She was about to end the call when a familiar voice responded, "Lincoln Steele here."

He sounded too alert to have been asleep moments before. "It's Kimberley. Sorry to call so early. I was out shooting and didn't realize the time."

"No problem. What can I do for you?"

"My brother phoned. His wife has gone into labor. If it's all right with you, I'd like to ask Matt to look after Lexi so I can be with them." She mentally kicked herself again. "But he's probably still asleep."

"He is, but bring the dog over. She can wake him up."

Five minutes later, she turned her Ranger onto Lincoln's access road. The gravel track wound through a grove of aspens, across a bridge over a trickling stream, and then through a sunny clearing. At the clearing's far edge, a parched lawn accented with blue spruces surrounded a cedar house and detached double garage. So this was Lincoln's lair. She pulled up beside his pickup in front of the garage.

A screen door opened, and the man in her thoughts stepped barefoot onto a cedar deck, attired in black nylon gym shorts and a red polo shirt, a white towel in his hands. His face was flushed, and sweat dampened his hair and gleamed on his bare limbs. Apparently, she'd interrupted a work out.

"You've got a beautiful spot." She stepped up onto the deck with Lexi beside her. "You must see plenty of wildlife."

"It's one of the reasons I built here." He wiped the towel across his face. "Terrence used to grumble about farmers and ranchers who drained sloughs and cut trees and then headed for water and trees on the weekend. I took his message to heart."

Remorse smacked her as she noted fatigue lines on his face. "Restless night?"

His smile erased some of the fatigue. "A late night, but one I needed. Any idea when you'll be back?"

She pulled a slip of paper from the breast pocket of her camo shirt. "Barring complications, I should be back well before dark. Here's my cell number in case you need to contact me." She handed him Lexi's leash and the pack containing her dog's dishes and food. Lexi looked up at her. "It's all right. Lincoln's all right. Go to him."

When he tugged firmly on the leash, Lexi walked to him and sniffed at his legs, tail wagging tentatively. "That's probably the most I can expect after the quill episode."

"Once she realizes you belong to Matt, she'll be more accepting." She flashed a grateful smile over her shoulder as she descended the steps. "Thanks a million. See you later."

At the hospital in Brandon, she watched the last stages of the labor, in awe at her sister-in-law's fortitude and peace. Wendy was already fully dilated, her dreadlocks drenched with sweat, every ounce of her being laser-focused on controlling her panting breaths. When the attending obstetrician gave the command to push, Wendy bore down, then gasped in air and panted again. Standing beside her, Gary gripped her hand, his face drawn. At 10:03 a.m., Damien Elliott Colter entered the world with a rousing wail. The doctor lifted him for Wendy to see. "Looks like you might have an opera singer here."

Kimberley snapped photos of Gary and Wendy's tired, entranced smiles as they celebrated their newborn's arrival: eight pounds, six ounces, twenty-one inches long, head lopsided and pointed, face brick red from howling. The birth had been so intense, so viscerally beautiful. An hour later, she cradled Damien, her heart tearing with joy at the miracle in her arms.

* * *

As a red truck emerged from his aspen grove, Lincoln looked up from flipping burgers on the barbecue. "Mission accomplished?" he called when Kimberley climbed out of her vehicle.

She mounted the steps, her face lit by a smile reminiscent of the one that had sent him to the old Steele place on a Friday evening. "One baby safely delivered. I now have a nephew."

Matt and Lexi bounded up the steps, the husky shivering with delight at Kimberley's touch.

"What's the baby's name?" Matt asked. "How big is it?"

"His name is Damien, and he's—" she spread her hands apart "—this long."

Matt frowned. "He's tiny."

Lincoln mussed his hair. "So were you when you were born. Got time for a burger, Kimberley? I can throw on an extra one."

Matt reached out to her. "Please stay. I want to show you something."

She paused briefly, suspended in time while testing her environment—in this case Matt and him—for its potential. He'd seen her do it before—in the meadow, on the diamond, in the hall before he'd taken her in his arms to waltz. Maybe it was a photography tactic. At any rate, she used it to size up a new situation fast. A fraction of a second later, the nearly imperceptible pause had evaporated.

"A burger sounds great," she told him. "I'm famished."

No storm watch in those blue eyes this time.

Matt took her hand. "Come with me."

She threw a surprised look over her shoulder before following, her black hair spilling over her shoulders.

Lincoln watched his son lead her into the house. The last time a woman with a thick mane of hair had entered his home, the color of that hair had been red.

* * *

Uncluttered and simply furnished, Lincoln's home bespoke the prairie, its large windows inviting Kimberley to view the expansive sky, meadow, and grove of nearby trees. She caught glimpses of a kitchen island topped with burger fixings, of an acoustic guitar leaning against a green leather sofa in a living room, and of carpentry tools scattered on the hardwood floor of an empty room.

Matt stepped through a doorway to his right. "Here's my room. Look!"

Photographs of a woman whose red hair spilled down her back in a wavy mane hung on the walls and perched on every furniture surface other than the bed. Some were casual snapshots; others, studio portraits. Matt led her to a set of shelves holding comic books and a half-dozen of the photos. "This is my mom."

Kimberley gazed into blue eyes the same shade as Matt's but holding none of his vulnerability. Instead, Gayle Steele's gaze was coy, alluring, bold, teasing, sweet in pregnancy, radiating love as a mother. How could Lincoln have ever doubted this woman's feelings for her son?

She smiled down at Matt. "She's beautiful. And she looks so happy holding you."

He nodded, his tight hand-clasp transmitting the joy that blazed through him. He showed her each photo in turn, reciting descriptions he'd undoubtedly heard from Terri, Lauren—or Lincoln, who in a wedding photo looked so young, so happy standing beside his bride. What had happened to transform that elation into bitterness?

"Burgers are ready."

She jerked away from the wedding portrait. Lincoln's exhausted expression early that morning had hinted at a battle with emotional demons the previous evening, yet now his gaze was calm. Apparently, he'd come out on top.

Matt scampered past his father. "Good. I'm starving."

Lincoln leaned against the door jamb, his jeans and

polo shirt smudged with white powder that looked like wallboard dust. When she didn't move, he raised his eyebrows.

"You're a good man, Lincoln."

"Once in a while I need a reminder that it's not all about me."

"I never assumed you thought it was all about you."

"Gayle did."

"Was she right?"

He shrugged. "I was sour at losing my chance at the big league and in over my head running the ranch. I wasn't always there for her. In fact, a lot of days I wasn't there for her at all."

"You paint a dark picture of yourself."

"It's who I was."

She imagined his lonely young wife feeling neglected. "Did she turn to someone else?"

Wariness entered his eyes. "She did."

The puzzle pieces snapped together. "And she was with him the day Matt got hurt. That's why she didn't pick him up."

Matt's shout from the kitchen startled them both. "Are you two *ever* coming?"

"Bingo." Lincoln pushed away from the door jamb, his face scored with pain.

Her emotions churned as she followed him to the kitchen. So, Matt wasn't the only one scarred by the abuse.

* * *

Lincoln carried a tray of buns and condiments onto the deck and placed it on the picnic table. Behind him, Matt and Kimberley followed with drinks, glasses, and a plate of rice crisp and marshmallow squares. What had Jake said? *You know, it might be a good thing if, one of these days, you talk to someone about what happened that day.* Well, he finally had, and now his broken marriage stood as exposed as a gopher standing on the dirt mound beside its burrow. He lifted the barbecue lid and slid thick burgers onto a plate.

Kimberley spread cucumber relish on a bun. "Are you renovating? You have white dust on your clothes, and I saw tools in an empty room."

Before he could answer, she extracted her cell phone from her pocket and checked the number. "Excuse me." Her black hair shifted from side to side as she walked a half-dozen steps along the deck. "Hi, Jake. Is it all right if call you back in half an hour? Thanks."

Speak of the man. Jake was nothing if not persistent. At Matt's age, he'd set his sights on becoming a veterinarian and had never wavered. After he'd graduated at the head of his class at veterinary school in Saskatoon, he'd come home to take over from a retired vet. In all the years Lincoln had known him, Jake had never had a steady girlfriend, which was why his announcement the previous evening about hoping to marry soon had come as a complete surprise.

Kimberley took a seat beside Matt at the table. "Sorry

for the interruption. I asked if you're renovating?"

"Dad's ripping apart his old bedroom." Matt squirted ketchup onto his burger and giggled when the plastic bottle blatted rudely. "He wants a church ceiling."

"A cathedral ceiling." Lincoln poured himself a glass of milk. "What's next on your shutterbug schedule? More burrowing owls? Mike's badgers?"

She savored a bite of burger and swallowed. "This burger's delicious. What's your secret?

"Soy sauce."

"I wouldn't have guessed. My schedule? Tomorrow I'll do a reconnaissance in the park."

"A what?" Matt's gaze swung up to her face.

"A look around to see what's there. I have a portable blind I can drape over myself and my camera gear if I find a good spot to set up. I'll show it to you next time you're over."

He nodded, the joyous K-light shining in his eyes.

"Oh! And I have pictures of the baby." She pulled a tiny black camera from her pocket. "Most of mine are on a different camera, but my brother took a few with this one. That's Wendy and Damien." She handed the camera to Matt.

"Matt, wipe your hands on your napkin first," Lincoln said quickly. "And mop the ketchup around your mouth."

His son grinned, wiped, and accepted the camera. "Gosh! His face is really red." He clicked the advance button and looked up at Kimberley. "Hey, you're holding the baby. Look, Dad."

Lincoln reached across the table for the camera and studied the image displayed on its screen. In it, Kimberley stood near a window with a red-faced infant bundled up in her arms. He barely glanced at the baby, his attention caught instead by the expression of wonder and longing on her face—she yearned for a child. And Jake was looking for a wife. He shoved away the potential connection. "You look good with a baby in your arms."

"Are you going to have a baby?" Matt asked, looking intently into Kimberley's face.

She laughed. "Someday, I hope to."

"But you have to get married first."

"Yes." She swung her gaze from Matt to him. "Will you do all the renovations yourself?"

He handed the camera back to her. "I'll gut the room and hire someone who knows what they're doing to install the new walls and ceiling."

"Dad's almost done, and he just started this morning."

"Then your father works fast." She poured a glass of lemonade. "Simply emptying a room can take hours."

"That room was empty ever since I was little."

As she paused infinitesimally, Lincoln could almost see the wheels turning.

"Want a square, Matt?" He passed the plate of sweets to his son, who in turn offered it to Kimberley. The kid was turning into a regular chatterbox and now he'd unknowingly conveyed to Kimberley what Lincoln had doubted he could ever tell anyone—that his wife had been unfaithful to him in their own bedroom.

Kimberley plucked a square from the plate and looked straight into his eyes. No flinching from what Matt had revealed, and no pity; instead, strength and encouragement. She raised her glass in a toast. "I think a cathedral ceiling is a great idea."

* * *

Kimberley steered her truck onto the access road to the old Steele place. In the yellow house, she dialed Jake's number and listened for his answer while mentally listing equipment she'd need for the next morning's shoot in the park.

Jake picked up after the first ring. "Hello. First off, let me apologize again for deserting you at the dance last night. Obviously you survived the ride home. How about Linc?"

She laughed. "We called a truce."

"Good. Things were getting a little too tense for comfort between the two of you." His voice took on a brisker tone. "The reason I'm calling is because I'll be doing my rounds at a wildlife rehab center north of town on Tuesday morning and thought you might find it interesting. The center has a collection of injured raptors, most of them hit by cars. They might make for some good photos, in context."

She pursed her lips. "Sounds like a possibility."

"I confess I have an ulterior motive for inviting you."

Did she detect a trace of shyness? "Really? What's that?"

"I'm writing an article about the center to garner publicity and support. I thought that a set of professional photographs accompanying it might go a long way toward piquing an editor's interest, especially with your reputation."

Her eyebrows lifted. "I didn't realize you're familiar with my work."

"I wasn't, but I did some research. Wildlife Photographer of the Year. Very impressive. Your photo of the polar bear drifting on that small ice pan, gazing up into the Arctic sky, is spectacular."

Like a jagged shard of ice, sorrow swept through Kimberley. Bryan had proposed to her on the Arctic shoot. After leaving Churchill, they'd flown to Ellesmere Island and camped at Alexandra Fiord, a deep, narrow inlet of salt water bordered on the south by an arctic oasis in what was otherwise polar desert. On a breathless night as bright as day, they'd photographed walruses in the fiord, the huge mammals' exhalations spilling out like steam over the still water. Glaciers had hung from Thorvald Peninsula in the background, and an ice floe that could have been a Henry Moore sculpture had caught the low sun and channeled a red beam through a perfectly circular hole eroded in its blue ice. Captivated by the moment's magic, she'd turned to Bryan and had seen love in his eyes. "Will you marry me?" he'd whispered.

"Kimberley?"

Her hand trembled. The phone jiggled against her ear. "Thank you."

"Some older links referred to tours you led with a fellow named Bryan March."

"Yes, we were partners."

"From your voice, I'd guess he's someone special."

"We were engaged."

A brief pause. "But no longer."

She drew in a deep breath. "He died during a shoot in the Rockies."

"I'm sorry, Kimberley."

"Jake, I'd like to visit the center. What time should I meet you, and how do I get there?

"Nine is good. It's a mile north of Seton on Highway 10, on the right. Look for the signs. You can't miss it."

After the call, she sank onto a kitchen chair, tears streaming down her face.

Chapter 16

The next morning, Lincoln watched sunshine gild the ranch horses in their paddocks and recalled Kimberley's comment about early sun being photo-friendly. Was she already shooting in the park, her blue eyes lit with passion, her glorious mane of hair tied back in a ponytail or spilling over her shoulders? He envisioned ticks crawling up her cargo pants and grinned as he recalled the frosty look she'd thrown at him. A man could lose himself in her eyes. They told a thousand stories. Perhaps it was her emotional sensitivity that made her such a good photographer.

He turned away from the horses and strode through the ranch yard toward the office to meet with his employees. His summer help, Dale, closed the office door and hurried away from the building, looking distinctly uncomfortable.

Lincoln intercepted him. "What's up, Dale?"

The thin, dark-haired student hesitated. "Thought I'd get an early start."

"That's all?"

Dale braced his feet shoulder wide. "No, sir. I left because I didn't want to listen to any more of Phil's comments about Ms. Colter." The young man's face reddened.

Fury knifed through Lincoln. He placed a hand on Dale's shoulder. "I'll take care of it."

"Yes, sir."

Stepping lightly, he covered the remaining distance to the office and eased open the door. Phil's words floated from the kitchenette, "…all over her arm. Gave me the creeps."

Alf's icy voice replied, "Then mind your own business. You don't have to look at her."

"But I like looking at her." A lewd laugh erupted. "Guess that vet will have to screw her with her clothes on."

Alf barked, "Keep your filthy trap shut!"

Lincoln glided into the kitchenette, as filled with adrenaline as when he'd anticipated big league hitters. "Phil's always had a hard time keeping his mouth shut, haven't you, Phil?"

The red-haired man jerked around in his chair. "What're you doing sneaking up on me?"

"Except this time, you forgot who you worked for." Lincoln took a step closer. "You've got one minute to get off Steele land before I throw you off."

"What the hell? You're *firing* me?"

"Fifty seconds. Leave your keys on the table. I'll mail your cheque."

Johnson stood, his hands clenching. "This is about that black-haired witch, isn't it? You want her for yourself."

Lincoln's hands bunched into fists. "Thirty seconds."

Alf rose from his chair and backed away from the table where he and Phil had been drinking coffee. "I'd get a move on if I were you, boy."

Johnson swore and threw a set of keys onto the table. He shoved his chair in Lincoln's direction and stomped out of the kitchenette. Moments later, the office door slammed. An engine roared to life, and tires spun gravel against the office wall. Loud horn honks blared through what had been a golden morning.

Alf rinsed his coffee mug in the sink and placed it in a drying rack on the counter. "He was good with the stock, but I can't say I'm sorry to see the back of him." His eyes narrowed. "Strikes me that he's got a mean streak when it comes to people. Sometimes seems a little bit crazy. We'd best keep a sharp eye out."

Lincoln paid attention. Thirty years his senior, Alf had patiently guided him through the first years that he'd managed the Steele Cattle Company when he'd been mired in grief and resentment. What the foreman didn't know about the ranch wasn't worth knowing. "If he steps on Steele land again, I'll charge him with trespassing."

Stoop-shouldered, Alf rubbed a hand over his chin. "I'd mention it to the lady photographer, her being out on her own all the time. Hate to see anything happen to her."

"Did he make threats?"

"Nah. Just talk. You heard him."

What he'd heard made him want to hit a punching bag. "We'll split the herd inspections. I'll take the north and west pastures. You take the east ones and then check the grass in the south pastures. I want to move the bred cows onto the nearest one this week."

Alf nodded. As he left the kitchenette, he settled a battered Stetson on his grizzled head.

Alone, Lincoln kicked Johnson's abandoned chair across the room.

* * *

Kimberley spread a Manitoba road map on the kitchen table and tapped a finger on the green irregular block that represented Turtle Mountain Provincial Park. She slid her finger across Highway 10 to neighboring William Lake Provincial Park. The smaller park east of the highway enclosed Turtle's Back Summit, the highest point in Manitoba's southwest corner. Perhaps the summit would offer a panoramic view of the rolling uplands and surrounding prairie. If so, that view might guide her explorations in the coming weeks and help clear her mind. So much had happened since her arrival at the old Steele place five weeks ago. She needed to find her bearings, both literally and figuratively.

Twenty minutes later, she parked her truck beside the trailhead for Turtle's Back Trail. A grassy clearing offered an unimpeded view over William Lake. Sunrise shot pink-gold light through misty tendrils wafting up from the water, and a common loon's eerie yodeled cry haunted the dawn air. Based on the cry's volume, the diving bird was close.

With the smooth efficiency of long practice, she chose a spot near the shore, erected her collapsible tripod and screwed her Nikon with the telephoto lens onto the tripod. She draped her portable blind—essentially a hooded poncho covered with camouflage designs—over herself and the tripod-mounted camera only seconds before the loon glided out of the mist. Excitement raced through her as she tracked the sleek black-and-white bird through her camera lens, adjusting shutter speed and snapping a series of images as the loon threw its head back, emitted another yodel, and arched its body forward into a dive.

She waited, motionless, scanning the lake surface. Seconds later, the loon surfaced closer to shore, its red eyes lit into rubies by the sun, a fish in its dagger-like beak wriggling and tossing glistening water drops into concentric ripples. *Perfect!* Two seconds and twenty pics later, the loon glanced in Kimberley's direction and disappeared beneath the water's surface. She waited for it to reappear, but her subject had vanished in the mist.

This was what she loved about her profession—the unplanned opportunities, the challenge of capturing the essence of a wild subject, the intimate connection with the natural world. Energy surged through her—she still had passion! But what would happen when that passion took her into danger?

She brushed the notion aside as she checked the trail map painted on a sign in the clearing. A side trail branched off the main track and reconnected with it near a steep ascent to Turtle's Back Summit. In no hurry, she decided to take the side trail and hike down from the summit on the main trail, making a loop.

The first mile of trail led her through deciduous woodland and community pastures beside the lake. As she approached an aspen grove, loud rustling and snapping sounds erupted, indicating heavy bodies moving through the bush. She froze, her pulse rocketing. The grizzly had charged from an aspen grove. Her hand darted to her pepper spray in the same instant that a Hereford cow bolted from the trees and hightailed it across the path, a gangly calf bucking and galloping at its side.

Get a grip, Kimberley. This was southern Manitoba, not the Rockies. Her hands shook as she reattached the spray canister to her belt.

Farther along the trail, she encountered muddy, rooted-up patches of vegetation and the cloven-hoof tracks of what could only be wild boars. She photographed the sign and continued along the trail, minutes later encountering fresh droppings—*steaming* fresh droppings—as well as more rootings and multiple tracks crossing the trail. One set of tracks dwarfed the others, meaning that the group consisted of a sow with young.

Bryan's "here-we-go" grin flashed into her mind. Countless times she'd walked at his side into whatever situation had awaited them, yet now she stood rooted to the trail, shaking. The voice inside her head mocked, *This is why you left Alberta, isn't it? Because you're afraid.* She envisioned Lincoln's pain-scored face the previous afternoon when he'd turned away from the door jamb of

Matt's room. He'd fought his emotional demons and won, but he'd paid a price. What price must she pay for freedom from her paralyzing fear?

Trust. The word came out of nowhere, like the loon appearing out of the mist.

She breathed in deeply and forced herself to look at her surroundings. Aspen leaves dangled like green hearts strung from pale, crooked twigs. A trio of crows cawed overhead, their wing feathers splayed like black fingers against the sky. Gradually, her trembling eased and faded. She glanced in both directions along the empty trail and then stealthily followed the wild pig tracks into the forest.

* * *

Lincoln parked in front of the calving barn supply room and left his pickup running. A steer in one of the north pastures was limping and oozing pus from a cut on its hock. He'd have to dart it with antibiotic. Normally, Phil would have taken care of the injury, but now the stockman's responsibilities fell onto Lincoln's and Alf's shoulders until a replacement could be found. At least they wouldn't have to squeeze in the harvest, too. The hail had taken care of that. As he climbed out of his pickup, he spotted Dale and Terri loping toward him.

The ag student waved toward the ravine. "We heard a ruckus over at the old house. The dog was barking like crazy, and then it started snarling and yelping. All of a sudden, the racket stopped. We were going to check it out, in case something's wrong."

Terri's forehead creased. "The only time I've heard Lexi bark was when she got excited over the porcupine."

Lincoln recalled the husky's wild barking the night Kimberley had run from him in the old Steele place. "And when she thinks Kimberley might be in danger."

His sister stared at him. "What do you mean?"

"Did you see a vehicle?"

Dale shook his head. "Too many trees, and the rise blocks the view of the road from here."

"I'll check it out."

"I'm coming with you." Terri ran around the front of the pickup and pulled the passenger door open. "You might need help."

"Where's Matt?"

"Riding with Mom."

He tossed his former employee's keys to Dale through the open truck window. "There's a steer in the far north pasture that needs a dart of penicillin. Ear tag ending in 8063. You'll see it limping. Use the new air rifle."

Dale straightened, a grin spreading over his face. "Yes, sir. 8063. Got it."

Gravel spit from beneath Lincoln's pickup's tires as he sped out of the ranch yard. Dust kicked up by a van ahead of him obscured his view of the road between the cattle company yard and the old Steele place. No clues there. He turned onto Kimberley's access road and roared into the ravine and up a rise into the yard. No red truck and no other vehicle.

"Linc, stop. It's Lexi."

A motionless black-and-white shape lay on the lawn.

Terri leapt from the truck. "Lexi!"

He pulled a first aid kit from under his seat and ran to the dog, a picture of Matt's small hands caressing the unconscious husky after the quills episode flashing through his mind. Terri dropped to her knees beside the dog and looked up at him, her face stricken. Blood was smeared over the dog's face, and red saturated the fur on its side. "Is she alive?" he asked.

His sister leaned forward and placed her cheek next to the husky's nostrils. "She's breathing, but she's lost a lot of blood." Her features firmed with determination. "Give me a pressure bandage for this gash on her shoulder. You deal with the one on her hip. And her front leg's broken. I'll need a splint."

After slapping a thick pad of gauze onto the hip wound and tying it firmly, he ran to the truck, stepped on the rear bumper, and vaulted into the box to retrieve a windshield scraper from the utility trunk behind the cab. The scraper's long wooden handle would suffice for a splint. Minutes later, he lifted the unconscious husky in his arms and carried the dog to the truck, settling its inert body on a folded tarpaulin his sister had spread over the bench seat.

Terri slid onto the seat beside the dog and gently elevated the husky's head onto her thigh. "Who would do this?" her voice shook as Lincoln reversed the truck. "Kimberley's only been here a few weeks. She hardly knows anyone. Do you think someone from Calgary followed her here, or was it a random act by some crazy person?"

He tossed her his phone. "Call Jake's office so they know we're on our way. Then call Kimberley. She's on the contact list. You'd better call Mom, too."

She alerted the clinic, then shook her head. "No answer from Kimberley."

"Keep trying. Reception in the park is spotty."

His sister's blonde curls bobbed as she turned to him. "How do you know she's in the park?"

"She said she'd be there today. Matt looked after the dog while she was in Brandon yesterday."

"Matt! What will we tell him?"

Lincoln glanced at the unconscious husky and recalled his son's laughter when racing Terri into the log house's yard with Lexi bounding beside them. "We'll tell him that the best vet in the province is looking after her."

At the clinic, Jake looked up after pressing the husky's abdomen with the flat of his hand. "A normal abdomen feels soft when you press it. Hers has resistance—tightening and hardening—indicating internal bleeding. She has three broken ribs plus the leg, lacerations, and a concussion, but the internal bleeding is my biggest concern. I may have to operate to save her, and it would be expensive. Have you been able to reach Kimberley?"

"No." Lincoln looked at the bloody dog, recalling Kimberley's words: *I bawled into her fur more times than I can remember.* He nodded to Jake. "Do whatever you need to do."

Jake's gaze sharpened. "You're offering to pay for it?"

"I could never face Matt if I didn't."

"Matt loves Lexi—absolutely *loves* her." Terri threw in, her riding breeches and shirt stained with blood. "She and Kimberley have made him so happy, it's like they've reset his joy button. Mom says it's a miracle. He'd be heartbroken if Lexi—"

"Okay." Jake lifted a hand and flashed a brief smile at Terri. "The two of you acted fast, and Lexi's young and healthy. She's got that going for her."

Lincoln saw the glow on Terri's face and knew his sister was courting heartbreak.

In the truck, he told her, "I'll drop you off and head to the park to look for Kimberley."

A stubborn expression settled over Terri's features. "I can go. You've got a million things to do. Mom told me you fired Phil. I wish you'd fired him ages ago. He was always trying to see through my clothes."

"*What?*" Lincoln stared at her. "Why didn't you tell me?"

"He never *did* anything. Do you think he's the one who beat Lexi?"

"We have no proof of that."

"But you suspect him, don't you?"

Lincoln didn't reply. Had Johnson blamed his job loss on Kimberley? If she'd been home, what would have happened? "Call Kimberley again."

A horrified expression spread over his sister's face. "He wouldn't go looking for her, would he?"

"Don't jump to conclusions." Yet, the possibility set

his heart racing. "Call Mom and tell her we're going straight to the park."

There was no red Ranger in the parking area at Adam Lake or at Bower Lake or Max Lake. Lincoln drummed his fingers on the steering wheel. "We must have missed her."

Terri ran her hands through her curls. "Did she say for certain she'd be in *this* park?"

"She just said she'd be in the park." Even as he uttered the words, the image of a panoramic view of the rolling uplands dropped into his mind. "She's gone to Turtle's Back."

A glimpse of red came into view as they approached the parking area at the north end of William Lake.

"There's her truck." Relief flared in Terri's voice.

He parked beside the Ranger at the same time that a man, woman, and two teenaged boys hiked into the clearing. Slamming his truck door, he hurried toward them. "Did you see a black-haired woman on the trail, probably carrying a pack? She may have been taking photographs."

The foursome paused, uncertainty on their faces as they eyed his and Terri's blood-stained clothes.

Terri jumped in. "I know we look a mess, but a dog belonging to the owner of that red truck has been critically injured and we need to find her."

The man spoke up. "The truck was here when we arrived, but we didn't see anyone on the trail."

The older teen pointed to the trailhead sign and map. "She might have hiked the loop."

Lincoln nodded. "Thanks. We'll leave a note for her in

case we miss her. What time did you start out?"

The man looked at the woman.

"It was around eight." Concern washed into the woman's features. "I hope you find her soon."

"So do I." Lincoln pulled a notebook out of his breast pocket, scribbled a message on a page, and slipped it under Kimberley's windshield wiper.

* * *

As Kimberley followed the wild pigs deeper into the forest, she scanned the ground for tracks pressed into soil or leaves and looked for broken stems and rootings. A musky odor hung on the still air. She eased forward one silent foot at a time and paused often to inspect her surroundings.

Thirty yards ahead, shrub leaves jiggled in an impromptu dance. She froze, half-hidden behind a thick-trunked aspen. The pigs had been moving away from her, so she'd expected to have to circle around to get ahead of them; yet, those jiggling leaves indicated movement in her direction. Slowly, she lifted her Nikon and steadied the telephoto lens against the tree. The faintest of breezes touched her face. Whatever was moving toward her likely hadn't detected her scent.

Snuffling sounds drifted toward her, and a grizzled black head appeared amid the jiggling leaves. The wild pig's small eyes scanned its surroundings as it lifted its snout and sniffed the air, revealing tusks curving upward on both sides of its long jaws. The deep-chested hog ambled into the open, rooting up soil and litter on the forest floor. Its path angled away from her, and instinctively—even before she noticed testicles bulging out from the pig's hindquarters—she knew this animal wasn't the sow she'd been following. It was a boar.

The hairs on the back of her neck rose, and adrenaline poured into her blood. *Relax. Gentle touch.* She drew in and released three calming, focusing breaths, readying herself for shooting and the possible consequences. Even at a distance of thirty yards, the boar might hear the multiple shutter clicks and explode into action. That motion might be away from her or toward her. How many seconds would it take a charging wild boar to cover thirty yards? Not many. She visualized reaching for the pepper spray on her belt. The other alternative was to climb a tree. Not the aspen—it had no low branches. Without moving her head, she scanned her immediate environment and noted a nearby bur oak with a fairly low, broken-off branch she could use to spring board higher into the tree. It would do if needed. She held her breath, zoomed in, and pressed the shutter release. The boar's head jerked up. Snapping its tusks, the wild pig flipped up its tail and hurtled toward her.

Chapter 17

The wild boar barreled past Kimberley and jerked its body around, swinging its powerful forequarters in her direction. She broke away at a ninety-degree angle and sprinted for the oak. *Spring onto low branch. Clutch trunk. Brace right foot against higher branch.* As she pushed off the branch, the boar clamped her left boot in its jaws. Jerked off balance, she lost the upper branch and slammed against the trunk, her camera digging into her chest, causing her to cry out. Scrabbling for a foothold on the lower branch, she yanked the pepper spray off her belt and fired capsaicin aerosol directly into the pig's rage-filled eyes. The boar squealed and released her foot then bolted erratically across the forest floor, tossing its head in an attempt to evade the blinding pepper spray in its eyes.

Freed from its grip, she scrambled up into the oak and pulled herself onto a thick limb, its furrowed bark rough beneath her hands. Pain shot through her foot. She gasped in breaths and watched the boar dash away in the direction from which it had charged, still shaking its head and growling. She waited in case it circled back, but saw no sign of it.

Quickly, she climbed down from her refuge. The pepper spray's inflammatory effects would last for twenty minutes, long enough for her to return to the trail and make a beeline for her truck. With senses on high alert, she scanned the forest for signs of movement. She jerked at a blue jay's ringing call and then calmed herself and limped toward the trail. *Triangular boulder. Broken-off aspen. Grassy clearing.* She recognized markers she'd imprinted in her mind. Bryan had taught her to look back periodically while hiking in order to create markers of a trail in reverse. To confirm her direction, she pulled a compass from her pocket, but before she could read it, a loud snap of breaking branches sounded directly ahead of her. Trembling, she yanked the pepper spray off her belt and aimed it.

* * *

Lincoln and Terri ran the trail and scanned the forest and pastures for sign of Kimberley. "We need to think like a photographer," his sister panted as she dodged a pile of wild boar dung on the trail.

He halted and stared at the dung. Like a sweet pitch blasting down the pipe, that pile of fresh feces was a marker as plain as day. "No, we need to think like Kimberley."

He inspected the ground more closely. The hog tracks crossed the trail and headed into the forest's dense thickets of hazel and wild cherry shrubs. He searched for compressed leaves or soil that might indicate Kimberley had followed the pigs. At the forest edge, he found what he was looking for—a fresh partial track on disturbed soil. It had been made by footwear bearing a rugged sole. *I'm more the hiking boot type.* He looked at Terri. "Bingo."

With his sister behind him, he followed the tracks through the forest as swiftly as he dared. A wild hog didn't compare with a grizzly, but a sow with young would be aggressive and potentially dangerous. So, Kimberley hadn't lost her nerve after all. He had to hand it to her. She had guts.

A high-pitched cry in the distance set his pulse racing. A second later, pig squeals rent the air. He broke into a run and shoved his way through the shrubs, branches swishing and snapping from his onslaught. As he emerged from a thicket, he caught sight of Kimberley, her face rigid with fear, her hands holding a canister of pepper spray aimed straight at him. He pulled up short, and Terri bumped into his back. "Kimberley!"

Recognition flared in her eyes. Her arm flopped to her side, and the canister fell to the forest floor. She began to shake violently.

He lunged toward her and caught her as she swayed into his arms. He held her against his heaving chest, her camera a hard barrier between them.

She trembled against him. "I can't do this."

"You just did." He hugged her tighter and kissed her hair. "The only way I'd go after a wild hog is with a gun in my hands. Is every wildlife photographer as gutsy—or crazy—as you are?"

"Probably not as crazy. Why are you—" She tensed and pushed away. "What's happened?" She stared at his polo shirt and Terri's riding clothes, both marred by the unmistakable red-brown residue of blood.

He slid his hands to her arms. "Lexi's been injured. She's with Jake."

"Injured? How? I left her in the yard."

"Someone beat her. We—"

"*Beat her?*"

"Jake's doing everything he can."

Her blue eyes widened. "How bad is she?"

"Internal bleeding. Broken leg and three ribs. Deep wounds. A concussion. Jake said he might have to operate."

She blinked back tears. "I tied her to the clothesline. She couldn't escape. I never thought—"

"Kimberley," he squeezed her arms gently, "we need to check the house in case there was a break-in."

"We didn't stop to look," Terri added.

Kimberley made an obvious effort to pull herself together. "All right."

He released her arms and bent to retrieve a compass and the canister from the ground. "I'm guessing this pepper spray accounted for the pig racket, but we heard you cry out. What happened? There's blood on your boot."

Kimberley tucked the compass in her pocket and clipped the canister to her belt. "I was climbing a tree when the boar bit me. I'll clean it up when I get to my truck. I didn't want to take the chance he'd come back."

"Boar? We saw tracks of a sow and piglets."

"Yes. I was following them when a boar came out of a thicket. He charged me." She looked over her shoulder. "We'd better go. The spray is only effective for twenty minutes, and with this foot, I can't outrun anything."

"Give Terri your camera. I'll take your pack and give you an arm to lean on. We can travel faster that way."

Terri slid her arms into the camera harness and cradled the Nikon in her hands. When Lincoln wrapped an arm around Kimberley, his sister threw him a searching look.

* * *

Relieved of the weight of her pack and camera, Kimberley's body seemed almost buoyant. She placed her left arm around Lincoln's waist and limped forward, a throbbing ache pulsing through her instep. Lincoln's momentum carried her with him, his fingers splayed across her midriff and his bare arm a warm band of strength around her. Right now, she needed his strength so much.

Who would beat Lexi? And why? Her mind circled as she and Lincoln did an awkward three-legged race through the forest. She came up with only three possibilities. The person who had attacked her dog could be a loose cannon, a would-be thief, or someone who had targeted Lexi because the husky belonged to her. The first two possibilities offered no clues. A perpetrator with either of those motives could be anyone. The third possibility limited the culprit to the small circle of people she'd met since her arrival on Turtle Mountain—the Steele family, Jake, the other ball players, and a few townspeople.

Lincoln helped her over a fallen tree. "Do you know anyone who might hold a grudge against you?"

"No. I have no enemies that I know of, and I've only met a handful of people here. I'm sure I haven't said or done anything to provoke someone to beat my dog."

Back at her truck, she poured hydrogen peroxide into the puncture wound on her foot and watched fizzing bubbles lift flecks of clotted blood. Although one of the pig's upper canines had shallowly penetrated her instep, her boot's thick sole had absorbed the impact of the corresponding, more dangerous lower tusk. She showed Lincoln and Terri the neat round hole in the sole. "Thank the Lord for Vibram."

"You should see a doctor," Lincoln told her. "A bite from a wild animal is nothing to mess around with."

Terri spoke up. "Do you want me to drive? Then you wouldn't have to put on your boot again."

The teen's eyes held a reserve she'd never seen in them before. "Thanks. I'd appreciate that, and I will stop by the hospital." In the yard of the old Steele place, her stomach twisted at the sight of dried blood on the parched lawn. Lexi's leash dangled from the clothesline.

"Terri and I probably destroyed any evidence around Lexi," Lincoln told her, "but it's unlikely she would've stayed in one spot and let herself be hit over and over."

"Unless whoever did it knocked her out first," Terri said. "She was unconscious when we found her."

Kimberley limped toward the yellow building. "I'll look later. Let's check the house." She unlocked the back porch door, and they examined every room, including the stone-walled cellar. The old farmhouse's doors and windows were undisturbed.

"Anything missing?" Lincoln asked.

"No, thankfully." She'd left equipment worth thousands of dollars in plain view in her workrooms and the living room.

Terri's riding boots clicked on the kitchen floor. "Maybe whoever beat Lexi got jittery because of all her barking."

"Could be." Lincoln strode toward the porch door. He stopped in front of Kimberley. "Let me know how she is. I told Jake to go ahead and do whatever needs to be done, so I'll foot the bill."

"No, you won't. I would have told him the same thing." She leaned against the kitchen wall to rest her foot. Lincoln stood close enough for her to relive his embrace in the forest. Had she really felt his lips in her hair? "And thanks—both of you—for dropping everything to help Lexi and find me."

"No problem." Lincoln opened the door to the July heat. "Report the beating to the police. For all we know, it might not be the first one in the area." His expression chilled. "By the way, I fired Phil Johnson this morning. If you see him on Steele land, he's trespassing. Let me know right away if you do."

Was there more to his statement than he was revealing?

"I will. When did you fire him?"

"First thing."

"Before Lexi was beaten?"

"Yes."

Terri spoke up. "Dale and I heard her barking and yelping at eight-thirty."

Kimberley examined Lincoln's set features. Phil had mentally undressed her in the wheat field and hauled her up against his body at the dance, but neither of those scenarios provided a reason for the paunchy, red-haired stockman to attack her dog. "I don't like Phil, but do you have any reason to think he'd hurt my dog?"

"Possibly."

"What is it?"

"I said 'possibly.' I could be completely off the mark." Controlled anger lurked behind the clipped words, although they cast no blame.

She took a chance. "I know this is a far-fetched idea, but does the reason you fired Phil have anything to do with me?" Her mouth dropped open when she read the answer in Lincoln's face.

Terri stared at her brother. "*What?* Why didn't you say so? So, Phil *would* have had a motive if he blamed Kimberley for being fired."

"A man is innocent until proven guilty." Lincoln stepped to the door, his gaze still fixed on Kimberley. "I know you don't do anything by halves, but keep the house locked and be careful when you're out on your own."

I'd rather get a whole lot closer. She pushed aside Phil's whiskey-soaked words. "I always am."

He eyed her foot.

"I took a calculated risk."

"Then calculate more carefully."

"For how long?"

"Until things settle down."

"That implies you think whoever did this isn't finished."

"Just be careful. Let's go, Terri."

Terri stepped past her and then paused. "Do you want me to go with you? I could give the police the details of how we found Lexi. And drive."

"That would be great, Terri. Thanks."

Lincoln touched his Blue Jays cap. "I'll have a quick look around."

Kimberley limped to a kitchen chair and removed her other boot. She slipped on sandals and locked the yellow house. During the drive to Seton, she envisioned Lexi as she'd seen her dog when driving out of the yard—the husky's ears up and tail wagging gently as though asking her to change her mind about leaving.

In Seton, tears welled in her eyes as she stared at Lexi's bandaged body. Terri stood on her left, offering silent support, and Jake, on her right, his brisk confidence comforting. "She came through the surgery with flying colors. I'm optimistic for a full recovery."

She slid a hand through the kennel's bars and touched Lexi's leg, its warmth a soothing indication of life. Her beautiful husky lay so still.

"She'll sleep for another hour or so and then should start coming around," Jake said. "I'll need to keep her here for observation at least until tomorrow."

"Thanks, Jake. Her injuries…how…?"

"They're consistent with being kicked and bludgeoned." His gaze dropped to her injured foot. "I see you're limping. Are we still on for tomorrow?"

"Of course. I'll see you at nine."

In her truck, she wiped a tissue across her cheeks. "Sorry I'm such a wimp," she told Terri. "Lexi was a gift from my dad after the mauling. She gave me a reason to try again."

"You heard Jake, "Terri said fiercely. "She's going to be okay. You have to believe him."

She stared at Lincoln's sister, unsure of what to make of Terri's sudden vehemence. "Of course, I believe him."

At the hospital, the same doctor who had tended Kimberley's cleat injury anaesthetized the bite wound, flushed and trimmed it, and smeared antibiotic ointment over it. "Wild boars carry diseases, but fortunately none that pose any threat to humans. Is your tetanus vaccination up to date?" The middle-aged woman looked over her glasses at her.

"Yes."

"Good. Don't bandage the wound. It needs to drain. Rest and elevate your foot. An ice pack will help relieve swelling and pain."

From the hospital, Terri drove her to the red-brick Royal Canadian Mounted Police detachment, where they reported the beating to a poker-faced corporal. Outside the detachment, Terri blew out a breath. "Life certainly hasn't been dull since you arrived."

Kimberley limped to her truck. "Is that good or bad?"

Terri hesitated beside the Ranger. "You and Lexi have done wonders for Matt."

In the truck, Kimberley turned to her. "Terri, I was under the impression that you and I are friends, but something's changed. What did I do or say to upset you?"

Terri looked straight ahead through the windshield. "You haven't done anything. You're amazing. Everyone loves you."

She studied the girl's aloof profile. "Not everyone. Someone beat my dog."

Back at the old Steele place, the yellow house yawned like a cavern without Lexi. She locked the door, raided her fridge, packed equipment for the morning's shoot at the rehabilitation center, and fell asleep while resting her foot.

After supper, she limped through the yard, the brown lawn crisp under her bare feet, the towering elms like columns holding the evening sky. She sat on the white fence at the yard's edge and glanced along its length. A flash of reflected sunlight in tall grass at the end of the fence caught her eye. She moved her head back and forth to try to distinguish its source and then abandoned her perch and limped toward it.

Chapter 18

Sunset rouged the sky as Lincoln turned his pickup onto the access road to the old Steele place, with Matt sitting beside him. Red-tinted mares' tails high above the elms and shelterbelt signaled fair weather and more heat to come. Last week's thunderstorms hadn't made a dent in the drought. The ranch's pastures lay bleached and dry, offering little nourishment for the stock. The hay that he and Alf had cut in May was disappearing at an alarming rate. He had a flashback of his stepfather inspecting herds and pointing out elements of good conformation. Terrence had gloried in any adversity the ranch had thrown at him and had steered the company through troubled waters with a smile on his face. The ranch had fit Terrence like a glove. Lincoln frowned. *But not me.*

Matt pointed to the yard as the pickup climbed out of the ravine. "There's Kimmie."

She hobbled across the lawn in a white T-shirt and green shorts, her loose hair swinging back and forth in time with her uneven steps. Without the husky by her side, part of her seemed missing.

A breeze caressed his face as he and Matt walked from

the truck to meet her, its sweet coolness a gift. Maybe he and his son wouldn't have to sweat their way through the night, with bed covers thrown off and bodies yearning for the relief brought by wind blowing through open windows. One of these years, he would have to install air conditioning.

Kimberley's blue eyes threw welcome light and lifted the edges of his fatigue, her direct gaze like steady rain on parched ground.

Matt touched her hand. "Is Lexi going to be okay?"

She caught his small hand in hers. "She lifted her head when Terri and I went to see her after we were done at the hospital and police station. That's a good sign."

Matt's quick smile flashed, erasing the crushing anxiety Lincoln had seen on his son's face ever since he'd told him about the beating. It was as though the kid had been transported back in time to the day before he'd blurted a question to Kimberley in Turtle Mountain Provincial Park. Even though Terri had told him about the husky lifting its head, he'd needed to hear it from Kimberley. Matt was healing, but he wasn't healed yet. It was plain that Matt's emotional recovery was still linked to Kimberley. And that meant the promise to stay away from her, to allow her to heal, had to be kept.

She looked up. "Would you like a cup of tea? You look beat."

Beat was a good word for it—beat by the heat, beat by the drought, beat by the unceasing demands of being a single father, and beat by the extra work he'd loaded on himself because he'd fired Johnson. Yet, he knew he wouldn't have acted differently. "Thanks, but we can't stay. I have stock records to update. Matt just wanted to stop in to see you."

She reached out to hug his son, and Matt moved into her arms like he'd been doing it all his life. "I'm sorry Lexi and I took you away from your work, Lincoln, especially since you have a heavier load now."

She made a pretty apology, her mouth soft in her tanned face, her vivid eyes offering. "Alf and I split the extra work, and Dale helped out. For a kid, he's got a good head on his shoulders. Next week we'll sell all the cattle except the breeding stock. That'll take some of the pressure off."

After discussing the situation with his mother, he'd arranged the stock shipments even though beef prices were rock bottom. No cattle were going to starve on Steele land. His mother had agreed to buy a shipment of hay from Alberta to feed the new Angus cows and fifty of the best of the other bred cows through the winter. With the demand for hay sky high and the supply low, that shipment had cost a fortune. The rest of the cattle had to go.

"Did you find any evidence this morning?" Kimberley asked.

He shook his head. "No vehicle tracks other than yours and mine. No weapon, and no obvious boot tracks that weren't mine, yours, or Terri's."

She removed a plastic bag from her shorts pocket and

held it out to him. "Look at this."

A tingle of recognition raced through him as he stared at the black-and-green snuff box. He knew a lot of ball players and a handful of farmers who tucked smokeless tobacco inside their lips for a nicotine hit, but he only knew one local who dipped Copenhagen Long Cut Wintergreen. "Where did you find this?"

She scrutinized his face. "In the long grass at the edge of the yard. I never would have known it was there except that I saw sunlight reflected from the shiny rim. I think it must have fallen out of someone's pocket."

He nodded. "I'd like to take it with me, if you don't mind."

"I picked it up with my pliers, so it doesn't have my fingerprints on it." She handed him the bag. "Do you know who owns it? You looked like you might."

"Maybe." A plan formed in his mind. "What did the police say when you reported the beating?"

"That it's almost impossible to lay animal cruelty charges without an eye witness."

"Which we don't have." He looked over the quiet yard and house. "Will you be all right here on your own?"

Her expression betrayed no hint of unease. "I sleep light, and I'll keep a canister of pepper spray handy. If whoever beat Lexi comes back, I'll be more than happy to let him have it."

"Judging from the pig racket this morning, that spray does its job."

Matt grinned up at Kimberley. "Dad told me you

scared a wild boar away. You're the queen of the bush."

She touched his nose with her fingertip. "Queen of the bush. That has a nice ring. I like it."

Lincoln flashed her an amused look before sobering at the possibility of the danger she might be in. "Call me if you need me, day or night."

"I will."

Matt hummed all the way home. In the bathroom, he pulled a new tube of toothpaste out of its box. "Dad, can I ask Kimmie to my birthday party?"

"'May' I," Lincoln corrected absently. "And yes, you may."

"I hope she never leaves." His son squeezed a dab of toothpaste onto a red Spiderman toothbrush. "If she got married, she'd stay, wouldn't she?"

Lincoln sat on the tub rim. "I guess she would, but you're a little young, cowboy."

Matt scrunched his face into a playful grimace. "I didn't mean to *me*."

"Then who do you have in mind?"

His son looked straight into his eyes. "You. Then I'd have her for my second mom, and she could have the baby she wants."

Lincoln spread his hands, a thousand images teasing him. "Well, that takes care of you two, but what about me?"

Matt looked at him like he was an idiot. "You'd have *Kimmie*. And she'd live with us."

He pulled his son onto his knee. He hated teaching

moments. "It's not that simple, Matt. When two—"

"Did you love my mom when you got married?"

He met his son's earnest eyes. "Yes, I did."

"Then you must love Kimmie." Matt's smile could only be described as beatific.

"I don't get that, cowboy. What do you mean?"

"When you look at Kimmie, you look just like in the picture of you and my mom. When you got married."

He opened his mouth to speak, but no words came out.

* * *

"You gorgeous creature!" Kimberley stepped closer to one of a dozen outdoor aviaries at the Seton Wildlife Rehabilitation Center.

Within the wire-mesh enclosure, a red-tailed hawk gripped a thick tree branch with one foot, its razor-sharp talons curved around the perch. Its other foot had been reduced to a scaly stub by amputation, yet the bird used it as a prop. The hawk's rusty-red tail contrasted sharply with its white feather leggings and brown back and head.

"That fellow was caught in an illegal leg hold trap." Jake shrugged on a white lab coat. "We call him Admiral Nelson." He placed a light hand on Kimberley's back and guided her to a smaller enclosure in which a male American kestrel perched on a dead branch. "This little fellow survived a collision with a tractor cab. Unfortunately, I had to amputate part of one wing, so Napoleon will never fly again, but he's an agile hopper."

The small falcon stared at Kimberley unwaveringly, its slate gray wings bracketing a cinnamon back and tail, its white face marked by a pair of distinctive vertical black stripes on each cheek. "He's beautiful."

Jake touched a rubber-sealed door set into the aviary wall. "All the aviaries have viewing portals that will accommodate your camera. If you have any questions, ask one of the staff or I'll answer them later." His eyes lit with enthusiasm. "Time to see my patients." He walked away with a boyish spring to his step.

Kimberley visited each aviary in turn, moving slowly and quietly so as to not startle the birds. No need for a telephoto lens here. Her challenge was to minimize the distraction of the artificial environments.

In addition to the red-tailed hawk and kestrel Jake had shown her, the aviaries housed dark-hooded Swainson's hawks, a juvenile Cooper's hawk with barred brown tail, a male merlin with gunmetal-blue back, and three more red-tailed hawks. Kimberley composed full-body shots, close-up portraits, and frames highlighting each raptor's infirmity. Some handicaps were obvious. Others she gleaned from a stocky, bearded young man in a khaki shirt whose name tag identified him as Raymond. Aside from their injuries, the birds looked strong and healthy, their feathers lustrous, their eyes bright.

"And last but not least, this is Mata Hari, our northern goshawk." Raymond led Kimberley to the only aviary she hadn't yet visited. The adult goshawk, with its red eyes and slate-colored back, was spectacularly beautiful despite the fact that it was missing two toes on one foot.

"Mata Hari?"

Raymond grinned. "Dr. Kruger is a military history buff."

"I'd like to observe him at work, please."

"He's tending a female harrier someone just brought in. I'll take you to him."

In a spotless examining room, Jake looked up from a brown-feathered bird of prey positioned on a shiny metal examining table. The harrier's head moved in weak, convulsive twitches, its feathers in disarray. "A car crash victim. Unfortunately, her injuries are too extensive to treat."

"May I photograph you?" Kimberley asked. "Given their injuries, the other raptors have happy endings to their stories, but this one doesn't. I think the public needs to see both."

"Shoot away." Jake gently brushed his fingers over the harrier's back before administering an injection. The bird arched its neck and, moments later, lay still. Jake nodded to Raymond, who gently lifted the dead raptor and removed it from the room.

Kimberley slid her daypack off her shoulders and placed her camera in it. "I'll take a look at what I've got and give you a disc of the best shots. You can use them with your article or for other publicity. Consider them a donation."

"Thanks, Kimberley. I appreciate that very much." Jake washed his hands and threw her a mischievous look while drying them. "I seem to always be putting this question to you in an examining room, but do you have plans for Saturday evening?"

Surprise skimmed through Kimberley as she slung her daypack onto her shoulders. "Not at the moment, no."

"Do you like stage plays? I have two tickets for *Les Misérables* in Winnipeg. Would you like to go? My plan is to leave early enough to dine out before the show." He grinned sheepishly. "Another vet will be covering for me, so there's no chance I'd have to bum you a ride home."

For an instant, Saturday night's storm held her in its grip—lightning flashing and thunder crashing against Lincoln's pickup while she let her hair down in more ways than one. He could have taken her gaffe about the dress and run with it, but he hadn't. And surprisingly, as she'd related the story of the grizzly attack, it was as though she'd been yearning to tell him.

"You're taking a long time to answer. Does that mean no?"

She jerked herself back to the present. Jake Kruger was a good man. True, he didn't share her love of the outdoors, but he was personable and had a great sense of humor. Definitely worth a second date. "Not at all. I've never seen *Les Mis*. I'd love to go. Thank you for the invitation."

"Good. The show starts at eight. We should leave by three to have enough time to enjoy our meal."

"Sounds good. I'll have the disc ready for you within a few days."

"Excellent. By the way, I checked Lexi over this morning. You can take her home. My assistant will explain the care she'll need."

"So soon? That's wonderful!" Impulsively, she hugged Jake. "You just made my day."

His arms tightened around her before she stepped back. "For a hug like that, I'd make your day every day."

As she drove away from the veterinary clinic with Lexi on the seat beside her, a startling possibility swept into her mind. Could the man in her future be Jake? He'd seen the web of scars on her arm after she'd been stomped on during the ball game but had never referred to it. And based on the comment he'd made in response to Sandra Aguilera's playful jab about him not being married, he was interested in settling down. Perhaps there was more on the line than just a second date.

Chapter 19

Matt unclipped the lead from Darby's halter and released the sorrel pony into its pasture. "Darby's cool, Dad, and I put away my tack. Can we drop it off now?"

Lincoln eyed his son's gleaming black boots and neat riding breeches. The show jumping outfit accentuated Matt's thin body and somehow made him look fragile and mature at the same time. "You should change first."

"Aw, Dad, I can change later. And it's lunchtime. You always take a break." The bright light in Matt's deep blue eyes was every bit as magnetic as the captivating gleam had been in Gayle's. Maybe he had some of his mother in him after all.

"Okay."

The kid almost danced to the truck. One woman had brought him so much joy. No, not one woman—two. If Lincoln had known how happy it would make Matt to have his room cluttered with pictures of Gayle, he would have borne the pain of their presence long ago. Or would he? No, it had taken Kimberley's discussion with Matt in the blind and her badgering at the dance to break down that locked door. She'd been the catalyst for his moonlit bout of soul-searching. He turned his pickup into the parking area at the old Steele place. No red truck.

Matt's shoulders slumped. "She's not here."

"We'll leave it for her. It'll be a nice surprise."

His son perked up. "Okay." He hopped down from the passenger seat and skipped to the back door.

Lincoln paused a moment to watch him. Except for the previous day's anxiety, Matt had metamorphosed into a different child since Kimberley had taken up residence at the old Steele place. It took some getting used to. The transformation was liberating, yet Lincoln found it hard to not guard his son as closely as he had for the past five years.

Matt bent to tuck a cream-colored Steele Cattle Company envelope partway under the door. "I hope she can come."

On hearing an engine rumble. Lincoln retrieved the invitation and handed it to his son. "You can give it to her yourself."

Matt raced from the door and waved. "Hi, Kimmie!"

Kimberley waved back before placing her finger to her lips. She idled her Ranger while Lincoln backed out of her parking spot and then pulled in close to the house before hustling around to her truck's passenger door. "I have Lexi."

Matt ran to her side, and the two of them peered into the truck, Kimberley's hair trailing in a thick black braid down the back of her yellow top. She wore sandals, and Lincoln noticed that she still limped from the pig bite. He looked over her shoulder. The dog curled awkwardly on the truck seat, its left foreleg in a cast. Shaved patches of skin bore white bandages on shoulder, hip, forehead, and belly, and an inverted plastic cone was positioned around the husky's neck. The dog's usual high-spirited energy was nowhere to be seen.

"What's that?" Matt whispered, pointing to the cone. "It looks weird."

"It's to stop her from chewing on her cast and stitches," Kimberley replied, her voice barely audible.

Lincoln touched her shoulder. "You're still limping. Let me carry her in for you."

She flashed him a smile. "Thanks. She was anxious earlier because I was lurching."

He cradled Lexi in his arms, entered the house, and gently placed the husky on a dog pillow in Kimberley's bedroom while she closed the room's drapes. In the dim light, her yellow dress hung beside camo clothes in an open closet—an intriguing combination like the woman herself.

When Matt knelt beside the dog pillow and reached out, Lexi flinched away from him.

Kimberley touched Matt's arm and moved to the door. In the kitchen, she said, "Lexi's scared and hurts all over, especially her head. She needs to rest and be in darkness for two weeks so her concussion can heal. We'll need to be very quiet and gentle with her."

"Let's go outside." Lincoln pushed open the porch door. "Matt's brought something for you."

"Oh, yeah." His son held the envelope out to Kimberley while the three of them trooped out onto the back porch step. "It's an invitation to my birthday party."

She opened the envelope and unfolded a sheet of blue paper, a spontaneous smile curving her lips. "Nice drawing of the burrowing owls, Matt. I'd be happy to come to your party. Thank you for the invitation. Let's see, it's on August fourteenth, so that's Monday, two weeks from yesterday."

"That's right." Matt's face shone.

Lincoln placed a hand on his son's shoulder. "Okay, cowboy, we need to get back."

Matt looked from him to Kimberley, yearning in his eyes. "Can—may—I stay for a while?"

"It's lunch time, Matt."

"And I bought pizza." Kimberley's gaze was as warm as a sweet evening breeze. "I'd love to share it with Matt. You, too, if you like Hawaiian and can wait five minutes. I'll nuke it."

He cast himself afloat on that sweet breeze. "I can wait."

They ate under an elm tree and licked pizza sauce and melted mozzarella off their fingers. Matt strained toward Kimberley as she described her morning at the rehab center. For fifteen minutes Lincoln forgot the crush of work waiting for him across the ravine. For fifteen minutes, he laughed and teased and conversed. During the brief interlude, the ranch's problems disappeared outside the coziness of the three of them sitting under the tree, knowing the injured dog was home and on the mend. It felt like family. Finally, he rose to his feet. "Thanks, Kimberley."

"You're welcome. Stop by any time."

"Just thought of something. First thing Sunday morning, we'll be rounding up cattle. A few of the neighbors are going to help out, and we'll top it off with a barbecue. Might be a good photo op."

Her eyes lit with interest. "I've never photographed a round-up. Where would be a good spot to take it in?"

"Want to ride? Although, come to think of it, the dust would be hard on your camera."

"I can cope with dust. I'd love to ride, but I'm no expert. I wouldn't have a clue where I should be in a round-up."

"Stick with me." He tossed her a grin. "I'll make sure you don't get run over."

"Deal!"

* * *

For the rest of the week, Kimberley stayed home to care for Lexi. In sweltering heat, she carried her pet outdoors to relieve itself. In order to eliminate the noise of walking up and down the uncarpeted stairs, she cropped, printed, and digitally sold photos at the kitchen table rather than at her desk upstairs. In early morning and evening, she read more from her portrait photography book while enjoying the kiss of dappled sunlight on her bare limbs as she sat beneath a favorite elm. Every night, she locked the yellow house's doors and windows before sliding between cotton sheets, a canister of pepper spray within easy reach on her bedside table.

Lincoln and Matt stopped in each day at lunch break, and she found herself listening for the blue pickup's arrival and hurrying to the door with a smile on her face. Before eating, Matt visited Lexi, sitting silently on the floor in the darkened bedroom with his hands in his lap. On Thursday, Lexi sniffed at him, ears pricked. On Friday, Lincoln brought venison stew and fresh bread his mother had baked, and Kimberley added a three-bean salad to his offering to create yet another impromptu picnic under their favorite elm. Matt chattered about Lexi and plans for his birthday party, finishing with, "Dad's going to barbecue a surprise for me."

She glanced at Lincoln and found his amber eyes focused on her rather than on his son.

"What's up?" she asked.

"I promised Matt we'd go to the lake this evening, probably around eight after I tie up some loose ends. Want to go?"

Water. "That sounds heavenly. How long would we be gone? I'm thinking of Lexi."

"An hour and a half."

"In that case, I'd love to."

When he rose to his feet, his eyes held the warmth that had so intrigued her the first time she'd seen him in Turtle Mountain Provincial Park.

"Good. See you at eight."

She leaned back against the elm's trunk as Lincoln strode to his pickup with his son skipping beside him. Did he even know how to walk slowly? His long legs were encased in jeans, his broad shoulders in a snug, rust-colored polo shirt that accented the feline quality of his eyes and made his shoulders look a mile wide. She'd sat beside him under the elm and had the impression that he was waiting. For what, she didn't know. As the pickup left the yard, she waved to her guests and then carried plates into the yellow house. After washing dishes, she tiptoed into her bedroom and smoothed the lightest caress over Lexi's back. Her dog didn't flinch.

* * *

Evening sunlight gilded desiccated pastures and stunted crops, transforming paucity into beauty as Lincoln drove toward the park with his son and Kimberley beside him. All week, tension had been building in him—tension derived from the overwhelming need to get the ranch's herds to market before the animals' condition deteriorated, and tension derived from his suspicion that whoever had beaten Kimberley's dog would strike again. Along with that suspicion came a gut feeling that the ranch would be the next target. He wouldn't rest until every animal other than the breeding stock was gone.

At dawn that morning, he and Alf had herded the ranch's hundred bred Angus cows onto the pasture south of the old Steele place, the best grazing the ranch had to offer. Even so, the cows had tugged eagerly at hay bales

Dale had transported to the pasture with the tractor and bale spear. It was going to be an expensive winter.

"You look pensive."

Lincoln glanced at Kimberley. Matt sat between them in the pickup, his nose in one of his Spiderman comic books. "Just thinking about the cattle."

"Are you worried? I saw hay bales in the pasture south of the house. This early, that can't be good."

He turned off Highway 10 onto the access road to Adam Lake. "The ranch will take a hit this year, but a new calf crop in spring will start the ball rolling again."

"What breed are the black cows?" Her voice took on a smile. "I know they're cows because they have udders."

"Purebred Aberdeen Angus."

"I have no idea what cows cost. Are they very valuable?"

He nodded as he steered the truck into the parking area. "The best I could buy."

"Your ace in the hole, so to speak."

She was a smart cookie. "My mother's ace in the hole. A black ace."

She slid her beach bag's straps over her shoulder. "Speaking of cows, when and where should I meet you on Sunday morning for the round-up?"

"Five-thirty, in the ranch yard. We'll trailer the horses to the starting point. By the way, my mother says hello and insists that you ride her mare. She'll be dealing with food for the barbecue, so won't be riding. You can use her boots, too, if you'd like. They're size eight. Will they fit?"

"I wear sevens but can make do with eights. My brother's family is going to drop in on Sunday afternoon. The round-up will be over by then, won't it?"

"Should be. Why don't you tell them to come at one for the barbecue? We're going to spit-roast a calf, so the more hearty appetites, the better."

"Sounds amazing. I'll do that. Should I bring something?"

"No need. There'll be plenty of food."

On the beach, he watched as Matt reached for his T-shirt to tug it up over his head and then hesitated with his hands on the hem, a haunted expression replacing his earlier happiness.

Kimberley tossed her towel onto a shrub. "I bet I have more scars than you do."

Matt's startled gaze jumped to hers. "Bet you don't."

"Bet I do." She tugged down white shorts and pulled her long pink T-shirt over her head, revealing tanned limbs and a turquoise one-piece swimsuit with a plunging back. "See?" She pointed to her shoulder, her chest, her thigh. "Oh, and there's this one." She ran a finger along her hairline and down behind her ear.

Matt's expression was a blend of shock and fascination. "They're big," he finally said, "but there aren't that many of them."

"What do you mean?" She tapped her thigh. "I've got a dozen right here."

"Well, I've got more than that right *here*." Defiantly, he tugged his shirt over his head and turned his back to her.

He poked his hand to where a field of short, white scars flecked his skin.

Lincoln's breath caught in his chest. All he could do was stand and watch, afraid any word he might utter would smash the scene playing out before him.

Kimberley pursed her lips, her gaze steady. "You're right. You do have a lot there. But I have others in unmentionable places."

"In...where?"

She pointed to her buttocks.

Matt's eyes opened wide. A huge grin split his face. "So do I!"

She broke for the lake. "Race you to the water."

"No fair—your legs are longer than mine."

"But I'm limping."

In marveling disbelief, Lincoln watched his son race Kimberley into the lake and slash a hand across the water's surface to splash her, to which she retaliated in kind. He felt the sand's heat on his bare feet, the sun's searing lick on his face, and knew he'd just witnessed a miracle.

Chapter 20

As Kimberley toweled her arms, Matt plopped onto the sand beside his father. "Dad, why didn't you come in?"

"I wanted to read for a few minutes." Lincoln leaned back against an aspen tree, his bare torso muscled and trim with a light sprinkling of blond hairs.

She recalled his gym clothes and sweat on the previous Sunday morning. So he *had* been working out. She glanced at the title of his book: *A Tale of Two Cities.* "Ah, one of your magic in the morning books." Clearing her throat, she quoted in a stage voice, "'It was the best of times, it was the worst of times.'"

He grinned lazily, a mystery hidden in his eyes.

She raised the towel to her hair and rubbed hard, sending the thick mass into a tangle she knew she'd regret. Maybe coming to the lake hadn't been a good idea after all. Lincoln's attractiveness was hard to ignore when the only thing covering his skin was a pair of black trunks.

"Kimmie and I are playing one question," Matt said. "We both picked a person and we get to ask one question about them."

Lincoln set the book on the sand. "So, who'd you

pick?"

"That photographer guy—Bryan. And she picked my mom."

His father's gaze sharpened.

Kimberley lowered her towel. "What's your question, Matt?"

"What was the *best* picture he ever took?"

"Hmm…" She rubbed the towel over her legs. "Bryan took a lot of great pictures. I think his best is a cheetah running at top speed. The whole background is blurry, but the cheetah is crystal clear. He caught it at full stretch."

"Neat!" Matt trickled sand through his fingers. "It's your turn."

"You told me your mom sang songs to you. Which was your favorite?"

"'Puff, the Magic Dragon.'"

"I've never heard of it." She turned to Lincoln.

"It's a Peter, Paul, and Mary hit from the sixties. Gayle wanted to revive some old songs and record them for kids."

"Then she must have been good."

"She was."

"I saw the guitar in your living room. Do you sing?"

He lifted a shoulder and let it fall. "I used to."

Kimberley returned her attention to his son. "Tell me about Puff."

"He was magic! He lived in a cave beside the sea. And he made friends with Jackie Paper, and Jackie brought him toys."

"Jackie Paper was a little boy?"

"Yes."

"Like you."

"Yes!"

"Sounds like a happy story."

"Some of it was."

"What happened in the happy parts?"

"They went places in a big boat, and Jackie sat on Puff's tail and watched for pirates."

"Nice. What happened in the not-so-happy parts?"

Matt looked down and dug his fingers into the sand. "Jackie went away."

"Ah."

"My mom always sounded so sad when she sang that part, like she was Puff." He set his jaw firmly, tears welling in his eyes. "I'm never going to forget my mom the way Jackie forgot Puff."

Kimberley glanced at Lincoln. He sat frozen, his eyes bleak. "I'm sure you won't," she told Matt. "Tell me some other songs your mom sang."

Before he could speak, Lincoln pushed to his feet. "I'll have that swim now." He sprinted for the water and plunged into the lake.

Matt's voice quavered, "Is Dad mad at me for talking about my mom?"

"No. He's not mad." Kimberley crouched in front of the child. "You didn't do or say anything wrong. It's just that sometimes your dad hurts inside when we talk about your mom. He loved her, too, you know."

"Then why did she have to go away?"

She took his small hands in hers like she had in the blind. "When you're all grown up, ask your dad. Love is a beautiful thing, but it's hard. Now, which of your mom's songs did you like second best?"

The drive home was quiet. Lincoln seemed distant, and Matt was immersed in his comic books. She hesitated before speaking, not knowing if her request would be an imposition. Finally she said, "I have a favor to ask."

Lincoln and Matt looked at her.

"I'm going to Winnipeg tomorrow afternoon and won't be home until around midnight. Would the two of you be willing to take Lexi outside after supper to pee? Then she'll be all right until I get home."

"No problem." Lincoln turned the pickup onto her access road. "Do you have a photography event of some kind?"

"No, I'm going to see a play. *Les Misérables*."

His dimples appeared. "Between that and the Dickens quote, we'll have you talking magic in the morning in no time."

At the old Steele place, Matt scampered into the house to visit Lexi.

Kimberley handed Lincoln a key. "It's for the sun porch. Thanks for the swim. I needed it."

"Let's walk." With a light touch on her arm, he directed her toward the lawn on the south side of the house.

She strolled at his side and paused to look out over the white rail fence. Sunset painted the tops of the bur oaks on the ravine slope flaming orange. Crickets' rapid-fire chirps droned into the hot evening air. Dusk wasn't far off. "I'm surprised there aren't any mosquitoes here," she murmured, resting her hands on the top rail.

"That's the one thing we can thank the drought for." He leaned forward to place his hands on the rail beside hers. "Most years, the little blood suckers feast on us."

She flashed him a smile. "It's strange, but I feel like I've been here longer than six weeks. This place has a way of soaking into a person's soul."

A teasing light lit his eyes. "Even with no cheetahs and crocodiles?"

"Oh, they're still out there in the world. A person can always find them."

His teasing changed to seriousness. "And will you always find them?"

She stepped away from the fence, suddenly restless. "I don't know. You saw me in the park. I'm not sure I'd be much good at going after the dangerous ones any more. It's different working with a partner. You have each other's backs."

He straightened. "Does that mean you're looking for a new partner?"

Dry grass crunched under her bare feet. "I can't even think about that until I get a grip on my...fears." She cast an ironic look at him. "Wildlife photographer afraid of wildlife. That's another reason I moved here. I couldn't face the Rockies."

He frowned. "Give yourself some credit, Kimberley.

You went after those hogs."

"After standing on the trail, shaking."

"So what? You conquered your fear."

"That time."

"Each time will be that time, and each time, you'll conquer it."

"You have more confidence in me than I do."

He brushed a stray strand of hair back from her forehead. "I've seen the look in your eyes when you're rigged out in your camo gear and ready to head out on a quest. You're completely in your element."

"A quest? It's hardly that." She spread her hands. "I just want to share the beauty and drama of nature with others."

"And you're exceptionally good at it. Did you get any pictures of the boar?"

"I did."

"And?"

"One shot of the charge is good."

"You see? You're braver than you knew." He traced a light finger along her hairline scar. "And you're incredibly generous. Thank you for what you did for Matt at the lake."

At his touch, her pulse rocketed into overdrive. "I don't like to see any child afraid, and I've benefited as much from being around Matt as he has from me."

"You're quite a woman."

She swallowed. "Even all rigged out in camo?"

"I like camo. I'm a hunter."

"What do you hunt?"

"Right now, this."

The warmth of his lips on hers ignited a yearning within her. She'd known, *known*, it could be like this.

For her.

She pushed away from him, a question searing her mind. Was the desire in his kiss genuine, or had every action he'd taken since her arrival been a manipulation to draw her closer to his son? An effort to help Matt heal? "I know you're feeling appreciative, but that wasn't fair."

His hands dropped to his sides. "What do you mean? You're unattached. I'm unattached. Why wasn't it fair?"

"Dad? Kimmie?" Anxiety laced Matt's voice. "Lexi wants to go out."

Kimberley waved to the child caught in the glow of porch light spilling onto the lawn. "Coming, Matt."

Lincoln caught her arm in a light grip. "Kimberley, we need to talk."

"Not now. Lexi needs me." She pulled away from his grasp and ran to where a red-haired boy waited in a pool of light.

The next morning, she punched Wendy's number into her cell phone. "I'm in the ladies clothing store in Seton," she told her sister-in-law. "Can you talk?"

"Yes. I'm plopped on the couch, nursing Damien."

"How's the cutest baby Colter in the whole world?"

"Stuck to me most of the time." Wendy's voice sounded tired but indulgent. "I feel like a milk cow."

Kimberley glanced at the racks of dresses, blouses, skirts, slacks, and sweaters surrounding her. Mild panic had assailed her when she'd walked through the shop's door, and another dose of it struck her now. "So far, I've found a pair of white pants and a blue blouse, like you suggested."

"What shade of blue?"

"Royal."

"It's not baggy?"

"No."

"Good. What are the pants made of?"

She muttered, "Ask me how to photograph a cheetah, and I'll tell you."

Amusement laced Wendy's voice. "I'm constantly amazed that you were raised by a tailor."

"I'm just not interested in clothes."

"The pants aren't denim, are they, or white cargo pants?"

"No, they're dress slacks, or so I was told."

"Good. You're getting the hang of this. They're not baggy?"

"No. Much snugger than what I'm used to."

"Then they're probably about right. As for shoes, white or blue sandals would work, and you can use the white clutch purse you bought to go with the yellow dress."

White or blue sandals? She looked at her feet clad in scuffed outdoor sandals with rugged soles designed for traction. "I noticed there's a shoe store down the street."

"Check it out. Before you leave the clothing store, look

for a lightweight cardigan or shawl—something to complement the pants and blouse."

She blew out a breath. "Is all this really necessary?"

"It is when you're going to see *Les Mis* with a man who drives a BMW." Wendy's intonation changed. "Out of curiosity, what does the rancher drive?"

"A blue Ford Supercrew pickup."

"No Sunday or special occasion car?"

"Not that I've seen."

"A real country man. Does he wear cowboy boots?"

"Yes, but not cowboy shirts or a cowboy hat."

"What then?"

"Polo shirts and a Blue Jays cap."

"What color polo shirts?"

"Black. Red. Green. Rust. Yellow."

"So, you're still interested in him."

Her mouth fell open. "I just happened to notice—"

"How hot he looks in polo shirts. I agree. He was wearing one that day at Adam Lake. The man is *built*."

She glanced around and spotted the store manager engaged in conversation with another customer. "Wendy," she said in a firm, hushed voice, "there is *nothing* between us. I've seen a fair bit of him because I've been helping his son get over a trauma he suffered as a toddler."

"What kind of trauma?"

"I won't go into it, but he has scars."

"Poor little fellow. And good for you. Do you miss your volunteer work with the kids in Calgary?"

"Sometimes. Matt and I even had an 'I've got more

scars than you do' contest when we went swimming yesterday."

"Then you must be healing, too. A month ago you wouldn't have worn a bathing suit in public."

"You know, that's true." Kimberley glanced at her watch. "I've got to go. Thanks a million. Love to you and kisses to Damien."

"Anything for my beautiful sister-in-law."

"Oh, I almost forgot." She relayed the invitation to the barbecue.

"Hmm. Except for the odd farmer's sausage, I'm not big on meat, but I'd make an exception for spit-roasted calf. And Gary would love it, so I'm going to say yes."

"Excellent. See you tomorrow."

A half-hour later, Kimberley placed a pair of strappy, blue, wedge-heeled sandals on the truck seat beside her. It was almost noon, and she'd spent far too much of Saturday morning in town. Soon Lexi would be getting restless. However, on her way into Seton, she'd noticed a ball tournament on the sports grounds and had promised herself a quick look at the action before driving back to the old Steele place.

A women's fastball game on the diamond nearest the sports ground's entrance caught her eye. She sat in the bleachers and watched Seton's team lose in the final inning, then she strolled past a canteen to a baseball diamond where a pitcher's duel held the score at zero to zero. Neither team was from Seton, but they were both good. A woman's faint, high-pitched yell jerked her attention from the baseball game. "Lincoln, I can't see it!"

She turned toward the sound and spotted the green-clad Seton slow-pitch team on the diamond farthest from the sports ground's entrance. She watched as Lincoln fielded a high fly directly over the second base player's head and lobbed the ball to the pitcher after checking runners on third and first bases. Drawn by his smooth grace, she hurried to the diamond and joined a cluster of people standing well back from the third base line. As a batter trudged away from home plate, a half-dozen players in the stands mimicked the second base player's earlier shout, one of the men cooing loudly, "Ooh, *Lincoln*, I can't see it." The others broke into guffaws. Kimberley caught a glimpse of Terri and Matt seated in the stands. Terri glared at the raucous men.

"Idiots," muttered a frizzy-haired teen standing beside Kimberley. "They're just jealous because he wouldn't play baseball for Seton."

"What inning is it? What's the score?"

Without taking her eyes off the game, the girl answered, "Bottom of the last. Two out. We're ahead by two."

As the next batter approached the plate, Seton's infield and outfield backed up. The team's curly-haired third base player—was his name Danny?—shot a look at Lincoln. At short stop, Lincoln nodded and settled into his ready position well back of the base line between second and third.

"What was that about?" Kimberley asked.

The teen swung a finger toward the batter who stood outside the batter's box, tapping dirt from his cleats with his bat. The man was a mountain of muscle. "He belted a home run over the fence first time up, but Lincoln snagged all three of his other hits. And they were *hot*, but not as hot as Lincoln. He's got wings on his feet." She darted Kimberley a self-conscious smile. "As you can tell, I'm a fan. That's my mom playing second base."

When the batter stepped up to the plate, a voice from the stands shouted, "Hey, Steele. Let's see if you can make it four for four."

Excitement raced through Kimberley as she slid her camera from her pocket.

* * *

Lincoln shut out Gordie Smith's taunt and watched the batter's every move as the big man stepped into the batter's box. A heightened sense of awareness swept through him, the sensation one of crystal clarity, of suspended time. He watched the pitcher deliver the ball as though in slow motion and knew it was an inside pitch as it left Tom's hand. His mind and eyes measured the batter's response to the pitch, and even before the slugger's bat contacted the ball, he was moving to his right and back.

The ball came off the bat in a climbing line drive that blasted over Danny's glove as Lincoln launched his body into the air and strained his glove hand upward. He felt the sweet smack of leather on leather and pulled the ball down to his chest for the third out, lobbing it to Danny before he touched ground. For a fraction of a second—for a thousandth of a second—a joy he'd thought he'd lost forever surged through him.

A movement at the edge of the crowd alongside third base drew his gaze to where Kimberley stood, a huge smile lighting her face. Then the Seton team mobbed him, and he lined up to shake hands with the opposition. As he gripped the slugger's hand, the other man grinned. "What the *hell* are you doing playing slow-pitch?"

"I could ask the same of you," he replied, his mind already shifting from the game to what was in his sports bag. Phil Johnson had avoided his eye during the entire game except when relaying balls in from left field. It was time to test a theory. At the Seton bench, he reached into his sports bag and pulled out a flat, green-and-black tin. He surreptitiously showed it to Jake. "Keep an eye on Phil's face when I give this to him."

Jake frowned. "I heard you fired him. What's this about?"

"Tell you later." He tossed the tin of Copenhagen Long Cut Wintergreen the length of the bench. It landed on Johnson's lap.

His ex-employee jerked, a mix of shock and fear spreading over his face.

Seated beside him, Danny whooped, "Phil, you look like you saw a ghost! It's nothing but a can of snuff!"

Lincoln made his voice deliberately neutral. "Kimberley found that at the edge of the yard at the old Steele place on

Monday. You must have dropped it sometime when you were over there."

Johnson shot him a venomous look. "What makes you think it's mine?"

He shrugged. "You were the only one working on Steele land who used that brand. I figured it must be yours. Throw it in the garbage if you don't want it."

Johnson's face closed into a mask. "Yeah, I guess I must have. What do you know?"

More than you think.

Jake murmured, "I'd say he looked guilty." He wiped his face with a towel. "And then like he wouldn't mind bashing your teeth in. Why did you fire him?"

Lincoln sucked up a mouthful of water from his bottle. "That's between him and me."

"Dad!" Matt ran along beside the bench and flung himself into his arms.

He dropped his bottle to the dirt and lifted his son high in the air. "Hey, cowboy."

"That was an *awesome* catch!"

"Thanks, buddy." He lowered his son to his hip in time to receive a hug from Terri.

"Way to go, bro." She kissed his cheek and turned to Jake. "How's your hand, Mr. First Base Man? Think you'll still be able to do surgery after catching Linc's throws?"

Jake gave an exaggerated wince and flexed his glove hand. "Maybe once the swelling subsides. Good thing I booked a couple of days off. I'd hate to think what would happen if your brother ever really let loose at me."

Terri's face glowed. "And what are you going to do with your days off? Anything exciting? At least one more game today, I suppose, since the team won."

Jake sat on the bench and reached down to untie his cleats. "Not for me. I'm heading into Winnipeg this afternoon for some culture."

"What kind of culture?"

"A play, if you must know, Miss Curiosity."

Terri laughed and asked, "Which one?"

Like the cylinders of a combination lock clicking into place, Lincoln knew what the answer would be. A tight sensation filled his chest. "Going to see *Les Mis*?"

Jake looked at him in surprise. "Kimberley told you?"

He lowered Matt to the ground and bent to retrieve his water bottle, acutely aware of Terri's sudden stillness. Straightening, he told Jake, "She asked Matt and me to check on her dog after supper." He shoved the bottle and his glove into his bag. "Enjoy the show. Come on, cowboy." He took Matt's hand. "We'd better get something to eat before the semi-final. Coming, Terri?"

His sister flashed Jake a cocky smile. "Sure. I want the biggest burger and greasiest batch of fries we can find."

"A likely story," Jake laughed. "See you, kiddo."

A few steps from the bench, Matt pulled away. "There's Kimmie. I want to talk to her."

"Be with you in a minute." Lincoln placed a hand on his sister's arm and guided her between two empty pickups in a line of vehicles parked beside the diamond. "Terri."

She turned to him, her chin high, tears shimmering in

her eyes. "I know what you're going to say. That he's ten years older than I am. That he treats me the same as when I was a kid. That if he wasn't interested in Kimberley, some other beautiful woman closer to his age would come along and he might marry her. And all that's true." She yanked her arm free. "But what about *you*? Are you just going to let him take her away from you?"

Lincoln tensed. "Hold on. She's never been *mine* for anyone to take, so are you saying that for me or for you?"

Anger flashed in his sister's eyes. "Don't tell me you don't care for her. I saw the look on your face when you kissed her hair. You *love* her, even if you won't admit it."

"Is that so?"

"Yes, it is. And do you know something else? You're *afraid* to admit it. Gayle scared you off women, and you've used Matt as a shield so you wouldn't have to be brave enough to love again. I might be a complete idiot, but at least I'm not scared to love." She gulped in a breath.

"Anything else while you're at it? Don't hold back."

"Yes." She flung him a scathing look. "You've been hiding out at the ranch since Dad died, licking your wounds because you lost your shot at the big league and regretting the fight you had with him before you went to Florida. You all thought I was asleep, but I heard it. And I think you fell in love with Kimberley the first time you saw her. And I'm not sorry I said all those things." Her head high, Terri walked away from him and waved to Kimberley.

Lincoln stared after his sister, his hands clenched.

When he stepped out from between the trucks, a trim man with graying hair and a tanned, creased face approached him. "Excuse me, son. I'd like to talk with you for a minute." The stranger removed reflective sunglasses and held out a hand. "I'm Bob MacLean."

The man had baseball written all over him.

Chapter 21

Kimberley watched Lincoln accept what looked like a business card from a man whose deep tan indicated that he spent a lot of time in the sun.

Jake joined her and Terri and Matt near the bleachers, his sports bag dangling from his hand. "Who's the stranger?" he asked in a low voice.

Kimberley shook her head, conscious of Matt's hand gripping hers, his eyes fixed on his father.

Terri shrugged. "Haven't a clue. I noticed him in the bleachers during the game, but I've never seen him before. He was sitting with Gordie Smith and the Seton baseball guys."

Jake's eyes narrowed. "Doesn't Gordie have an uncle who coaches Brandon's Senior Triple A team?"

"I wouldn't know. Could be he's visiting family."

"Or maybe he's heard about Seton's reputation."

"For what?" Terri placed her hands on her hips. "Our blazingly fast painted turtle races?"

Jake grinned. "I was thinking more along the lines of cheeky—I mean *pretty*—girls."

Terri touched her curls and pursed her lips in a

photogenic pout. "Flattery will get you everywhere."

Kimberley noted—not for the first time—that Lincoln's sister and Jake seemed to have a special bond.

"She's a brat, isn't she?" Jake asked, avuncular indulgence in his voice.

She smiled at Terri. "Not in my experience." She squeezed Matt's hand gently and released it. "I have to go. Lexi will need to go out. I'll see you tomorrow."

Matt smiled up at her. "Dad told me you'll be riding in the round-up with us."

"That's right." She turned to Jake and Terri. "Bye, both of you."

The teen smiled her lovely, warm smile. "Bye, Kimberley."

"I'll see you at three," Jake said, a sudden intensity in his eyes.

"Right." Warmth stole into her face. "At three."

At the old Steele place, she tended Lexi and unpacked her purchases. She hung the pants and blouse next to the yellow dress in her bedroom closet and ran her fingers over a cropped, silvery sweater she'd found after speaking with Wendy. The sweater was a bolero style, she'd been told by the store manager, and both she and the other woman had noticed that the metallic blue threads zigzagging through the silver fabric were the exact shade of Kimberley's eyes.

After hanging the sweater in the closet, she ate the remainder of the three-bean salad she'd made the previous day, along with Brie on two slices of crusty French bread she'd bought from Seton's bakery. Then for two hours, while Lexi rested in the darkened bedroom, she immersed herself in work. She analyzed the portraits she'd taken of Terri, excited at the way the teen's unguarded expression in the final indoor shot showed the girl caught between two life stages: child and woman. That was a keeper, as were two outdoor shots. She matted and framed an eight-by-ten print of Matt and Lexi romping under the elms, which she intended to give Matt as a birthday gift. Then she submitted a black-and-white version of the photo she'd taken of Lincoln and Matt in the wheat field to National Geographic's annual photography contest. She'd opted for black-and-white because that format intensified the poignancy of the scene.

Finally, she uploaded and scrolled through the action shots she'd snapped of Lincoln at the ball game. Most were a little out of focus, but in one clear, crisp image, she'd captured him in the air after the catch—glove hand in front of his chest, the ball in his right hand, his face lit with an expression of pure, adrenaline-fueled joy. As she stared at the image, she realized how much Lincoln had given up to manage the ranch. On the heels of that realization came the idea that perhaps she could expand portrait photography to include sports photography. As she shut down her laptop, it occurred to her that every image she'd examined that day had featured Terri, Matt, or Lincoln. In the short time since she'd moved to Turtle Mountain, the Steele family had become embedded in her life.

At three o'clock, Jake greeted her with a kiss on the cheek. He appeared every inch the successful vet, in gray dress pants and a navy, pin-striped, short-sleeved shirt. "You look beautiful!" he told her. "How's Lexi doing?"

"Thank you. She's been quiet all week but seems more comfortable—she doesn't scrunch into herself as much when I carry her out, and Matt said she sniffed his hand on Thursday." She switched on the exterior porch light, locked the door, and handed Jake a disc. "Here are the pics from the rehab center."

"Thanks again for donating your work." He accepted the disc and placed light fingers under her elbow. "Terri mentioned that Matthew loves Lexi."

"It's mutual. He's been over to visit her—quietly—every day this week except today."

"And he'll see her this evening."

She shot a look up at Jake's face. "How do you know that?"

"Linc mentioned it after the game. I suppose Terri brought Matthew over to visit Lexi during the week?"

"No, Lincoln did on his lunch breaks."

His gaze swung to the ravine and beyond it, the Steele Cattle Company complex of barns and shelters. "So, the truce is holding."

More than holding. Flashes of the past week reminded her that she'd spent hours with Lincoln, hours that had included revelations, rescue, camaraderie, and an unexpected kiss. "Did you think it wouldn't?"

Jake's gaze took on the same intensity it had at the

sports grounds. "Maybe I was hoping it wouldn't."

"What do you mean?"

"In some ways, I'd rather think of you at odds with Linc than not."

"Is that a subtle way of asking if something's going on between us?"

"Not so subtle, I guess. I know how—"

"He's your best friend." She fixed Jake with a warning glance. "When you trusted him to drive me home, your trust wasn't misplaced."

Her date hesitated and then nodded. "Good."

She sank into the convertible's luxury. "At the rehab center, Raymond mentioned that you're a military history buff."

Jake reversed the BMW out of the driveway. "I am. When I was a kid, I got hooked on Dudley Pope's *Ramage* series. I still read a fair amount on the subject in my spare time, but no doubt that will change in the future when I'm married." He gave a good-natured grin as he drove out the access road. "Hello, diapers. Good-bye, Admiral Nelson and Napoleon Bonaparte."

"And Mata Hari."

He chuckled. "Do you mind if we make a short detour? I want to show you something."

"No, I don't mind. What is it?"

"A piece of land I bought last week, four miles east of Seton. I finally convinced the farmer who owned it to sell me a quarter section."

"My city girl roots are showing. What's a quarter

section?"

"On the prairies, land was divided into sections a mile long and a mile across. A quarter section is a quarter of a mile long by a quarter of a mile wide. It holds one hundred and sixty acres."

"That's a lot of land."

"Compared with city lots, yes, but not compared with the farms around here. Most of my quarter is bush, but there's a slough and pasture and a nice rise with a good view."

"Are you planning to build?"

"I am. On that rise."

Twenty minutes later, Kimberley stood beside Jake on the rise, her sandaled feet pricked by dry prairie grasses. A patchwork of farm fields dotted with sloughs stretched away to the south, and aspen and oak woodland curved around the rise on the north. "It's a gorgeous spot. I can see why you wanted to buy it. Congratulations!"

His eyes shone. "They say a man's home is his castle. My castle will be here."

"What kind of castle do you have in mind?"

"I'm still working out the details, but I'm hoping to move into the house after Christmas." He smiled into her eyes. "All I need is someone to share it with me."

Before she could frame a witty response, he glanced at his watch. "Speaking of moving, we'd better go. I'd prefer to not have indigestion while watching the play."

"Of course."

As she started downhill, Jake placed his right arm

around her waist. "Don't want you to turn an ankle. Those sandals weren't made for this kind of terrain."

"If I'd known we were going to hike up a hill, I'd have worn boots."

"I'm glad you didn't. Gives me a chance to show you my gallant side."

"That sounds like something out of one of your historical novels. Did Admiral Nelson have a gallant side?"

"Definitely, but after the Battle of Santa Cruz, it was always his left side."

"Why is that?"

"Because he lost his right arm in the battle. Have you considered doing other types of photography?"

Surprised by the quick change of topic, she replied, "I'm considering branching into portrait photography. Maybe even sports photography. Why do you ask?"

He met her eyes. "Wildlife photography is a dangerous occupation, isn't it?"

"It can be, but probably not as dangerous as being a logger or a pilot."

"Still, once you settle down with a family, won't you want to stick closer to home?"

"Perhaps, or maybe I'll take my husband and kids with me sometimes. I hope the man I marry will support my career, whatever path it takes."

In silence, Jake guided her the rest of the way through the bleached, rustling grass to the convertible parked in a farm field access lane. Inside the BMW, he turned to her. "Your idea of portrait and sports photography is exciting.

I'd like to see some of your work when you get started."

"Actually, I've done a little experimenting already. Terri modeled for me a few weeks ago, and this morning, I got one good shot of Lincoln making that final catch."

"You did? I'd love to see that."

"I'll show it to you sometime. Tomorrow I'm shooting the round-up, which isn't exactly a sport, but I'm hoping for some interesting images."

His gaze sharpened. "Matthew mentioned that you'd be riding with him and Linc."

"Yes. Lincoln thought it might be a good photo op." She studied Jake's face. If she didn't know that he and Lincoln were best friends, she'd suspect him of being jealous. "I hope my horse is a calm one so I can focus on the shoot. Lincoln told me I'll be riding Lauren's mare."

"Jaycee Queen. JQ, for short. She's a sweetheart and pretty as a picture—a palomino. You should be all right on her, and I'll see you tomorrow, too."

"Are you riding?"

"No. Linc invited me to the barbecue, and no one in their right mind misses a Steele Cattle Company barbecue."

"I'm intrigued."

He took her hand lightly in his. "I know this is really short notice, but would you like to attend my cousin Lisa's wedding with me next Saturday? The ceremony's at one-thirty, and the reception's at six, with a dance to follow. I'd be honored if you would."

Another date. Where was their relationship headed?

And what exactly *was* her relationship with Jake? For that matter, what exactly was her relationship with Lincoln? "Thank you for the invitation, but I couldn't leave Lexi for the whole afternoon and evening."

Jake nodded. "Then how about joining me for the reception and dance? Would you feel comfortable with that?"

She took a deep breath. Maybe there was only one way to find out where her relationship with Jake was headed. "As long as I'm home by eleven."

"Does that mean you'll come?"

"Yes."

"Excellent. Now for *Les Mis*." The BMW purred as he backed out the access lane and steered the convertible toward Winnipeg.

Seated beside him, Kimberley enjoyed more anecdotes from the Battle of Santa Cruz, yet peace of mind evaded her. Mental pictures of Lincoln kept intruding—the ball game that morning, the swim at the lake, the kiss under the elms, the embrace in the forest after she'd pepper-sprayed the wild boar, the waltz that had led to her telling him of the grizzly attack.

She ran her gaze over Jake's profile. He looked serene, confident, on track in life. In her present state of finding her feet again—both as a photographer and a woman—his air of serenity and confidence was immensely appealing. She was tempted to cling to it, to ride the track with him. But would she want that forever?

* * *

In his mother's log house, Lincoln paced back and forth past the dining table several times before placing the card Bob MacLean had given him that morning on the polished oak surface.

Seated at the table, his mother stopped in the act of turning a page of her gardening catalogue. "What's this?" She picked up the card and read it. Emotions flitted across her face—curiosity, surprise, joy. When she smiled, it was as though sunshine radiated through her. "How exciting!"

"It would mean I'd have less time for the ranch."

"Of course. Your father would be so pleased."

He stared at her. "Terrence? You must be kidding."

"I didn't mean Terrence. I meant Andy."

He stopped pacing. "You haven't mentioned my biological father for a long time."

She shrugged lightly. "That doesn't mean I don't think about him. He shared your love of sport. Do you remember me telling you that he competed for Canada as a heptathlete and decathlete while at university?"

"I remember thinking that those two words had something to do with marching until you explained that 'hepta' meant seven and 'deca' meant ten."

A nostalgic smile curved her mouth. "You remind me so much of him. If you grew a mustache and beard, you could be his double."

He studied her face. "Do you still miss him?"

"Always."

"*Always?* I thought you loved Terrence."

His mother leaned back in her chair. "There are many kinds of love, Lincoln. Terrence was a good man. I cared deeply for him and miss him, but Andy was the love of my life."

He glanced through the log house's wall of windows to where his son and sister zinged a Frisbee to each other on the lawn. "Don't let Terri hear you say that."

"I won't." His mother closed the gardening catalogue. "Darling, despite the terrible argument you had with Terrence before you left for Florida—which he regretted, I might add—you are everything he wanted you to be. I always knew you didn't love the ranch like he did, and I believe he knew it, too. Be that as it may, he couldn't have asked—nor could I ask—for a more competent and dedicated manager than you've been." She stood and pushed her chair in. "You paid such a high price to help Terri and me. You lost your dream and then your marriage. Now you have a second chance to follow that dream—perhaps not to the Majors but at least to a level that does justice to your abilities."

"And the ranch?"

She spread her hands. "God has given you this opportunity. He'll find me a part-time manager if playing takes too much of your time. At least, you'd still be here in Manitoba. We have no crops to harvest this year, and all the stock except for the bred cows will be gone. If you want to play, this is a good time to do it."

He ran a hand through his hair. "I'm rusty as hell."

His mother picked up the business card and handed it to him. "Bob MacLean saw something in you that he wants." She tilted her head, a quizzical smile curving her mouth. "I have to admit that I've always wondered why you chose to play slow-pitch."

He slid the card into his polo shirt pocket. Today seemed to be a day for revelations, so why not jump onboard? "Remember how clingy Matt was, especially after Gayle died?"

"I certainly do."

"One day when I was in the bank, he was all over me. I could barely deal with the transaction. The teller happened to be Carol Dueck."

"Does she still play second base on your team?"

"She does. Anyway, she gave Matt and me one of those deep, slow looks of hers and then invited me to throw a few balls with the team. Told me to bring Matt along, that her gang would look after him for me."

His mother's eyes danced. "Were you insulted?"

"Flabbergasted is more like it, but she looked me straight in the eye."

"And you went for Matt's sake."

"I never even put on my glove. He panicked and started screaming when I tried to leave him with the other kids and Terri, so we just left."

"But you went back."

"I did, and the team adopted Matt and me, one painful inning at a time."

"Terri told me she was at her wit's end with Matt more

than once."

"She was amazing, God bless her. I can never thank her enough. The poor kid basically collapsed into my arms after every game." And Jake had seen her efforts and made a point of bantering with her. Now, look where that had led.

His mother spread her hands. "It's not the same situation now. Matt will be all right. He's healed an incredible amount, particularly since Kimberley arrived."

Kimberley. He glanced at his watch. He'd missed his chance to talk with her after the game, and now she was watching *Les Mis* with his best friend. Jake came with no strings attached, no garbage from the past. How fast would he move in his pursuit of a wife? "Did you know that Terri's crush on Jake is more than a crush?"

His mother's brow furrowed. "I suspected. She'll be heartbroken when he marries. It seems he's interested in Kimberley."

"He is." Lincoln walked to the French doors and then paused to look over his shoulder at the woman who had guided his life. "And so am I. That means I'm breaking my promise to stay away from her."

"I see."

He touched his cap brim and opened one of the doors. "Matt and I need to check on her dog. She's in Winnipeg."

"Don't forget to take the boots for her. I hope she enjoys the round-up." Sudden amusement lit his mother's eyes. "Cattle. Dust. Horses. Dust. Cowboys..."

"Dust," Lincoln supplied, grinning wryly. "No shortage

of that this year. I have to say that I'll be relieved when all the cattle other than the breeding stock are gone."

His mother's levity evaporated. "So will I. You know I'm not superstitious, but for the past week, I've had the feeling that something is looming over us, and I don't know what it is. The grass is so dry, it's like tinder. A fire could get started so easily, accidentally or…"

A knot formed in his gut. So he wasn't the only one who suspected that the ranch might be a target. "We'll set a round-the-clock watch on the herds. I'll ask Tom McCorquodale and Mike Ransom to help out, and I'll do my best to get the stock out of here before the end of the week. The plan is to load from daybreak until mid-morning every day. It's too hot to load later than that."

"I know. I'll pray for the temperature to take a nosedive."

"Ask for rain, too, while you're at it. Goodnight, and don't worry. We'll get through this."

At the old Steele place, the yellow house stood solid and bright, made even more cheerful by the presence of Kimberley's red truck parked beside it. Lincoln unlocked the sun porch door, and he and Matt quietly entered the house that he would forever associate with the woman who had freed his son. As they stepped into the darkened bedroom, Kimberley's husky lifted its head, still encircled by the plastic protective cone.

"It's okay, Lexi. Kimmie asked us to take you out." Matt crouched beside the dog and stretched out a hand. The husky licked his fingers, and he grinned. "Now Dad's gonna pick you up."

Lincoln gently carried the dog outdoors onto the lawn. The cast on the husky's foreleg caused it to limp awkwardly, but the dog pricked its ears forward and managed a half-dozen steps before squatting to do its business. Matt whispered encouragement, and Lexi limped toward them before stopping to rest, tail hanging. Lincoln carefully lifted Kimberley's pet into his arms and returned to the bedroom. As he set the husky on its pillow, Lexi's blue eyes met his—blue as the prairie summer sky, almost the blue of Kimberley's eyes.

He looked around the room. Pepper spray on the night table. A framed photograph of Gary Colter and his wife and an older man who resembled Kimberley and her brother too closely to be anyone other than their father. A photograph of a teenage Kimberley with a blonde woman, their arms around each other, love radiating from their smiles. Her mother?

The yellow dress in the closet teased him with images of Kimberley wearing it. If he'd taken her in his arms in his truck after the dance—breaking Jake's trust—would she be with his best friend now?

Chapter 22

At dawn, Kimberley lifted the strap of a waist pack onto her shoulder and locked the back porch door, remembering she'd have to ask Lincoln for the sun porch key. Fatigue rolled over her as she walked to her truck. A late night and less than four hours of fitful sleep weren't the best ingredients for a successful morning shoot. Fighting to clear her mind, she backed her Ranger out of the driveway and drove away from the yellow house.

It had been nearly one in the morning when Jake had walked her to the door, a full moon painting shadows on the driveway. The three-hour drive from Winnipeg had been quiet. Drained—almost overwhelmed—by the emotional intensity of *Les Misérables*, she'd found it difficult to make light conversation. After a few attempts, Jake had lapsed into silence. Before saying goodnight, he'd kissed her. When he'd pulled away, his face had looked flushed in the light spilling onto the back porch step.

During the night, she'd tossed and turned, her mind racing with images from the play and shadowy questions about her future. Did a person ever know where life would lead? The convict character in the play, Jean Valjean, could not have foreseen his redemption. A year ago, she never would have imagined she'd now be living in a farmhouse in southwestern Manitoba and dating a veterinarian. When she'd moved to the old Steele place, she hadn't even known Jake existed. She'd come because of the need to make a new start and because she'd been intrigued by a trio of strangers she'd met in the park. During the weeks after her arrival, the entire Steele family had welcomed her—almost adopted her. Even so, was it possible that Jake, rather than the Steeles, was the key to her new life? She acknowledged that it was possible, yet a niggling doubt refused to leave her. When Jake had kissed her, she'd only felt the barest hint of response.

* * *

Lincoln led Jaycee Queen across the ranch yard, the saddled palomino mare clopping sedately behind him. JQ was an easy loader, which was why he'd chosen to load the mare into the double horse trailer first. JQ sniffed at the ramp, pricked ears forward, and then climbed the incline and entered the trailer's left compartment. "Atta girl."

A flash of red caught his eye, and he watched Kimberley drive her Ranger into the ranch yard. He waited until after the engine had died and she'd exited the truck before calling calmly, "Stay there, would you, Kimberley? Matt's pony is a little shy about loading." He nodded to his son. "Okay, Matt. Bring her up."

When Matt handed him Darby's lead rope, the sorrel danced to the side. "Easy, girl. You know how to do this.

Matt, go say hello to Kimberley." Making kissing noises, he walked to the right side of the trailer's door, allowing the pony plenty of rope. After two false starts, Darby stepped forward onto the ramp, sniffed at JQ, and hesitantly entered the trailer. "Good girl."

Lincoln secured the pony, locked the trailer's back door, and then strode to where Matt and Kimberley stood beside the Ranger. She wore snug jeans tucked into his mother's tall black riding boots and held a small camera in her hands.

"Good morning, *Ms. Colter*. Ready to ride?"

"As ready as I'll ever be, *Mr. Steele*." She tucked the camera into a waist pack.

He looked at her closely, taking in her shadowed eyes. "Late getting back?"

"Around one."

"How was *Les Mis*?"

"Amazing, but it didn't make for a peaceful sleep. My imagination was in overdrive all night. Thanks for taking Lexi out."

"No problem." He retrieved the sun porch key from his jeans pocket and handed it to her.

She eyed his black straw Stetson. "So you *do* own a cowboy hat, and so does Matt. I feel out of place, with my baseball cap."

"We can fix that. Terri's hat's in the office. Want to try it? "

"Terri's not riding?"

"She has to work the early shift, pumping gas. I'll text

her about the hat."

"Why not? I may never have another chance to wear a cowboy hat and ride in a round-up."

"Cow*girl* hat," Matt chipped in.

"I stand corrected."

Moments later, with permission, Lincoln handed Kimberley his sister's brown straw hat, with its tooled leather band and turquoise-studded underbrim design. She settled it atop her black mane. "Looks good." *Better than good.* From the first instant he'd seen Kimberley taking pictures in the park, he'd thought she was beautiful and strong. Now she looked like she belonged to the land in a whole different way.

He led the way out of the office. "Alf and Dale already headed out. Alf's pulling the trailer that has my horse. We'll bring in the cattle from the north pasture first, then the west one. Tom McCorquodale—pitcher on our slow-pitch team—and his crew will bring in the east herds. Tom's cutting horse is a world champion. She and Tom like to get out and play."

A fresh breeze blew through the open truck windows as Lincoln drove out of the ranch yard. His tired round-up guest inhaled a deep, time-to-wake-up kind of breath and looked at him over the top of Matt's Stetson. "Is there a reason why you chose this morning for the round-up?"

"Less traffic on a Sunday. We'll drive the north herd down Sanderson Road. My mother called the neighbors to warn them."

"How many cattle will we be rounding up, in total?"

"Do you remember, Matt?" he asked.

His son yawned. "Five hundred…and fifty-three."

"That's right. Tom'll bring in five hundred and ten. We sorted the stock last week. We'll bring in the groups separately."

She frowned. "Which groups?"

"Cows. Steers. Heifers. Weaned calves, sexed."

"Each of those groups goes into a separate pasture?"

"That's right. We have shipping pastures next to the loading corrals."

She looked through the windshield at the parched land. "The pastures look so dry. Will that many cattle have enough to eat?"

"Dale's already put out hay. Once we've brought in the cattle, we'll settle them so they can fill up and rest."

"Settle?"

He grinned. "You're getting a crash course in ranching. When cattle, especially calves, have been trailed, they often keep on walking, and that takes off weight. We hang around with them, soothing them until they settle down and start eating."

"When will you ship them?"

"Four loads early tomorrow morning, and the same for the next three mornings."

"Sounds like all this might be stressful for the cows—steers—calves—whatever."

She was quick on the pick-up. "All of the above. And yes, it is stressful. Every time you move cattle, it causes some weight loss. That's called shrinkage. Since the price we get is based on weight, the goal is to minimize shrinkage. That's why we'll do everything nice and easy. No yelling or scaring the stock."

She eyed the waist pack resting on her lap. "Are you sure taking pictures will be all right?"

"Should be. We'll be riding at the back of the herd." He sent her a cautioning look. "That means dust."

She nodded. "Rule number one in dusty conditions: protect camera until needed. Rule number two: never change lenses in the field. Rule number three: clean camera thoroughly after the shoot."

Matt looked up at her, "How many cameras did you bring?"

"Two. My little go-everywhere, autofocus Sony and my Nikon with a short zoom lens, not the telephoto lens we used with the burrowing owls. My challenge today will be to take steady shots."

"We can stop now and then," Lincoln told her. "Just say when. And Jaycee Queen is as quiet as they come."

"Thanks, I appreciate that."

At the north pasture, he introduced her to Alf and Dale and then quickly unloaded Jaycee Queen and Darby. After seeing Matt and Kimberley safely mounted, he swung his leg over Batlock's back. Early sunshine gilded the dry pasture and a herd of sleek Angus steers that stared at them curiously. At his nod, Dale opened the pasture gate and then mounted a quad to act as a road block to prevent the steers from turning in the wrong direction onto Sanderson Road.

With Matt and Kimberley beside him, Lincoln circled behind the steers and nudged them toward the gate. The herd flowed through the opening, filling the road and ditches, dust rising among the muscular black bodies. A few steers bolted into short-lived runs and then slowed to the brisk walking pace set by the herd leaders. Alf led the way south, driving his pickup slowly. Dust billowed from beneath the truck's tires and wafted across fields in a pale plume carried on the morning breeze.

Adrenaline coursed through Lincoln. He'd taken every precaution to ensure the safety of both humans and cattle, but a hundred things could go wrong during a round-up. It was up to him to see that everything went right. So far, Kimberley was doing okay. She threw him an excited smile, and he touched his hat brim, saluting her. This gorgeous woman riding beside him thrived on adventure, blossoming in the outdoors. He could picture her someday leading her kids into wild places. On the heels of that thought came another—he wanted to be the father of those children.

* * *

When they reached a rise, Kimberley drew in a quick breath at the scene before her. The herd looked like a black snake slithering through sun-bleached pastures. "This is a great view," she called to Lincoln over the rumble created by the cattle. "Go ahead. I want you and Matt in the picture. I'll catch up."

He nodded, and she eased Jaycee Queen to a halt.

Exhilaration raced through her as she removed the Nikon from her waist pack. "Easy, girl. Nice and still." She patted the mare on the neck and then quickly snapped images of the scene before her—river of black cattle, Lincoln and Matt nearly silhouetted against a backdrop of dust-infused, golden light. When Lincoln turned his head to speak to Matt, she fired off a burst of twenty shots of father and son outlined in profile. *Perfect!* She returned her camera to her waist pack and urged Jaycee Queen into a fast walk. Her last ride had been a trail ride with Bryan in the Rockies. There, the rugged majesty of lofty peaks and forested valleys had stretched into the distance as though seeking eternity. On the Manitoba prairie, she was close to the earth, to the here and now, to the parched land and dusty gravel.

For hours, she rode at Lincoln's side, with Matt next to her. Knowing she might never have another chance, she immersed herself in the round-up—the rocking motion of riding, the grit of dust on her skin, the pungent smell of fresh manure, the thud of hooves, the rasping bawls of cattle. Throughout it, she helped keep the cattle moving, first the steers from the north pasture and then weaned calves from a west pasture. More boisterous than the steers, some of the calves bucked and ran, tails high, until they settled into a jogging walk to their allotted shipping pasture.

"This has been wonderful," she told Lincoln when they approached the shipping pastures for the last time. "What a fantastic way to spend a morning! Thank you so much for inviting me."

Sitting tall and easy in the saddle, he grinned, his amber eyes teasing beneath the black Stetson. "You might not say that when it comes time to dismount."

Her breath caught in her throat, and in that instant, she completely understood why cowboy movies continued to be made and why thousands of women read western romances. Cowboy charisma was hard to resist. A sudden hope soared within her. Maybe Lincoln really *did* care for her. Maybe his kiss had been genuine. If that were true, where did it put her relationship with Jake? Questions ricocheted in her brain.

Lincoln turned to his son. "It's getting hot, cowboy. You and Kimberley untack and cool down Darby and JQ. Snacks are in the kitchenette. I'll meet you after I settle the calves and check the rest of the stock." He nodded to her and then entered the calves' shipping pasture, breaking into a song as he rode Batlock slowly around the perimeter.

She strained to hear the words and melody but couldn't distinguish more than a few snippets amid the background noise. As she and Matt rode toward the ranch yard, her attention shifted to Tom McCorquodale mounted on a wiry brown horse that moved with quick grace among black cattle in an adjacent shipping pasture. More cattle filled other pastures. *Black gold.* It was a sea of beef. She couldn't even guess at the herds' value. Lincoln had said the ranch would take a hit this year, so that meant a lot depended on getting these cattle safely to market.

Hopefully the next four days would pass without incident. In the ranch yard, she groaned as she swung out of the saddle.

* * *

Lincoln parked his pickup outside the ranch office, a huge burden lifting from his shoulders. The round-up had gone as planned and with no injuries. However, another weight—guarding and loading the stock—still rested on him. His cell phone jingled in his shirt pocket. The boss. "Hello. I just finished a final check. Cattle are settled. No problems."

"Excellent. That's such a blessing. We're all set here. Will you be much longer?"

"Just a minute in the office, then I'm on my way." Settling the calves had taken longer than expected. Matt had grown tired of waiting and texted to ask if Kimberley could drive him to his grandmother's house. He'd agreed, knowing he was holding up Kimberley, who by then had probably needed to tend her injured dog. Again, he'd missed an opportunity to talk with her privately. "Dale offered to take the first watch, as long as someone brings him a cold drink, a plate piled high, and two pieces of pie—preferably coconut cream and apple with ice cream."

"Done. I'll take his meal over right after grace."

Grace. Throughout his life, his mother had seen grace in places where he'd only seen hardship and pain. "Learn to see with the depths of your heart," she'd implored in the months after Gayle's betrayal and the abuse. "We may not understand why things happen, but God's grace is everywhere, and God's grace is sufficient."

Maybe he'd always been blind, his heart closed to that inner voice. He hadn't seen his wife's unhappiness. He hadn't seen how much his son needed to have pictures of his mother. He hadn't realized how hard he'd become until Kimberley had pushed him into taking a critical look at himself. She'd broken his world—and his heart—wide open.

In the ranch office, he phoned the livestock shipping company, confirming the time the trucks would arrive in the morning. Then he strode to his pickup, singing Neil Young's "Harvest Moon." A memory flashed into his mind. On a moonlit August night, the little band he'd somehow found time to be part of in high school had performed the hit at a benefit dance in Seton, with Jake at the keyboard, Jack Bos on electric guitar, Tom McCorquodale on drums, and Gayle's clear, warm voice backing up his own lead vocals. Could it have been ten years ago? The memory held no pain or bitterness, only sweet nostalgia. God had set him free.

Chapter 23

"This looks amazing," Wendy whispered. Damien rested against her chest, asleep in a fabric baby carrier. Beside Wendy, Gary pushed a stroller.

"It does." Kimberley took in the sight before her. Covered with red-and-white-checked tablecloths, four tables stood end-to-end in dappled shade cast by the windbreak at the edge of Lauren's yard. Wine glasses and white cloth napkins complemented an assortment of dinner plates on the tables, and vases of flowers added bright splashes of color. Clear pitchers of water and bottles of wine rested among the plates, as did condiments, baskets of buns, plates of butter, and dishes of pickles. Off to the side, in the shade of a spreading willow tree, coolers held cans of soda pop and beer on ice. A round table with a white tablecloth held bowls of salads, and another bore dessert plates and a dozen pies. A third table was laden with cutting boards topped by chunky, foil-covered shapes. "Must be the meat," Kimberley murmured.

"That's quite a set-up." Gary nodded toward a concrete fire pit flanked by two sturdy wrought-iron stands holding a steel spit. An extension cord trailed from the log house to a motor connected to the spit, now motionless. "Motor turned the spit. I wonder how many hours they cooked the calf."

"I wonder how many people are here." Kimberley scanned the yard and counted Lauren, Matt, and twenty-eight guests. Adults stood in clusters in the shade provided by the windbreak while teens and children explored among the trees. The tables were set for thirty-six, which meant that three people hadn't arrived yet—Lincoln, Jake, and Terri.

Smiling, Lauren approached. "Welcome to our annual Steele Cattle Company barbecue. Did you enjoy your ride this morning, Kimberley?"

"So much." Kimberley hugged Lincoln's mother. "Thank you for the use of your boots and for allowing me to ride Jaycee Queen. She was the perfect mount for a riding shoot."

"Excellent. Are you stiff?"

"Terribly, but the ride was worth it. Do you remember my brother, Gary Colter?"

"Of course." Lauren reached out to shake Gary's hand. "As I told Kimberley, we're so pleased with the arena you designed. How are you, Gary?"

"Very well, Mrs. Steele. This is my wife, Wendy, and the newest addition to the Colter family, Damien."

"I'm happy to meet you, Wendy, and please, both of you, call me Lauren." She gently touched the sleeping baby's dark hair. "What a darling child! How old is "Damien?"

Wendy smiled proudly. "One week."

"You're brave to be out and about so soon after the birth. Would you like a cushion to sit on?"

"I have one in the stroller, but thank you."

"Let's walk into the shade. It's becoming unbearably hot."

"How long did you roast the calf?" Gary asked as they strolled toward the windbreak.

"Eight hours. Lincoln was here at three-thirty to light the fire and help Terri and me spit the calf. We had a good bed of coals by four-fifteen, after which it was just a matter of feeding the fire and basting the meat with drippings."

Wendy extended a hand toward the tables. "Everything looks so welcoming, so marvelously abundant. Did you make all those salads and pies?"

"The pies, yes, with Terri's help. The salads and buns, no." Lauren nodded in the direction of the other guests. "Jenny McCorquodale baked the buns—hers are always mouthwatering—and Paula Ransom and other friends and neighbors brought the salads. Let me introduce you around."

As Kimberley shook hands with the other guests, a number commented, "You're the lady with the big camera and red truck." That phrase was inevitably followed by, "How's the photography going?" Surprised by the level of interest in her work, she briefly recounted some of her recent sightings before Lauren tactfully moved to another group of guests.

"You're a hit," Wendy whispered.

"Much to my surprise."

"Ah, here's Jake." Lauren lifted a hand in greeting. "And Lincoln will only be a minute. Then we can start. Terri doesn't get off work until two, so she'll be late."

Jake set a bowl on the salad table before kissing the ranch owner on the cheek. "Hello, Lauren. The sun shines yet again on Steele Cattle Company barbecue day."

Lauren laughed. "Hello, Jake. You always arrive precisely at the appointed hour. Did you bring your famous coleslaw?"

"I did. Hi, Kimberley." He bent to kiss Kimberley lightly on the lips and slid an arm around her. "How was riding in the round-up?"

Heat bloomed in her cheeks. "Wonderful! I might have some good shots. I haven't gone over them in detail yet." She introduced Jake to Gary and Wendy, acutely aware of the warmth of his bare arm on her back. Instinctively, she glanced at the house and saw Lincoln striding across the lawn toward them.

* * *

Lincoln walked through the breezeway between his mother's house and garage and stepped onto the back yard lawn, his boots crunching the dry grass. He'd washed his hands and face and swatted some of the dust off his clothes but hadn't had time to drive home and shower. He scanned the yard and spotted Jake approaching his mother, who stood with Kimberley and her brother and sister-in-law. Jake kissed Lauren on the cheek, and she smiled in return. It looked like he'd just arrived. About to call out a greeting, Lincoln paused when his best friend kissed Kimberley and slid an arm around her. So, Jake was staking a claim.

He took a deep breath and kept on walking.

"Good. You're here." Lauren glanced from him to Jake, questions in her gaze. She called for everyone's attention, prayed over the food, and invited guests to choose a place at a table and fill their plates. "Would you slice the meat?" she asked. "It's all set up on cutting boards."

"Sure. Hi, Jake." He shook hands with his friend and then extended his hand to Kimberley's brother. "I saw you with Kimberley at Adam Lake in May, but we haven't met. I'm Lincoln Steele."

"Gary Colter. This is my wife, Wendy."

The two of them had the tired, elated look of brand-new parents. "Good to meet you." For a moment, the baby in the carrier reminded him of Matt sleeping against Gayle, his red hair sticking straight up, the softest of crowns. "And this must be Damien."

"Yes." Gary's voice held surprise.

"My son looked after Lexi when Kimberley was with you for the birth. She gave us a full report when she got back." He smiled at Kimberley, noting the high color in her face, and then nodded to Gary and Wendy. "Catch you later. I'd better slice that beef."

Jake stepped away from Kimberley. "Want some help?"

Lincoln eyed his friend. "As long as you don't name every muscle we're eating."

"I'll restrain myself."

He stood side by side with Jake behind the table, cutting thick slices of hot, succulent beef. As they served it, they chatted with friends and neighbors about the weather, the crops and gardens, the livestock, the kids. To Lincoln's mind—and to his mother's, he knew—the Steele Cattle Company's annual barbecue represented more than a meal, even more than a celebration. It embodied rural community, a sharing of food and, along with it, a sharing of life tied to the land.

When Jake burst into laughter at a comment Tom made, a mix of joy and pain cut through Lincoln. There was no man he was more honored to stand beside than Jake, yet he hoped that for once in his life, his best friend would fail at something, just one thing—his pursuit of Kimberley.

* * *

"Those two seem close." Seated at the table, Wendy nodded to where Lincoln and Jake stood behind the meat table. "One, the rugged cowboy, the other, the successful vet."

Kimberley followed Wendy's gaze. Lincoln still wore the navy polo shirt and jeans he'd worn for the round-up. Perhaps he hadn't had time to change. Jake had paired a cobalt short-sleeved shirt with cream pants. Only a few remaining guests stood in line, waiting to be served.

"They're best friends."

Wendy lifted an eyebrow, her voice thoughtful. "That'll make it harder."

"What do you mean?"

"Choo—"

Damien's heart-wrenching cry rent the air.

"I wondered if I would make it through the meal. *Shh*, sweet baby." Wendy pushed her chair back and rose to her feet, looking around her. "Maybe I'll nurse him in the car," she told Gary. She smiled self-consciously at the other guests at the table. "Sorry for the disturbance."

An older man shook his head, empathy in his features. "Don't you worry. A baby's got to eat when it's hungry. Look at us. We've all got our meal."

Damien's cries grew louder and more insistent.

Lincoln approached and gently touched Damien's back. "You're welcome to use the house," he told Wendy. "No one's in there, and it's cool and quiet."

"Thank you. That would be wonderful." A tear slid down Wendy's cheek.

Startled at the sight, Kimberley rose from her chair. "I'll come, too. I'll bring our plates, and we can finish eating inside." She caught Gary's look of thanks before following Lincoln and Wendy across the lawn and into the living room of Lauren's log home. She set the plates on the dining table.

Lincoln remained by the French doors. "If you'd like more privacy, there are bedrooms upstairs. Bathroom's up there, too."

"Thank you, this is fine," Wendy's voice rose above Damien's cries.

He nodded and stepped out onto the stone patio, closing the door behind him.

More tears rolled down Wendy's cheeks as she sat on the floral-patterned sofa, removed Damien from the baby carrier, and guided his mouth to her breast. Screaming, the baby made several unsuccessful attempts to latch onto the nipple before he finally succeeded.

In the sudden quiet, Kimberley's shoulders relaxed. "Are you okay?" she asked Wendy.

"Hormones." Wendy wiped a hand across her face. "One minute, I'm Supermom and the next, I'm a mess."

"Here." Kimberley pulled two tissues from a box on a sideboard and handed them to her sister-in-law.

"Thanks." Wendy wiped her eyes and blew her nose. "You know, if I didn't love your brother so much, I could seriously fall for that cowboy, especially when he looks at my baby as though he's just seen an angel. I know it's none of my business, but I think you should go after him. He's a keeper."

Kimberley stared at her sister-in-law. "Wendy, it's not that simple."

"Meaning the scars or the vet?"

She sat on the sofa beside Wendy. "Meaning Jake, I suppose. Lincoln and I sorted out the scars business— more or less."

"Good." Wendy brushed fingertips over Damien's hair. "Was he the one who mentioned vanity?"

"Yes. I did *not* appreciate it at the time, but now I think there might be something to what he said. I can't go through the rest of my life hiding my scars and hiding *behind* my scars.

"You know what your dad would say about all this, don't you?"

"'Follow your heart.'"

"Exactly. The question is, what's your heart telling you?"

What's my heart telling me? The question haunted Kimberley. After the barbecue ended and Gary and family departed for Brandon, she paced through the yellow house, reviewing every interaction she'd had with Lincoln and Jake. Jake asked her out on dates, entertained her, and pursued her. Lincoln shared everyday life with her, had her back, and was always there for her. Both were good men who intrigued and attracted her in different ways. Mired in analysis, she grew frustrated and forced herself to take a step back. She really didn't know where either of those relationships was headed, and anyway, what was the likelihood she'd ever have to choose between the two men? Zero.

Dismissing the comparison, she edited the photos she'd taken during the round-up, thrilled that three of the images of Lincoln and Matt backlit by the sun had captured what she'd hoped they would—a bond between father and son set against the backdrop of nitty-gritty rural life. At least with her photography, she had control. *Really?*

the taunting voice in her head jeered. *You've never returned to the Rockies. You're still scared, aren't you?* She quashed the voice, immersing herself in work.

For the next three mornings, the sounds of bawling cattle and revving stock trailers drifted across the ravine as the ranch's shipping pastures emptied. Lincoln and Matt joined her for hurried lunches, Lincoln's tenseness easing during the brief intervals of food and camaraderie beneath their favorite elm. Jake phoned each day and stopped in briefly one afternoon after attending a case at a nearby farm. In mid-week, a raging thunderstorm had Lexi cringing on her pillow as wind and hail pounded the yellow house, shattering two windows. The loud crack of a breaking tree split the night, and, petrified with fear, Kimberley waited for the thud of it hitting the house—a thud that never came.

The next morning, Lincoln looked worn and harried as he inspected the damage to the house and yard. One of the majestic elms had broken off at the base, its massive trunk lying across the crushed white rail fence. He removed his Blue Jays cap and raked a hand through his hair. "As if this isn't enough, a tornado touched down north of Winnipeg and damaged the livestock sales complex. That means we have to wait until Sunday to ship the calves."

She touched his arm lightly. "It's just three days, Lincoln. Then it'll be over and you can relax."

He caught her hand in his. "Three days can be an eternity. Kimberley, I need to talk with you, but all I can think about right now is the cattle. I'll come over as soon as I can." He released her hand. "I'll pick up replacement glass for the windows later today and send Dale over with a chainsaw to cut up the elm."

She watched him stride to his pickup, his shoulders rigid. An image swept into her mind, that of Lincoln and Jake standing side by side, cutting beef for guests at the barbecue. The two men were so close. Was it possible that her presence on Turtle Mountain would drive a wedge between them?

* * *

Lincoln stared at Terri. His sister looked every inch a beautiful, desirable woman. She'd swept her blond curls back from her face in an elegant, playful style. Tastefully applied makeup accented her smoky green eyes, and glossy scarlet lipstick shone on her lips. A sleeveless, ankle-length dress the exact shade of her lipstick clung to her youthful curves, and gold, spike-heeled sandals graced her feet. "Wow! You look amazing." He dropped a light kiss on her cheek. "What's the occasion?"

"Paul Engbrecht's sister is getting married this afternoon, and he asked me to go with him." She raised a hand quickly. "Just as a friend. We're not dating or anything."

"I'd forgotten it's Lisa's big day. The last time I talked to Jake, he mentioned he was going to be an usher at his cousin's wedding, but it slipped my mind that it's today. When's the ceremony?"

"One-thirty. Paul's the other usher, so we have to be

there early."

"It's only eleven."

"I know, but I'm not very good at this primping stuff, so I wasn't sure how long it would take to transform myself into…" She shrugged, her expression marked by uncharacteristic uncertainty. "I had to practice a lot."

"Well, I'd say you hit the ball out of the park. I hope you make it to the church in one piece. Paul may not be able to keep his eyes on the road."

His sister's quick grin flashed.

He drove to the old Steele place at noon. Would Kimberley be there? Maybe Jake had asked her to attend the wedding with him. The red truck was parked beside the house, but that didn't mean she was home. He carried a casserole dish to the back door and knocked. The door opened, and Kimberley stood before him, dressed in green cargo shorts and a white tank top. *Forget Jake and the calves. Forget everything except Kimberley.*

"Hi." She looked around him. "Matt's not with you?"

"He's at a birthday party."

"Ah, and his party's on Monday." She smiled and glanced at the casserole dish. "What's on the menu today?"

"Farmer's sausage."

"Excellent. I have French bread and my favorite salad." She led the way into the kitchen.

He set his dish on the kitchen table. "Can I help?"

"You could slice the bread." She handed him a cutting board. "I'll get the butter. What would you like to drink? Hot or cold?"

She seemed a little flustered. "Cold water's fine. My mother says hello and asked me to tell you again how much she enjoyed having you and Gary and Wendy at the barbecue. She was quite taken with little Damien."

"Your mother is an incredibly kind and generous woman."

"She is." He sliced thick slices of bread. "Her motto is that God put us on this earth to be a blessing to others, and she lives by that motto. She has the kind of inner strength I've never seen in another woman." He glanced at Kimberley. "Except for you."

Astonishment flashed across her face. "*I* have your mother's strength?"

"With an added dose of hot sauce."

"Is that a polite way of saying I have a temper?"

"It's a polite way of saying that you're a kind and generous woman in a different way. A spicier version, if you'd like. By the way, a blush looks good on you."

Her blue eyes flashed. "Now you're flirting with me."

"A little, but it's all true." His amusement faded. "Kimberley—"

"Let's eat." She popped off the salad bowl's lid, her movements jerky, as though she was on a leash.

"What kind of salad?" he asked, studying the brightly colored contents of the bowl.

"It has spinach, rice, cashews, red pepper, celery, and a bunch of other ingredients, with a garlic and soy sauce dressing. It's unusual."

They ate outdoors, seated on the sun-browned grass in

the shade of an elm. He ran his gaze over her features.
"You seem restless. Are you feeling cooped up?"

She blew out a breath. "That's putting it mildly. I'm so
tired of being indoors, I don't know what to do with
myself. And that's why..." she scrambled to her feet, "I
baked a chocolate cake. Do you like chocolate cake?"

"My favorite."

"Good. I'll bring us some."

He placed a light hand on her ankle to detain her.
"Kimberley, the cake can wait. I'd like to talk with you for
a few minutes. Please sit down."

A storm of emotion lit her eyes. "All right." She
lowered herself to the grass at his side. "What do you want
to talk about?"

"Us." No sooner had he uttered the word than tires
crunched on the gravel driveway, and sunlight glinted off a
white pickup. Frustration formed a knot in his gut. The
timing couldn't be worse. He touched Kimberley's cheek.
"We're about to be interrupted, so I'll come by tomorrow
after the last shipment. Will you be here?"

A tendril of hair blew across her face, screening her
gaze. "I'll be here."

He stood and gave her a hand up.

Dust rose from under the white pickup's tires as Jake
pulled into the yard. He frowned as he exited the truck.
"Linc." He shook hands with Lincoln. "Your shadow isn't
with you today."

"Matt's at a birthday party."

"I had a case down the road, so thought I'd drop in to

see Kimberley for a few minutes."

Lincoln glanced at his watch. "You're running close to the wire, aren't you? The wedding starts in a little over an hour."

"I know, but I wanted to confirm with Kimberley what time to pick her up for the reception."

He glanced at Kimberley. She had that flustered look about her again, as if her thoughts were going in different directions. "Well then, I'd better be off. I'll just grab my dish. See you tomorrow, Kimberley."

"Yes. And I'll send cake so you and Matt can celebrate the last shipment."

He touched his baseball cap. "Looking forward to it." He retrieved his dish and strode to his pickup. *Just one more day*. He glanced across the yard, his steps faltering as Kimberley smiled up at Jake. Then he pushed ahead strongly. After the last shipment, nothing—*nothing*—was going to stop him from telling Kimberley what was in his heart—that she'd brought light back into his life. That he loved her.

* * *

At the wedding reception in the Seton Community Center, Kimberley had the impression that she was playing a supporting role in a movie. Terri, seated at the same table as she and Jake, looked as strikingly beautiful as a scarlet rose suddenly opened. Jake's cousin Paul, a good-looking blond boy with an air of entitlement, draped his arm around Terri's shoulders. Jake, handsome in his beige suit, looked annoyed with Paul and, surprisingly, with Terri. His banter with her had a decided edge to it, and Terri responded in kind.

"What's up?" Kimberley asked him when he took her in his arms to dance after the meal. "You seem out of sorts today." Not only was he annoyed with Terri, he'd been annoyed when he'd seen Lincoln at the old Steele place. He'd asked her if Lincoln had joined her for lunch before without Matt. The question had sounded like an interrogation.

"Sorry." Irritation faded from Jake's gaze. "I haven't been good company, have I?"

"No, you haven't. You spent the whole meal sniping at Terri, to say nothing of Paul, and you've been glaring at them ever since we started dancing. What's bothering you?" She glanced across the dance floor to where Paul held Terri in a tight embrace. "Are you upset because of the way Paul is acting toward Terri?"

Jake's jaw tightened. "He's taking liberties."

"Jake, Terri is a very smart young woman. If she doesn't want Paul's attention, she'll tell him."

"He's a spoiled brat. It irks me to see him with Terri. She's a special person."

Kimberley suppressed a wry smile. *Definitely a supporting role.* "You've probably known her all her life."

"Since she was a baby. Linc and I used to carry her around. She wanted to go everywhere with us."

"And now she wants to stand on her own two feet, so let her be the adult she is."

He shook his head as though to clear it. "Sometimes it's hard to let go." He ran his gaze over her face, his expression softening into tenderness. "What an idiot I am! Here I have you in my arms, and we're talking about Terri."

"You care about her."

"Well, it so happens that I care about you, too." He eased her into a tighter embrace, his gaze filled with sudden intensity. "In fact, I care about you very much."

The night was mild and dreamy. At eleven o'clock, Jake held her hand as he walked her to the back door of the old Steele place. In the light shining onto the step, he took her in his arms and kissed her deeply, his touch filled with passion. Breathing fast, he stepped back, his expression intensely focused. He reached for her hands and gripped them lightly before lifting her left hand to his lips. "I know this is sudden. I'd planned to wait a while longer, but I'm going to ask you now. Will you marry me, Kimberley? I love you and would be honored if you would be my wife."

Chapter 24

Before dawn, Kimberley carried Lexi outdoors and then back inside. Her emotions in chaos, she desperately needed to clear her mind, which was why—as always when troubled—she sought the outdoors. She left the kitchen light on, locked the porch doors, and struck out on foot with her Nikon clipped to the camera harness, her pack on her back, and her binoculars around her neck. Anyone who approached the yard would see the light on and her truck parked beside the house and assume she was inside.

Calves bawled from across the ravine—the last shipment. Lincoln would be so relieved.

Lincoln.

All night, she'd tossed and turned, her mind racing. A thousand times, she'd relived the events of the previous day. First, Lincoln's visit and how he'd wanted to discuss their relationship, only to be interrupted by Jake's arrival. Then, later, Jake's proposal. She'd stood frozen, caught completely off guard. She'd only met Jake a month ago. In a crazy way, it seemed as though the emotional intensity of *Les Misérables* had infused her own life.

First light softened the darkness as she descended the

slope below the house and hiked south beside the creek bed in the ravine bottom. From earlier study of a topographic map, she knew that the gentle ravine slopes near the house compressed into high walls a mile to the south, creating a narrow gully. On the map, closely spaced contour lines indicated a bluff with a sheer cliff on the gully's west side. Perhaps the gully and cliff would offer good subject material, and maybe the outing would give her insight as to how she should answer Jake.

Grass swished against her boots as she pondered her heart. She was twenty-seven years old, and although she wanted children—*yearned* for children—she wanted love, too, the kind of deep, soul-sure love her parents had shared, the kind of love she'd thought she'd found with Bryan. Did she love Jake like that? No, not now. *Could* she love him like that? In all honesty, maybe with time she could. Did that mean her answer was yes? She didn't know.

On the south side of the access road, grass gave way to a ribbon of forest. She trod softly among lofty aspens beside the creek, the morning air cool and fresh in the deep shade cast by the trees. She breathed deeply of it, glad to be outdoors with her camera. *This is who I am.*

She skirted the pool where she'd photographed a beaver reinforcing its dam a few weeks after her arrival on Turtle Mountain. Two blue jays voiced strident alarm calls from atop the ravine edge and swooped into view ahead of her. What had set them off? An owl? A fox? With the awareness of someone who spends hours outdoors on a daily basis, she noted a sudden difference in the feel of the ravine. She froze into stillness in the shade, knowing that as long as she remained motionless, she would be virtually invisible. Her camo clothing and cap were a leaf-and-twig design, and her pack, camera, and binoculars were also covered with camo designs. She'd even daubed camo makeup on her face and hands and tucked her long ponytail down the back of her shirt, heeding Lincoln's advice to be careful when she was out on her own. Without moving her head, she scanned the ravine banks and creek bed. Her senses pricked. She wasn't alone.

After thirty seconds, a man carrying a rifle stepped into view fifty yards ahead of her. He picked his way south beside the creek, his back to her, an over-the-shoulder canvas bag bumping against his side. Not Lincoln. She would have recognized his broad shoulders and athletic build instantly. She froze as the figure swung around to look behind him. The face turned in her direction was familiar, as was the paunch revealed in a side view. Phil Johnson.

She remained absolutely motionless while Lincoln's former employee swept his gaze over the ravine. When he resumed walking away from her, she noted that he wore moccasins rather than the cowboy boots he'd worn on the day he'd mentally undressed her at the wheat field. She slid her cell phone out of her pocket and checked for coverage. Only one small bar. The ravine walls blocked the signal. She texted a message to Lincoln, not knowing if or when he would receive it.

What was Johnson up to? No good, undoubtedly, but what? She envisioned the topographic map she'd studied earlier that morning, and then pictured the land ownership map. A chill ran through her. Lauren's purebred Aberdeen Angus cows—her black ace, as Lincoln had called them— were pastured south of the old Steele place on land adjacent to the ravine. If Johnson had beaten Lexi, what might he do to those cows?

With every sense heightened, she silently followed the trespasser. Caution told her to move only when he turned his back to her. Johnson worked his way south along the creek for another half-mile and then crossed the stream and disappeared from sight behind what looked like a bank of soil. Seconds later, his head reappeared. He was climbing the steep ravine slope but was in a depression of some sort—perhaps a small drainage channel eroded by a tributary emptying into the creek. As quickly as she dared, she traced the creek to a position near where she'd seen Lincoln's ex-stockman cross the stream and then paused, motionless in the shade, knowing she'd be more obvious when she crossed the running water.

After thirty seconds, she quickly crossed the creek on stepping stones and ducked down against the stream bank. Again she waited, counting out another thirty seconds. Then she peered up the dry, V-shaped, rocky depression, but detected no sign of Johnson. Had he topped out? Or had he ducked into cover, conscious of another human presence, as she had been? If Johnson was somewhere at the top, checking his back trail, she'd be a sitting duck in the drainage channel. Her camouflage was leaves and branches, not rocks and soil.

Step by careful step, she climbed the boulder-strewn ravine slope beside the drainage channel, grasping tree branches and saplings' trunks to pull herself higher. To her left, past the eroded channel, a precipitous cliff reared up to a bluff. When she reached the top of the slope, she paused in an aspen grove to catch her breath. Where was Johnson? Her heart pounded as she scanned the bush in all directions. A man with a rifle wasn't someone to underestimate. She crept to the edge of the trees and looked out over the pasture.

And there he was, fifty yards away. He stood beside a fence post and held what looked like heavy-duty pliers in his hands, now gloved. Light glinted off a strand of wire as Johnson used the tool to cut it and then carefully hauled it aside. His movements were smooth and natural, as though he was doing a ranch job and didn't want to startle the nearby cows clustered in a curious herd. Ebony heads raised, the sleek animals crowded closer together, a few stepping toward him, their ears cupped forward, their eyes fixed on the man who had cared for them.

She faded behind an aspen and raised her camera, popping off ten shots as Johnson cut and hauled away the remaining three strands of wire, creating a gap. Did he intend to steal the cows? Was he a rustler? She did a quick estimate. There were about a hundred cows. It was impossible to believe that Johnson, on his own, would be capable of herding that many animals to a waiting truck hidden somewhere. So, what was his plan? She lowered her camera and texted Lincoln an update. He hadn't replied to her earlier message. Perhaps he hadn't received it.

When she looked up, Johnson was striding in her direction along the fence line, inside the pasture. She drew farther behind the tree, her pulse rocketing. Had he seen her? It was possible he'd noticed the round shape of her camera's lens when she'd been snapping photos. She waited, expecting him to appear in her line of vision. When he didn't, she peeked out from behind the tree.

He was circling around behind the cattle. The entire herd was on alert now, hooves shifting restlessly as the animals turned to follow his progress. When he reached a point opposite the gap in the fence, he lifted his rifle to his shoulder.

Hardly able to believe what she was seeing, she raised her camera and snapped photographs while Johnson repeatedly fired at the herd. Loud bawls of pain rent the air as cows went down. Like a black wave, the remainder of the herd wheeled away from the man and thundered into a run, picking up speed as the cows arrowed toward the gap in the fence.

Then she knew Johnson's plan.

The cliff.

Lincoln!

* * *

The last stock trailer roared out of the ranch yard as

Lincoln lifted his cap and wiped dirty sweat from his brow with his hand. In this case, the calm came *after* the storm— a storm of milling and bawling calves. "You're good to go." He nodded to Alf and Dale as he pulled his cell phone from his pocket to call in a report to his mother. "Thanks for coming out again on a Sunday. I've got it from here."

A notice flashed across his phone's screen, saying he'd missed a text message. In all the commotion of loading the calves, he hadn't heard his phone's jingle. Kimberley's name and number came up, and he read:

0610 following Phil Johnson in ravine south of beaver dam. He has rifle.

Johnson. Fear for her surged through Lincoln. "Wait! Phil's got a rifle in the ravine, south from the beaver dam. Kimberley's following him." Unbidden, an image of the red-haired man pulling her into his arms at the dance entered Lincoln's mind. She was bush savvy, but if Johnson got hold of her, what would he do to her? She'd sent the text twenty minutes ago.

Alf's brow furrowed. "Where's she now?"

"I don't know. Hold on." Lincoln read aloud a second message that had appeared on his screen:

"0630 He's cutting fence beside gully where cows are. Took pics."

And took chances. *Dangerous* chances.

"She's gotta get outta there." Alf's body language radiated urgency. "You know what he's doin'. She could get trampled."

Rapid-fire, Lincoln texted:

Get somewhere safe. Stampede.

He shoved the phone into his chest pocket. "Alf, call the police and then alert my mother and patrol the ranch yard. If Johnson shows up, don't take any chances. Dale, grab the .3030 and ammo. I'll pick you up at the supply room. If the cows stampede, this could be ugly."

He sprinted to his pickup and revved the engine, his hands trembling on the steering wheel. Alf's gut feeling about Johnson had been right. The man was off his rocker. If she was hurt... Instinctively, Lincoln did something he hadn't done for longer than he could remember. He prayed. *Protect her. Please, God, protect her.*

* * *

Kimberley ducked behind an aspen tree and felt the ground shake. Pounding hooves thundered in her direction. In a split second, she weighed her options. If she moved and the crazy man with the rifle was watching, he might get a bead on her. If she didn't move, she'd be trampled. She cast a frantic look around her and homed in on a truck-sized boulder ten yards away at the top edge of the ravine. To get to it, she'd be in the open and would have to cross the path of the stampeding cows.

She sprinted for the rock, every ounce of her being straining toward it as the black cattle galloped straight at her. An instant after she ducked behind the boulder, the panicked cows hurtled past it. She cringed against the rock, knowing her next actions might mean life or death. Then she pushed away from the boulder and slid over the ravine edge.

* * *

With Dale beside him, Lincoln raced the pickup from the ranch yard onto the gravel road.

"I hope he didn't see her." Anxiety flooded Dale's voice.

"So do I." Kimberley had guts, but a thin line existed between bravery and foolishness. Her photographs would provide irrefutable proof of Johnson's actions, but was that proof worth the danger of obtaining it? *Not in my mind.*

Gravel spurted from beneath the pickup's tires as he turned onto the dirt road leading to the south pasture. A memory took him farther along that road to a meadow where Kimberley had waited for him amid sun-gilded grasses and wildflowers. Four loud, sharp cracks sounded through the open truck windows.

Dale tensed. "I hear gunshots."

Lincoln floored the accelerator, his heart almost bursting through his chest. At the gate to the south pasture, Dale sprang out of the cab to open it. "Look!" The student pointed to motionless black shapes on the ground in the distance.

"I see them." Cattle down. How many? And where was Kimberley? For that matter, where was Johnson? "Keep your head down. Phil might still be around."

He braked beside the downed cattle and leapt out of the truck, rifle in hand. Three cows were obviously dead.

Another's side twitched while its glassy bovine eyes stared straight ahead and its lifeblood trickled out of a gunshot wound in its chest. Anger and shock rolled over him as he loaded a bullet into the rifle, placed the tip of the rifle barrel against the cow's forehead, and pulled the trigger. How could Johnson, who'd cared for these animals meticulously, have now carried out such a reprehensible act?

At the pasture's edge, barbed wire curled on the ground and arched into the air in spiky coils beside the cut fence. Cattle tracks in trampled grass headed into aspen woodland beyond the fence. He knew that past the trees, a cliff plunged twenty yards to the ravine's creek bed. "If the cows went over the edge, it'll be bad."

Beside him, Dale nodded, the young man's larynx bobbing up and down.

Lincoln scanned the pasture and forest edge. No sign of Kimberley or Johnson. He slung the rifle's strap over his shoulder and pushed bullets into his pockets, praying that his cell phone's jingle would bring him a message from Kimberley saying she was safe. Johnson would have heard the rifle discharge. Would he hightail it away or sneak back to take a potshot at whoever was at the scene? "Take the truck and get out of here. Call Alf and direct the police."

"Yes, sir."

"If you see Phil, stay away from him."

"Believe me, I will." Dale climbed into the pickup and spoke to Lincoln through the open window. "If I were you, I'd put my phone on vibrate."

"I was just about to do that." As the truck roared away, Lincoln punched in a quick text to Kimberley:

    At the cut fence. Are you safe?

Then he ran through the bush toward the bluff. At his feet, some of the hoof prints veered left or right. Others led straight to the cliff edge.

"Dear God!" The scene before him looked like a modern-day buffalo jump. He counted ten motionless cows in the dry creek bed; their black bodies piled one on top of the other. Movement caught his eye, and he watched another cow attempt to lurch up the ravine's opposite bank. The animal's right foreleg dragged, and a broken-off branch protruded from the cow's belly. He loaded the rifle and fired. Blood exploded from the cow's head, and the animal collapsed onto the bank.

He turned away from the carnage. There might be more injured cows, but he had to find Kimberley. She'd followed Johnson from the north, so there was a good chance she'd taken her pictures from a position north of the cut fence. A chill speared him. If Johnson had seen her, he might be pursuing her. And now he knew that someone else was on the scene, someone with a gun. Lincoln had hunted ducks and deer, but he'd never trailed an armed man. He melted into the aspen woodland alongside the fence and scanned the bush and pasture. Then he followed the cattle tracks north.

* * *

Kimberley skidded down the steep ravine slope beside the drainage channel, grabbing onto tree trunks to slow her descent. She could barely stay on her feet, but she had to get away. A gun shot ripped the air, and then, less than a minute later, another shot. What was Johnson doing now? The enormity of the danger she'd placed herself in rolled over her. Why had she followed him? Why hadn't she left the ravine immediately after seeing he was armed? What was she trying to prove—that she wasn't afraid?

As she made a lunge toward a big aspen below her, a loose rock rolled out from under her foot, sending her falling headlong. She managed to turn her body sideways before she hit the ground to protect her camera. Pain shot through her right elbow as it slammed onto a rock. She stifled a cry and curled into a ball, wanting to scream from the agony that coursed up and down her arm. *Keep going!*

She lunged to her feet and nearly fell again, pain stabbing through her right ankle. She stumbled against the aspen and cradled her right arm, her breath tearing out in sobs. There was no way she could outrun Johnson like this.

Slow down, Kimmie. Think. Be invisible. The calm words flowed through her mind. Bryan. He'd spoken those words to her more than once. Stalking a bull elk. Waiting for hours near a red fox's den.

She scanned the slope. Ten yards away, an aspen's broken-off crown had lodged against a boulder, creating a tangle of branches and drying leaves. Hunched over, she limped toward it, placing her left hand on the bank to keep her balance. Twice, her feet slid out from under her, leaving skid marks. She hastily covered the skid marks with fallen leaves. She could only hope that Johnson hadn't seen her and wasn't looking for her. Pain coursed through her right arm. She couldn't straighten her elbow.

When she reached the tangle, she fell to her knees and began to crawl between two branches, only to feel a sharp tug on her back—her pack. She backed out and awkwardly slid the pack off her shoulders, nearly crying out when it jolted her injured elbow. She unclipped her camera harness, wiggled out of it, and shoved the camera and pack under the broken-off tree crown. Panting, she squeezed between branches and lay on her back, knees up. Twigs poked her, and leaves dangled in her face.

The memory card. If Johnson found her and checked her camera, he'd see the incriminating images she'd taken. She reached around a thick branch and tugged her camera toward her. Only then did she feel her cell phone vibrate in her pocket.

* * *

Broken trees. Pulverized grasses. The stampeding cows had trampled everything in their path. His chest tight with dread, Lincoln searched for Kimberley amid the devastation. The cattle had obliterated any sign she might have left. He zigzagged across the trampled ground, hoping to find something, a hiking boot track, *anything.*

A shallow, half-inch-long depression in the disturbed soil caught his eye. The depression had one soft, gently contoured edge, like tracks made by the moccasins he'd worn as a preteen running around in the bush. Soil particles obscured the rest of the depression, *soil particles that had been swept across it*. He scanned the ground and located more mostly obscured moccasin prints in a series that crossed the trampled earth. At the ravine's edge, he found a leafy aspen branch with soil clinging to the leaves. Bingo. Johnson was wearing moccasins and had swept the branch over his footprints in an attempt to conceal them. The soil particles were still damp, which meant that the ranch's ex-stockman was close by.

Lincoln crouched low to minimize his silhouette against the skyline. Johnson was likely below him, descending the steep bank or already following the creek bed away from the bluff. He'd still be experiencing a hunter's high, his senses incredibly alert. Not a man to mess with.

Where was Kimberley? Not with Johnson. Perhaps she'd escaped ahead of Phil and was well on her way back to the old Steele place. That was the best case scenario. The worst case scenario was that she was lying somewhere in the bush, dead or injured.

Anger at Johnson boiled up in him. He forced himself to channel the emotion into heightened awareness as he traced the moccasin prints along the top of the ravine. When his cell phone vibrated in his chest pocket, he nearly jumped out of his skin. Relief flooded through him as he read Kimberley's message:

```
Under broken-off treetop lodged against
boulder north of drainage channel.
```

That channel lay twenty yards ahead of him. Johnson's tracks pointed straight toward it.

* * *

Find me, Lincoln! Pain throbbed through her right arm, her elbow tight and swollen. Did she dare drag her pack closer? It held a vial of Tylenol. Kimberley reached for the pack and paused, the hairs lifting on the back of her neck. A dislodged leaf rustled, and fabric brushed against wood as nearly silent footsteps approached. She removed her canister of pepper spray from her belt and hid it from view under her left thigh.

Moccasins and a rifle barrel appeared in her line of view as Phil Johnson crouched beside her refuge. "Not bad, Miss Nosy Photographer," he hissed. "You beat the cows, but didn't cover your tracks well enough." He grabbed her uninjured ankle and yanked her toward him.

Kimberley gripped the pepper spray canister, knowing it was her only hope. She allowed her body to slide over it as Johnson pulled her toward him, until the canister rested under the small of her back. She cried out as her injured elbow jammed against a branch before sliding past it.

"Shut up, you black-haired witch!" Johnson clamped a bare hand over her mouth and knelt over her legs, pinning her body to the ground. He reeked of sweat. "Your lover boy's around here somewhere. He found the present I left him. Now, I'm going to take what he's been getting, real quick. Then I'll kill you, trash your camera, and be on my way."

Through waves of pain, Kimberley forced herself to remain motionless as she stared into the maniacal glitter in Johnson's eyes. She would only have one chance.

The red-haired man gave a groan of lust. He placed the rifle on the ground beside him and began to unzip his pants. The zipper caught, and he removed the hand over her mouth, swearing as he used both hands to free the fastening.

"Stop right there, Phil."

Lincoln!

Johnson flinched, his attention diverted toward the drainage channel.

She whipped out the capsaicin canister and sprayed her attacker point blank in the face.

He screamed and clutched at his eyes.

She dropped the canister and shoved him off her.

Blinded, Johnson scrabbled for his rifle.

She rolled onto the weapon and cried out in agony when her assailant grasped her injured elbow and yanked on it.

Then Lincoln knocked him off her. The two men clutched at and punched each other, rolling down the incline until Johnson slammed into a boulder ten yards below her. While he lay momentarily stunned, Lincoln wrestled him face down and pulled his arms behind his back. "Why did you do it, Phil? You loved those cows."

Johnson groaned and spat out a mouthful of leaves. "Damn you, Steele!" He rolled onto his side, trying to escape Lincoln's grip. "Why d'ya think? To get back at you. You had everything on a silver platter—women, the ranch, that black-haired witch. Then you robbed me of my job."

Lincoln shoved Johnson's face into the leaves. "Let's get a few things straight. There's only ever been one woman in my life, and she was my wife. I only ever had one dream, and it was to play ball. I lost both, and now the ranch is on the verge of bankruptcy, thanks to you."

"Think I give a damn?"

"No, but if that's your definition of a silver platter, you'd better spend your jail time reading a dictionary."

The world froze around Kimberley. How could such emptiness be? She stared at Lincoln. During the round-up, she'd allowed herself to hope again, to believe that he cared for her. Now even the taste of her own saliva seemed bitter. *There's only ever been one woman in my life, and she was my wife.* So his supposed interest in her really had been no more than a ploy, his kiss under the elms just another step in his strategy to help his son. He was a good actor, a *very* good actor. Tears stung her eyes. He'd told her that he'd never lied to her. *Right.*

He looked up at her. "Do you have anything we can use to tie his arms?"

"A rope."

"Get it."

She cradled her aching arm against her waist and

crawled to the broken treetop. She dragged her pack out from within the tangle of branches and clumsily, with one hand, unzipped it and rummaged inside until she found a hank of green nylon rope she carried in case of an emergency.

"What happened to your arm?"

She winced at his icy tone. "I lost my footing and fell on a rock." She limped toward him, propping her good arm against the slope as she slid downhill.

"And your leg?"

"Turned my ankle." She fumbled to extricate the rope's end. As she handed it to him, her thoughts flew to the morning Lexi had attacked a porcupine in Lauren's yard. After Jake had removed the quills, his gaze had been warm and welcoming, filled with genuine interest. Witty and generous, he'd shown her sincere affection on the dates that had followed, and last night, he'd said he loved her... She dropped the rope and backed away from Lincoln and his struggling captive. "There's nothing between him and me," she told Johnson. "I'm going to marry Jake Kruger."

Lincoln's head snapped toward her, the muscles in his jaw bunching. "Is that so?"

"Yes, it is."

He whipped the rope round and round Johnson's wrists. "Lucky man! Well, from now on *he* can rescue you when you get into scrapes."

Indignation exploded inside her. "Of all the arrogant...I never *once* asked you to rescue me. I don't *need* to be rescued. I can take care of myself."

"So she says, as she stands there with a wrecked arm and barely able to walk." Anger radiated from his every pore. "You risked your life unnecessarily by following an armed man. What were you trying to prove? That you're the tough outdoorswoman? The great photographer? Everyone but you already knows that."

She flinched as though he'd slapped her. Johnson's insane guffaw rubbed the air, the sound as raw and mocking as the gaping emptiness inside her.

Chapter 25

Lincoln made the dismal tally: fifteen cows dead and a dozen with injuries requiring attention. All the live cows were exhausted and stressed from stampeding. Half of them had ended up in the shallow grassy ravine adjacent to the barns and corrals. The rest had galloped in the opposite direction, into the oak forest on the block of land where he'd caught Kimberley trespassing in a golden meadow.

His memory jolted back to the ravine. White-faced after his tongue-lashing, Kimberley had handed him her camera's memory card, explaining that she'd figured Johnson would destroy any evidence if he'd found her. Instead, Johnson had almost destroyed *her*. The sight of the red-haired man atop her, unzipping his pants, had sent Lincoln into a cold fury. Kimberley, however, was full of surprises, as Johnson had discovered when she'd blasted him with pepper spray. She'd played her one card perfectly.

Still, if he hadn't come across her and Johnson when he had, would she still be alive? She couldn't have fought off Johnson or run from him. And he'd thrown that fact in her face. His anger, bred out of concern for her safety and her startling announcement about the engagement, had led him to speak words he shouldn't have spoken, words that had caused her to go white with shock. He'd wanted to hurt her because her news had hurt him. Not something to be proud of. Once again, he owed Kimberley an apology.

She's going to marry Jake. The knowledge pierced him. He couldn't believe it. In putting Matt's and the ranch's welfare first, he'd waited too long, and his best friend had won her love.

He ran his gaze over the black cows standing listlessly with heads down in the corrals beside the calving barn. Jake was attending the injured animals inside, with Alf and Dale assisting him. After the police had arrested Johnson, it had taken three hours, plus Tom and Sandy McCorquodale's help, to round up the scattered cows and bring them home. Now the danger was that the cows would abort, since the stress they'd endured would have stimulated the production of cortisol, a steroid hormone that could cause them to go into labor.

"Linc?"

He turned toward the calving barn. "Give me the bad news."

Jake walked toward him, bag in hand. "I stitched up the lacerations and took blood samples for cortisol levels."

"Which are probably sky high."

"Judging from the herd's condition, yes. I'll call you with the test results, but in my opinion, they'll abort."

"I expected as much."

First, no crops, and now, no calves next spring. It was a ranch manager's nightmare. The cows would become receptive again after their condition improved, but breeding them late in the year would mean shifting to a completely different calving season that could interfere with other ranch work. "Thanks for coming out, Jake. I'm not looking forward to telling my mother."

His friend's gaze held empathy. "Are she and Kimberley back from the hospital?"

"I haven't heard." Lincoln forced himself to reach out to shake his best friend's hand. "By the way, congratulations on your engagement."

Jake's eyebrows shot up. "Thanks." He gripped Lincoln's hand.

"You look surprised. Was it supposed to be a secret?"

Happiness spread across Jake's face. "Not at all—just brand new. I didn't realize Kimberley had told you. She was very subdued when I saw her at the hospital. She seemed really shaken up. It was good of your mother and Terri and Matthew to stay with her." He hesitated and then asked, "What exactly happened in the ravine?"

"What did Kimberley tell you?"

"Not much. She fell and twisted her ankle and hurt her arm."

"Johnson tried to rape her."

Shock blanked Jake's expression. "*What?*"

"He didn't get anywhere. She used her pepper spray on him, and then I was close enough to tackle him and restrain him until the police arrived."

"No wonder she's shaken up. I hate to think what would have happened if you hadn't been there. Phil had a rifle, didn't he?"

"There's no point in speculating. I was there."

"Thank God for that."

Lincoln dredged up a smile. "She's yours to look after now."

Jake nodded, frowning. "She told me she's interested in portrait and sports photography. I'll encourage her to pursue those."

"Clip her wings?"

"More like concern for her safety. Since we're on the topic of the engagement, I might as well ask you now. Will you be my best man?"

Lincoln stepped back, the request like a blow. *Stand beside Jake as he made forever vows with Kimberley?* Matt had seen what he'd refused to admit. Terri had seen it, too, and had called him on it. Why had he been so reluctant to acknowledge his love for Kimberley? Deep down, he knew that his sister had voiced the reason during her tirade after the ball game. His painful experience with Gayle *had* scared him off women. He *had* been afraid to love again. By the time he'd admitted his feelings for Kimberley to himself, Jake was already on the scene, and now they were engaged. It was too late. He'd lost his chance to tell Kimberley that he loved her.

"You're taking a long time to answer. Is something wrong?"

He pulled himself together. Jake had been his closest

friend since third grade. He couldn't let that friendship down now. "Of course, I'll be your best man."

* * *

"Thanks, Kimmie." Matt grinned as he held up the photograph of him and Lexi romping in the yard at the old Steele place. "Look, Dad."

Seated in a deck chair on Lincoln's cedar deck, Kimberley tensed as Lincoln studied the picture.

His amber gaze lifted to her, steady and charming, the perfect host. "It's beautiful, like joy caught on the wind."

"Doesn't it kill you when he talks like that?" Seated beside her, Sandy McCorquodale leaned toward her, blonde hair swinging gently. "Our high school English teacher always asked him to read Austen or Shakespeare or whatever poet aloud to the class." She raised her voice a little and directed a teasing smile at Lincoln. "All the girls were crazy about him, but he only had eyes for two things: a baseball and a certain pretty redhead."

Lincoln tossed Sandy a quick grin and handed Matt another gift.

Matt's three friends—two boys and Sandy's daughter, Ashley—crowded around him as he ripped off wrapping paper. "A Spiderman book. Grrr-eat!" His dark blue eyes shone. "Thanks, Ashley."

Mixed emotions flitted through Kimberley. It was so good to see Matt laughing and surrounded by friends. Looking at him, she could hardly equate the happily self-confident nine-year-old with the anxious child she'd first met three months ago in Turtle Mountain Provincial Park. How often would she see him after she and Jake were married? Would she fade from his affection and become only the wildlife photographer who had lived at the old Steele place with her dog for a few months, someone he occasionally met on Seton's streets?

"He's like a different child," Sandy said quietly. "This summer, something good—and I don't know what it was—gave him a whole new outlook on life. I'm so glad it did."

"Yes." Kimberley cleared huskiness from her voice. "Every child deserves joy."

Sandy probed her with a look and nodded toward her left hand. "That's a stunning engagement ring—diamond solitaire flanked by sapphires. Wow! I was beginning to think that Jake was a confirmed bachelor, but it seems he was waiting for you to come along. Have you known him long?"

"No, just a month."

"Love at first sight, eh?"

Matt's excited voice rang out, "A multitool! Thanks, Dad." He sprang onto the picnic table bench and hugged his father.

As Lincoln enfolded his son, an expression of love so strong it was almost pain flitted across his face. He released Matt and called out, "Anyone for more dessert?"

"Not for me," Kimberley replied when he looked in her direction. With her severely bruised elbow supported in a sling, she'd awkwardly eaten the birthday meal using her left hand. He'd grilled teriyaki steaks, and Terri and Lauren had contributed herbed potato salad, red cabbage and apple coleslaw, and home-baked bread. Matt's barbecue surprise had been grilled banana splits comprised of a piece of coconut cake sandwiched between two lightly charred half-bananas and topped with ice cream, fudge sauce, strawberries, pineapple, and whipped cream.

Voices flowed around her. Matt asked for more ice cream and fudge sauce. Terri and Lauren, seated at the picnic table, conversed with the parents of the two young boys. Sandy wished her a quick recovery before departing with Ashley.

She eased her swollen ankle into a more comfortable position on the foot stool that Terri had smilingly provided for her earlier. Unable to drive because of her injured elbow, she'd caught a ride to the party with Terri and Lauren and had watched the lively goings-on from the comfort of the padded deck chair. Would Matt's party be the last time she'd be part of a Steele family gathering? The possibility filled her with a sense of desolation. Lincoln's family had given her so much, had cared for her and Lexi. She hadn't even met Jake's family. His sister, Amanda, lived in England, and his parents were traveling.

She tensed as Lincoln walked toward her and sat beside her in the chair Sandy had vacated.

"You look pensive." His amber gaze searched her face. "How are you feeling?"

"Sore, but I'll heal." Other than party pleasantries, she hadn't spoken with him since the ravine incident the previous day. She had no idea what to say. He'd been so angry. *And so right.*

He held her gaze steadily. "I came down hard on you yesterday morning. I owe you an apology for that. I'm sorry."

She swallowed, her heart aching. "No need to apologize. What you said was true. Before you arrived, I'd already begun to question why I was there."

"Then I hammered it home with a big hammer."

"You did."

"I hope you know I was angry because I was concerned about what might have happened to you."

"I know." She tried to smile. "And what I said wasn't true. I *did* need to be rescued. Thank you for being there for me."

His gaze drifted to her left hand. He looked as though he was about to say something about her ring and then changed his mind. "I have a favor to ask."

"Name it."

He moved restlessly, and she read uncertainty in his eyes.

"Matt wants to see the house where he was abused. He'd like you and my mother and Terri to come along with us. We'd drop you off at the old Steele place afterward."

"Of course." She touched his arm lightly. "Some of the traumatized kids I volunteered with in Calgary did similar things. It can be part of the healing process. Your son is incredibly brave."

"But what if—"

She shook her head. "No what ifs, Lincoln."

He took a deep breath. "You're right. No what ifs. Thanks, Kimberley."

* * *

Lincoln steered his mother's Lexus onto a road he'd avoided for the past five years. Matt sat between him and Terri, and Kimberley and his mother sat in the rear seat.

"Where is it?" Matt asked.

He smiled down at his son. "We'll see it soon. It's just around the bend." Five years ago, he'd driven to the house, filled with rage at Gayle's perfidy. He'd left it, crying, with his traumatized son in his arms.

As the car rounded the curve on the gravel road, he steeled himself for the sight of the boxy farmhouse with white vinyl siding, but it never appeared. Instead, a graceful two-story home with dormer windows and an addition, all clad in pale green siding with white trim, met his gaze. A covered porch stretched along the front of the house. He pulled over to the roadside.

"Does it look the same?" Matt asked, his brow furrowed as he peered through the windshield.

"No, it doesn't." He could hardly find his voice. "Someone new lives there. They've changed it."

His son flashed a look up at him. "It's just a house, and it's pretty. Look." He pointed. "There's someone on a swing."

A muffled sound emanated from the back seat. Lincoln glanced in the rear-view mirror and saw tears streaming down Kimberley's face.

The guests were gone, the party cleaned up, and Matt's wish fulfilled. Lincoln drew in a deep breath. There was one more thing he had to do. "Mind if I cut some of your flowers for a bouquet?" he asked his mother. "Matt and I are going to the graveyard. I'll drop him off at the Stewarts afterward for his sleepover."

"Of course I don't mind." His mother's startled gaze held a thousand shards of joy. "Give my best to Rose and Paul."

Evening sunshine gilded gravestones in the cemetery on Seton's outskirts as Matt led him to the polished black marble headstone engraved with the name Gayle Antonia Steele.

"I'm nine today, Mom." Matt knelt and laid a yellow rose on the grave. "I miss you, but I have lots of pictures of you now, and that helps. I wish you could have been at my party. I'm going to stay with Nana and Papa tonight. I know they miss you, too."

The past broke into pieces inside Lincoln. He knelt on one knee beside his son and placed the bouquet of his mother's Shasta daisies, purple coneflowers, and perfumed Stargazer lilies—always Gayle's favorite blossom—on the grave. He could hardly speak. "Thanks for the good times we had and for our wonderful son. I know you loved him with all your heart."

"It's about time you admitted that."

The raspy voice jolted Lincoln to his feet. His former

father-in-law stood nearby, glaring at him. "Hello, Paul." He prepared himself for a barrage of hard words of the kind the Stewarts had thrown at him ever since he and Gayle had separated. "I guess I'm a little slow in some things."

"I guess you are."

Lincoln placed a hand on his son's shoulder, hoping against hope that Gayle's father wouldn't ruin Matt's birthday with sarcasm and anger.

More stooped with the years than Lincoln had realized, Paul Stewart eyed him and Matt and then drew himself up tall. "Maybe we're all a little slow in some things. Rose baked a cherry pie. I seem to recall you liking cherry pie."

"Yes, sir."

"Then let's not stand here jawing. I just came by to say hello to my little girl on my grandson's birthday. Don't you worry, sweetie," he said gruffly as he placed a single stalk of Stargazer lilies on the grave. "He's doing fine. He's doing real fine."

Chapter 26

By the end of August, Kimberley could walk normally and fully straighten her elbow, but she couldn't carry Lexi. The Steeles had come to her rescue yet again. Lauren and Matt or Terri and Matt had stopped in four times a day to carry Lexi outdoors. Always, Matt had encouraged Lexi, and her pet had responded with more steps each day.

"We're quite a pair, aren't we?" She gently brushed her fingertips over Lexi's back. Not only had the Steeles cared for Lexi, Lauren and Terri had also brought food—easy meals she could cope with using one hand. Jake had spent a half-dozen evenings with her, and on the others, he'd telephoned. The only person she hadn't seen or spoken with was Lincoln. "Back soon," she told Lexi. "I need some fresh air."

Gray clouds scudded across the sky, moving as quickly as her life had during the two months since her arrival at the old Steele place. The shelterbelt trees north of the yard waved in the wind, leaves whipping back and forth, flipping pale undersides into view. They were like her emotions, tossed this way and that by recent circumstances, revealing aspects of her character she would have preferred to not acknowledge—her impulsiveness that sometimes bordered on recklessness, her lapse of good judgment in the ravine. Lincoln had driven those flaws home to her.

Dust puffed from beneath her sandals as she walked toward the shrunken pond north of the yard. Hail-broken grasses formed a rough scalp on the prairie. Despite the thunderstorm that had broken the elm two weeks ago, drought still claimed the land. Her blind remained near the clump of wolf willows, and she recalled how hail had pounded down onto her, Matt, and Lincoln as they'd run for the pickup. Inside it, Lincoln had stared at her as though drawn to her by an immeasurable force… She shook her head and raised her face to the wind. Why did her thoughts persist in going to him?

The day after Matt's party, she and Jake had set a wedding date—the third Saturday in September. His brown eyes filled with warm intensity, her fiancé had told her he wasn't one to wait around. His kiss had held passion and promise.

An image surfaced in her mind, of Lincoln standing rock solid between Terri and Matt in the calving barn supply room after Jake had removed Lexi's imbedded quills. She knew his stance would be as rock solid beside Jake waiting at the altar. Unaccountably, her throat tightened. Tears pricked her eyes as she walked into the wind.

* * *

Lincoln rested his head on the back of his mother's sofa and closed his eyes, exhaustion rolling over him. Physical exhaustion from training for baseball and the workouts with the Brandon team. Nothing wrong with that—his body gloried in the challenge. Mental exhaustion from putting the breeding herd to rights after Phil Johnson's dirty deed. The remaining cows again looked glossy with health, but as Jake had predicted, they'd aborted their fetuses. Lincoln had decided to keep the cows and shift them to a fall calving schedule, which meant that for the next year, the ranch's finances would be down to bare bones.

He exhaled a long breath, knowing he had much to be thankful for. The ranch was running peacefully, he'd re-established a civil, if uneasy, relationship with Gayle's parents, and for the first time Matt was excited about attending public school. His son had healed so much.

"Kimberley doesn't seem happy."

"What?" As Lincoln opened his eyes, a vision that had haunted him ever since Kimberley had announced her engagement clobbered him again. *The wedding.* In six days time, the woman he loved would walk down the aisle and marry his best friend. "Sorry, I beg your pardon?"

Seated in an armchair, his mother searched his face. "I said that Kimberley doesn't seem happy. Most young women planning their weddings radiate joy. They don't look as if they're still seeking."

He frowned and sat up straight. "What makes you say she looks like that?"

"She walks and walks. No camera. Face lifted to the wind."

"You and Terri have been over at her place a lot, helping with wedding preparations. How's she been?"

"Preoccupied." Lines formed in his mother's brow. "I wonder if she's feeling rushed or having second thoughts. The engagement *was* rather sudden, and she's only had a month to plan since she and Jake picked a date."

He shrugged. "Some weddings happen a lot faster than that, and you know Jake—he goes straight from A to B."

"That's true, he does. Still, I sense that Kimberley's emotions are in turmoil. Have you spoken with her?"

"Only at Matt's party."

His mother clasped her hands. "She loves your son."

"I know."

"And…I've seen the incredible attraction between her and you. It's as though the two of you are linked by an unfailing energy. I've never seen that between her and Jake."

"He's a good man."

"One of the best, but that doesn't mean he's right for Kimberley."

Lincoln leaned forward, forearms propped on his thighs. "What exactly are you saying?"

"I'm saying that Kimberley needs to realize that what she's seeking is *you*."

"You told me to stay away from her."

"And you said you were breaking your promise. Did you tell her how you feel about her?"

"I never had the chance. She was with Jake until late on the evening that you and I talked, and then I was up to my eyeballs in cattle. I planned to tell her after the last shipment, but that was the day Phil went nuts, and then in the ravine she announced her engagement to Jake."

Surprise skimmed across his mother's face. "I didn't know that. She announced her engagement *in the ravine*? In the midst of that chaos? Doesn't that strike you as odd?"

He ran a hand through his hair. "Well, the whole situation was pretty crazy. She was shaken up, and I was angry because I thought she'd been reckless. Then she just came out with it—told Phil there was nothing between us and she was going to marry Jake."

His mother's brows drew together. "Why on earth would she say that to a man who'd almost raped her?"

He shrugged. "He thought we were lovers, so I told him there was only ever one woman in my life, and—"

Revelation leapt into his mother's eyes. "She was your wife." She bounded to her feet, her smile radiant. "Don't you see? That could be it. Put yourself in Kimberley's place. If you heard that, what would you conclude?"

He ran the scene through his mind. "That I didn't care for her." What his mother pointed out now seemed so obvious. Could it really be that simple? He stood and paced through the living room. "If she thought that, she might also have thought I'd been stringing her along because of Matt."

His mother's expression sobered. "In which case, she would have been terribly hurt. It's easy to understand how, in the heat of the moment and perhaps as a sort of retaliation for what you'd said, she might have made the decision to marry Jake."

He stopped pacing. "God knows I've said the wrong thing to her often enough, but could it really be something so simple as a wrong turn of phrase?"

"Well, you probably weren't editing your words in the ravine, and, yes, it could be that simple. It's easy to take words the wrong way or misunderstand their intent, particularly when a person is feeling vulnerable like Kimberley was." His mother touched his arm lightly. "There's still a chance, darling. Show Kimberley you love her, truly love *her*, not just because of Matt. Then all you can do is hope and pray."

A nearly unbearable burden lifted from his shoulders. *The game isn't over until it's over.* "I'll stop by her place right after the school bus picks up Matt in the morning."

"If you need an excuse, I can do my shopping in Winnipeg, leaving you to volunteer to help with her dog. Lexi's cast is supposed to come off first thing tomorrow, and since Kimberley still can't carry her, she'll need someone to put the dog in her truck."

He grinned. "I never knew you were such a schemer."

Mystery veiled his mother's glance. "I still have some surprises."

* * *

"Just a minute." Kimberley hurried through the living room and darted around the corner into the kitchen and back porch. That would be Lauren. She swung the door open. "Hi. Oh! Hello."

Lincoln stood on the back porch step. Dressed in blue jeans and a black polo shirt and wearing a Toronto Blue Jays baseball cap, he was attired exactly as he'd been one morning in his golden meadow. His amber eyes were filled with the same warmth they'd held the first time she'd seen him in Turtle Mountain Provincial Park. "Hi." He dipped his head in an acknowledging nod. "My mother's in Winnipeg, so she can't help with Lexi. Will I do?"

She stepped back from the doorway, her heart racing. "Of course. Come in. How have you been? I haven't seen you since Matt's party."

"Oh, I had a rough spell after the ravine business, but I see new hope."

His gaze held secret laughter so rich and inviting, she felt an ache inside her. The magic she'd sensed in his golden meadow still surrounded him.

He lifted his eyebrows. "Shall I carry Lexi out?"

She was staring. "Of course. You'll want to get back to work."

Dimples appeared in his cheeks, a teasing light in his eyes. "I'm in no hurry, but I thought you might be, to get her cast off."

She gave him an edgy smile and hurried into the living

room, wishing Lauren hadn't chosen that day to drive to Winnipeg. "You're right. And Lexi's restless. She'll need to pee before you put her in my truck."

Restless. Since the birthday party, she'd been dogged by that emotion. She and Jake had planned their wedding ceremony, reception meal, and a square dance to follow and had discussed plans for the house to be built on Jake's quarter section. She'd consulted Wendy about a wedding dress and had chosen a simple white gown with elbow-length sleeves and a boat neckline. Terri and Lauren had helped her design table decorations consisting of burlap runners, beveled mirrors, tea light candles in mason jars, and clear glass vases that would be filled with flowers on the morning of the wedding. After expressing surprise, Terri had agreed to be her bridesmaid, and Wendy, her matron of honor. Despite the short span between the engagement and wedding, preparations were falling into place surprisingly smoothly, *yet she had no peace.* Each day she walked until her body was as weary as her racing mind.

"How's Lexi doing?"

She tensed at Lincoln's voice close behind her. "Much better, but she still gets exhausted from walking, and her neck is chafed from wearing the cone. Thankfully, both cast and cone come off today."

In her bedroom, he gently lifted Lexi into his arms. Then his gaze traveled around the room, seeming to linger on the yellow dress in the open closet.

Overwhelmed by his presence in the small space, she quickly led the way outdoors.

As they watched her dog hobble across the lawn, he turned to her and smiled straight into her eyes. "In no time, she'll be back to her old self."

Her breath caught in her throat, her heart yearning to the point of breaking, yet impaled by the bitter realization of what she knew to be true. "Please don't look at me like that. You're too good a man to play games, and we both know that look is a lie."

* * *

Lincoln drew in and released a slow breath. *God, don't let me mess this up.* The rest of his life would depend on his next words. "Kimberley, the way I'm looking at you is not a lie."

Pain scored her face. "How can you tell me that? In the ravine, you said—"

"A poor choice of words—not for the first time. I wasn't thinking straight, but in no way was I referring to my relationship with you. I should have said that I only ever *had* one woman, and she was my wife. Past tense."

Her beautiful eyes implored him. "Why are you telling me this?"

"Because I want you to give me a chance."

"A chance for what?"

"To share my life with you."

"I'm going to marry Jake!"

His heart nearly burst. "Is that what you really want?"

Her mouth opened and closed. Tears filled her eyes.

He threw all caution to the wind. "I love you,

Kimberley. I've loved you since the first time I saw you in the park, with ticks crawling all over you. I intended to tell you that the day we shipped the calves, but before I had a chance, you announced your engagement to Jake. Please, *please* believe me when I say that, more than anything, I want to be the man to see you off in your camo gear and rescue you when you get into scrapes. I want to be the man to take you in my arms and give you the baby you want." He ran a finger lightly along her hairline scar. "And in case you have any lingering doubts about my reaction to your scars, just give me the chance, and I'll show you exactly what I'll do with them."

She stared into his eyes, emotions buffeting her features like the prairie wind.

"It's your decision." He touched his cap brim and walked to where Lexi lay in a pool of September sunlight.

Chapter 27

"The x-ray looks great. Radius and ulna are completely healed." Jake removed Lexi's cast and carefully observed the husky's movements while Kimberley led her dog in a slow walk around the examining room. He nodded. "The limp should disappear within a week or two. Her muscles have atrophied, so she'll need to rebuild strength in that leg. Let her take things at her own pace. I'll prescribe more antibiotic cream for the sores on her neck."

"Thanks, Jake. It's so good to see her recovering."

Her fiancé draped an arm around her shoulders, his gaze warm. "Why don't we eat out in Seton this evening? We can discuss last minute wedding details, and I've got something to show you."

"Is it a surprise?"

"No." His gaze took on the intensity Kimberley had learned to recognize. "It's a small building that went up for sale on Friday. It used to be a gift shop. I thought it might make a good studio for your portrait photography."

Her eyebrows lifted. "I'm not at the studio stage yet. Most of my subject material is still wildlife."

"You haven't used your camera for weeks."

"No, I haven't."

His brow furrowed. "Don't you think it might be wise to start focusing more on portrait and sports photography?"

"You've mentioned that before." Unsettled, she moved away from him, his arm sliding down her back. "Jake, I'm a wildlife photographer with an interest in other subjects, not the reverse."

"I'm concerned for your safety. Look what happened with the wild boar and in the ravine." He held her gaze. "And you have scars."

She took a deep breath. "I've had work-related injuries, as have people in many other occupations. I'm sure vets aren't exempt from on-the-job injuries."

"You're right, however—"

"And to clarify, getting hurt in the ravine had nothing to do with wildlife."

"You went there to photograph wildlife."

"So what? Something unexpected happened. Life is unpredictable." Bryan's words jumped into her mind: *Slow down, Kimmie. Think.* She studied Jake's familiar features. She respected him so much, and he was unfailingly considerate and open-hearted—except with regard to her profession, and with regard to Lincoln visiting her. "Jake, I've never said that I would give up wildlife photography. It's a big part of who I am. I need you to understand that."

He took her arm. "We can discuss it again this evening. Would you like me to carry Lexi to your truck?"

"That would be wonderful, thank you."

"I assume Lauren carried her out for you?"

"Actually, Lincoln did. Lauren is away."

Her fiancé gave her a sharp look. "Has Linc been over other times, too?"

"I hadn't seen him since Matt's party."

Tension eased from Jake's face. "The last time I talked to him was after the cows stampeded. How's he doing?"

"I asked him that. He said he had a rough spell after the ravine incident but sees new hope." She envisioned the warmth she'd seen in Lincoln's eyes and smile. "He looked...happy."

Jake studied her face. "Good. I'll see him at the stag party on Wednesday." He dropped a kiss onto her lips. "And I'll see you this evening."

As Kimberley walked with Lexi through the yard before dusk, it seemed that her life was spiraling into a scenario out of her control. During supper, she and Jake had again disagreed—no, they'd quarreled—about her giving up wildlife photography. He hadn't demanded that she give it up—he had no right to do that—yet his stance on the subject had been firm—wildlife photography was dangerous. Their heated words had left her tied in a knot. She loved nature and the thrill of photographing it—the hidden glimpses, the transcendent beauty. She'd always envisioned having a husband and children who would support her in her chosen endeavor.

Had she made a mistake in accepting Jake's proposal? A hundred times that day, she'd relived her conversation with Lincoln. *The decision is yours*, he'd said. He'd placed his future in her hands—as had Jake.

The next two evenings—Tuesday and Wednesday—she traced the familiar path through the hayfield, with Lexi walking slowly at her side. She sat amid prairie grasses near the shrunken pond and looked out over the water, where dabbling ducks fed voraciously in preparation for migrating south to their wintering grounds. Her thoughts a whirlpool of indecision, she wrapped her arms around Lexi. *Jake. Lincoln. Jake. Lincoln.* Tormented, she buried her face in her hands. *God, please show me what to do.* Of one thing, she was certain. By the end of the week, she would deeply wound one of two men she cared about and possibly destroy a lifelong friendship.

On Thursday, two days before the wedding, dawn came on a light breeze that drew her outdoors after a fitful night. As she watched the sunrise spill pink-gold light over the bur oaks on the ravine slope, she knew she'd made the decision she'd had to make. Part of her was at peace, and part of her strained toward resolution. After rushing through breakfast, she removed her blind from its site by the pond, ignoring the throb in her elbow. Then she drove to the burrowing owl site and removed her second blind.

Back at the old Steele place, she dismantled her desk and packed her photography equipment. Energy surged through her, and memories raced through her mind: Terri bringing her a saskatoon berry pie; the wild boar's charge;

Phil Johnson carrying a rifle in the ravine. Lovingly, she touched Matt's drawing of the burrowing owls before tucking the party invitation inside her portrait photography book. She placed a copy of her second-place-winning National Geographic contest entry—the black-and-white image of Lincoln and Matt standing in the hail-crushed wheat field—in an eight-by-ten envelope, along with color copies of three portraits of Terri, a color print of Lincoln's catch at the ball game, and one of him and Matt riding in the round-up. Then she filled her truck with everything she'd brought from Calgary. Lastly, she hung a white dress in the kitchen and placed the burlap table runners, beveled mirrors, tea light candles, mason jars, and vases in cardboard boxes in the living room.

Everything was ready. Her heart pounded with joy and resolve as she drove to Seton to meet Jake.

"Hi, beautiful," he greeted her outside Seton's Chinese food restaurant, his lips warm on hers. He glanced at her truck. "Looks like you got everything packed up. We can take it to my place after supper." A frown creased his brow. "You brought Lexi? I thought you were going to stay with her at the old Steele place until Saturday."

"Let's walk for a minute." Kimberley took Jake's arm and led him to a small park edged with balsam poplar trees, their leaves golden. "There's something I need to say."

"This sounds serious."

"It is." She stopped and released his arm before turning to face him. "Jake, I want you to know how incredibly

honored I am that you want to share your life with me...
But you also need to know that I've been in turmoil for
the past six weeks, knowing that I made a decision at a
moment when I never should have made such an
important decision."

Wariness entered his eyes. "Are you referring to your
decision to marry me?"

"Yes."

He scrutinized her face. "You never did tell me when
you decided to accept my proposal."

She glanced away, her mind filled with images. *Cattle
stampeding toward her. Broken-off aspen. Johnson's moccasins and
rifle barrel. Lincoln pinning her assailant to the ground.* She
looked straight into his eyes. "In the ravine."

His eyebrows shot up. "I'm flattered that while your
life was in danger, you decided to share the rest of it with
me." His gaze sharpened. "Or did you make that decision
after Linc rescued you?"

"The whole thing was a crazy situation. I was injured
and in emotional shock. I wasn't thinking straight, I was
just reacting, reaching for some light. I—"

"You know what I think?" He laid a light hand on her
arm, the tension in his face easing. "I think you've got
wedding jitters. That's normal, Kimberley. Everything will
be fine. You'll see." His smile held comfort and
encouragement.

"No. Please listen to me." This was so hard. She placed
her left hand over his. "I don't have wedding jitters. I'm
not doing a good job of explaining, but try to understand.

In that crazy moment in the ravine after Phil's attack, I thought my decision to marry you was the right one, but given the circumstances I shouldn't have made *any* decision of that kind. I have thought this over every waking hour, and I've come to the conclusion that you deserve so much more than what I can give you."

His face went blank. "Are you breaking our engagement?" He looked at her hand on his arm. "You're not wearing your ring."

Aching with sympathy for him, she reached into her cargo pants pocket and removed the exquisite diamond and sapphire ring. "I'm sorry." She handed it to him.

His expression tightened. "Does this have anything to do with Linc? I wondered why you told him we were engaged before you told me."

"I did it all wrong. I did *everything* wrong that day. Now I'm trying to fix part of what I did wrong."

"By breaking our engagement two days before the wedding? Tell me, is Linc involved in this?"

"Jake, this is about *me*."

Holding up the ring, he snapped, "In case you've forgotten, it's about *us*. An engagement involves two people."

"You're right. All I can say is that I realized I was wrong to have made the decision I made and I'm sorry for the hurt I'm causing you."

He stepped back from her, the ring gripped in his fist. "You're the woman I chose to spend my life with, and all you can say is that you're *sorry*?"

"Jake, I have to go."

"To Linc?"

She shook her head, her heart filled with peace. "No. To the Rockies. I have demons to fight, and I won't be whole until I do."

Chapter 28

Lincoln closed the door of his pickup and gazed up at the stars. The rhythmical chirping of crickets played through the night air like a thousand tiny strumming musicians. For a few seconds, he stood with his eyes closed, allowing the soothing sound to quiet his heart. He hadn't heard from Kimberley. Jake's stag party the previous evening had been torture. Tomorrow would bring the wedding rehearsal, and the following day, the wedding.

"Thank goodness you're back," his mother whispered when he stepped into the log house. "I don't know what's got into Matt. He's beside himself with anxiety. He keeps saying that Kimberley might get hurt. He burst into tears and told us he has a message for you from her. He's in the living room with Terri."

Lincoln's heart thudded. *A message.* He kicked off his sneakers and walked through the short hallway and into his mother's living room.

His son sat cuddled up to Terri on the floral sofa, *Nim's Island* playing on the television. On seeing him, Matt bounded off the couch and ran into his arms, tears streaming down his face.

"Hey, cowboy. What's wrong?" He lifted his son into his arms and hugged him tightly.

"She's going away," Matt sobbed.

"Who's going away?"

"Kimmie. And she might get hurt or killed."

"Kimberley's fine," Lincoln soothed. "She's leaving the old Steele place because she's going to marry Jake."

"No! She's going *away*. Back to Alberta. To that place with the grizzly bear."

"Easy, Matt." Lincoln rubbed his son's back. "Something's got you muddled up. Kimberley's not going back to Alberta. After she and Jake are married, she'll be living a few miles from Seton."

His son grabbed handfuls of his baseball uniform and bunched the fabric in his fists. "You're not *listening* to me. She's not going to marry Jake. She's going *away*."

Every movement in the room stopped, as though time had been suspended. Lincoln stared into his son's imploring eyes. Then he glanced at his mother and at Terri, who'd arranged to take her Brandon University classes off to help with the final wedding preparations. Both stood frozen. He turned back to Matt and tried to make his voice neutral. "How do you know that Kimberley's not going to marry Jake?"

"Because she told me." Matt released his shirt.

"When?"

"After supper, when you were gone to the ball game."

Lincoln questioned his mother with a look.

She shrugged. "I didn't hear her truck or see her."

Terri shook her head.

Matt wiped a hand across his face. "She came when you and Terri were in the basement. I went outside and saw her. She came to tell me that she has to go back to the mountains. She said it's like when I had to see that house." His face crumpled as he looked up at Lincoln. "But what if there's another bear? It might kill her, and you won't be there to guard her."

Lincoln hugged his son tightly before pulling back. He searched Matt's face. "Matt, are you absolutely sure that Kimberley told you she's not going to marry Jake?"

Matt nodded, his face blotchy from crying. "She showed me her hand—she wasn't wearing that fancy ring anymore—and she gave me an envelope with a message for you. It's over there." He pointed to a brown envelope on the dining table.

Lincoln's heart raced as he slid his son to the floor. He opened the sealed envelope and pulled out several photographs. A folded piece of blue paper rested on top of them—blue as Kimberley's eyes. Slowly he unfolded the paper and read:

If you still want that chance, I'll come back.

He whooped a joyous laugh and hugged his startled son. "No bear is going to kill Kimberley. I *will* be with her."

His mother lifted her hands, palms up, her eyes moist.

Tears streamed down Terri's face.

He released Matt. "Back in a minute." He pulled his

cell phone from his pocket as he strode to the French doors of his mother's living room. Outside the log house, autumn warmth filled the evening air as he punched in Kimberley's number. Her phone rang four times before a beloved voice answered it.

"Hello. Kimberley Colter here."

He smiled at the happy lilt in her words. "Hello, *Ms. Colter.*"

She laughed the delightful, husky laugh she'd laughed in his golden meadow at dawn. "Hello, *Mr. Steele.* Do I take it you want that chance?"

"I do. Where are you?"

"In Brandon, with Gary and Wendy. Lincoln, I have to go to the Rockies."

"I know. Matt told me. Let me come with you."

"I was hoping you'd say that."

Aspen leaves trembled like gold coins in a fresh wind that swept over Jasper National Park's Skyline Trail in the Canadian Rockies. Mountain peaks reared up, already crowned with new snow, even though it was still September. Lincoln hiked at Kimberley's side and watched for tension building in her face. So far, he'd perceived none, just quiet, steady resolution.

They'd flown to Calgary two days after Kimberley had broken her engagement with Jake. There, Lincoln had met her father, Elliott Colter, whose penetrating blue gaze had assessed him like a rapier before easing into welcome. From Calgary, he and Kimberley had driven to Banff and then north to Jasper.

"It's up ahead." She nodded to where the trail passed between an aspen grove and a rock outcrop. When they reached the outcrop, she halted and slowly scanned their surroundings. "It looks different in autumn." She took a few more steps along the trail. "This is about where Bryan and I were when the bear charged. She came from the trees. I think it was there." She pointed to a dense aspen clone and then walked briskly to the fractured outcrop riddled with crevices. "After she knocked us down, I rolled and crawled into one of these crevices." Her brow furrowed as she placed a hiking boot toe at the edge of a cleft in the outcrop. "Maybe it was this one. I'm not sure. Everything happened so fast."

She turned to look over her shoulder, as though seeing something invisible to him, and then stepped away from the crevice and knelt on one knee. She touched her fingertips to her lips and then to the rocky ground, and he knew that was the spot where a man who'd loved her so much he'd stood between her and a charging grizzly had died.

After a few seconds, she rose to her feet and gazed at the snow-clad peaks and rustling aspens, her eyes clear. "The mountains are so beautiful, aren't they? We should come back."

"We will. I'm sure you'll find plenty to photograph."

"I'm sure I will."

* * *

Six weeks later, Kimberley watched Lincoln stride into the horse barn in the ranch yard and could tell things hadn't gone well between him and Jake. Her shoulders slumped. "What did he say?"

Her fiancé enfolded her in a hug, resting his chin on her hair. "Nothing. He just walked away."

"I was afraid this might happen. I'm sorry." She hugged Lincoln closer to her.

He kissed her hair. "Not your fault. Come with me." He showed her the caulking gun he held in one hand. "I need to caulk a leak in the loft roof. Terri noticed rain dripping this morning when she went up for hay. Should be dry enough now to caulk."

She followed him up the narrow wooden stairs to the loft filled with sweet-smelling hay bales and sat on a bale to wait, glad of her warm jacket and wool gloves in the cool late October air. Engaged for a week, she and Lincoln had settled on a December wedding, allowing two months to take care of the details.

"There it is." He pointed to the peak of the roof. "I can see two specks of light. This will only take a minute." He scrambled up onto the stack of bales, positioned the caulking gun, and pressed the lever to discharge caulking compound. The bales were so soft, he made barely a whisper of sound as he moved.

The clip-clop of a horse's hooves sounded on the cement floor, accompanied by the rap of riding boot heels.

That would be Terri bringing in Restless Moon. Home from university for the weekend, Terri had been riding in the arena next door.

Jake's angry voice rang out. "I told you I need to talk to you."

Kimberley gave a start.

Lincoln put a finger to his lips.

Terri's footsteps halted, her voice cool. "Please keep your voice down in the barn. As a veterinarian, you know that stress is bad for animals."

"What's gotten into you?" Jake's volume lowered several notches. "You're like a different person since the summer."

"Well, maybe you don't know me as well as you thought you did."

"I'm beginning to see that—especially when it comes to my cousin."

"Yes, and what *about* Paul, Jake? I'm tired of you glowering at us. I've known him for years at school. He's good-looking, funny, really smart, and enjoys my company. What's wrong with that?"

"Enjoys your company? It that what you call what the two of you were doing in his car in Seton this morning?"

Terri's voice took on a coat of ice. "As a matter of fact, Paul and I were discussing our university classes."

"With your arms around each other?"

"Yes. We're huggy types, not that it's any of your business."

Kimberley spread her hands, sending Lincoln a silent

question. Should they let Terri and Jake know they were in the loft?

He shook his head.

Below them, Jake's voice bit out, "Paul's a spoiled brat."

"Is he? Well at least he's not consumed by jealousy like you are."

"*Jealousy?* If you mean your brother—"

"I *do* mean my brother. I think you've been jealous of him for years—maybe ever since you've known him."

"You don't know what you're talking about."

"Don't I? I watched you when you and Linc and Kimberley were in the same room or at the ball park or the barbecue. You couldn't take your eyes off the two of them. What were you afraid of? Did you think he would steal her away from right under your nose?"

A harsh laugh rang out. "Well, he certainly did that, didn't he?"

Terri's voice heated up. "No, he didn't. The simple fact is that Kimberley chose Linc, and you can't accept it."

"I don't have to listen to this." Jake's footsteps snapped on the barn floor.

"*My brother* agreed to be your best man when his heart was breaking."

The footsteps halted.

"He would have stood beside you in that church while you married the woman he fell in love with the first time he saw her. But *you*..." Terri's voice throbbed with emotion. "When he asked you to do the same for him, you walked away. I saw it."

"Your brother—"

"Is named Lincoln, in case you've forgotten. Linc, to you, for what, twenty years? He's the brother you never had, and you're the brother *he* never had. Are you going to let that go, let all those years of friendship and love disappear because Kimberley chose him?"

"You don't know what you're asking."

"Oh, believe me, I *do* know what I'm asking. I also know Linc. The last thing he would ever want to do is hurt you." Her voice softened. "If you truly feel that you can't do this, he won't hold it against you."

"But you will?" Jake's voice was calm.

Seconds of silence fell like stones before Terri spoke. "I've always thought the world of you. Please don't make me think less of you now."

Kimberley stared into Lincoln's eyes. Silence screamed from below the loft.

Jake's footsteps faded away.

Terri's riding boots clicked on the barn floor as she spoke softly, reassuring Restless Moon.

Lincoln gave a jerk, reached inside his jacket, and held up his cell phone. His eyebrows shot up as he read the screen. He stepped silently from one bale to another and handed her the phone, mouthing the word *Jake*.

She read :

I'll do it. Tell me where when and what to wear.

Tears streamed down her face. *Thank you, Jake.*

Epilogue

Kimberley looked at Wendy in exasperation. "It doesn't matter if *every* hair is in place."

Her sister-in-law spoke around a mouthful of hair pins, "If Lincoln wants your hair styled the same as at that dance last summer, that's the way it's going to be. There." She stepped back, eyeing Kimberley critically from head to toe. "It was pure providence that we found a dress so similar to the daffodil. At least this time it's white, so I didn't have to paint your pumps."

"Wendy, I'm ready!"

"I knew that the moment I saw you two exchange that hot look at the lake." Wendy briefly checked her own appearance in the mirror in the church's basement bathroom. "What I don't know is what took you so long."

"Misunderstandings."

"And the vet."

"Yes, and Jake."

Wendy met her eyes in the mirror. They both turned to Terri, who'd been standing quietly nearby. "Do you think he'll show?" Wendy asked.

"For Linc's sake, I hope so."

The wedding rehearsal had been an uncomfortable affair the previous evening. Jake had stood between Lincoln and Tom McCorquodale, with his jaw clenched, and had disappeared immediately after the practice ceremony.

A knock sounded on the bathroom door, and Kimberley heard her father's voice, "It's time, ladies."

They hurried up the stairs to where Matt—ring bearer—and his young friend, Ashley McCorquodale—flower girl—stood outside the sanctuary doors. Ashley's eyes opened wide when she saw Kimberley. Matt gave a huge grin and a thumbs up.

Wendy peeked into the sanctuary and whispered, "Jake's here. Not looking happy, but he's here."

Kimberley hugged her father and then Wendy, Terri, and finally, Matt and Ashley. How was it possible to feel so much happiness? "Okay, let's do this."

Wendy handed her a bouquet of pink and scarlet roses and white lilies. A piano rendition of Pachelbel's *Canon in D* swept through the church. Terri took a deep breath before walking slowly down the aisle, wearing a scarlet, knee-length dress and carrying a bouquet of white baby's breath and pink roses. Dressed to match and carrying a similar bouquet, Wendy followed. In a miniature version of the same dress, Ashley stepped into the sanctuary and scattered white and pink rose petals from a basket while Matt—clad in a gray suit like the groom's and groomsmen's—walked proudly beside her, bearing the wedding rings on a cushion.

When the music changed to Beethoven's *Moonlight Sonata*, Kimberley's father smiled into her eyes. "You're so beautiful. Your mother would have been proud of you." He held out his arm.

She placed her hand on it and walked slowly down the aisle, her gaze fixed on Lincoln, who stood rock solid at the front of the church, tenderness in his gaze. She'd come to Turtle Mountain hunting a glimpse of the rest of her life. Now that future stretched joyfully before her, the gift of courage and the healing power of love.

Dear Reader,

Thank you so much for reading *Braver Than You Know*, the first of my Prairie Hearts novels. I hope you enjoyed Kimberley and Lincoln's love story—I was thrilled to write it! If you enjoyed this book, please help other readers discover it by posting an online review with your favorite retailer.

If you would like more information about the series, the writing of *Braver Than You Know*, or my author life, please visit my website at www.katieardea.com. While you're there, sign up for my email newsletter if you'd like to receive news about works in progress, upcoming releases, special events, and discounts.

And if you love to cook, turn the page for some delicious Prairie Hearts recipes.

Best wishes to you all!

Katie Ardea

Terri's Saskatoon Berry Pie

(makes a 9-inch pie)
8 cups saskatoon berries
1 cup sugar
5 1/4 tablespoons cornstarch
1/2 teaspoon cinnamon (optional)
1 tablespoon butter
pastry for a double crust pie
Combine sugar, cornstarch, and cinnamon and sprinkle over berries. Stir lightly and allow to rest 15 minutes.

On a well-floured surface, roll out dough for pie bottom and place in pie plate. Trim edge. Add berry mixture. Top with dabs of butter. Wet pastry rim with cold water.

Roll out dough for pie top and place over filling. Trim edge. Press top and bottom pastry together at rim and turn edge under. Flute pastry rim between fingers to create an attractive border. Cut a design into the pie's top crust to allow venting. Sprinkle crust with sugar (optional).

Preheat oven to 450°F. Place pie in oven and immediately reduce heat to 350°F. Bake for 50-60 minutes or until crust is golden brown and juices bubble in the pie's center.

Matt's Nibblies

Place leftover rolled pastry scraps on a cookie sheet. Sprinkle with cinnamon and sugar and bake at 350°F for 12-15 minutes or until pastry is lightly browned.

Lauren's Hearty Bread

(makes 4 loaves)

4 3/8 cups boiling water

2 cups rolled oats

5/8 cup molasses

1 1/4 tablespoons salt

5/12 cup olive oil

5/8 cup sunflower seeds

5/8 cup flax seeds, ground

Pour boiling water over other ingredients in a large bowl. Stir. Cool to lukewarm.

1 1/4 cups lukewarm water

6 cups whole wheat flour

4 cups all-purpose flour

2 1/2 tablespoons active dry yeast

Add water, flours, and yeast to lukewarm mixture. Stir until nearly completely blended. If dough is very sticky, add a little more flour. Tip dough onto a well-floured surface, cover with the bowl, and allow to rest for 15 minutes.

Knead dough until smooth and springy but not hard. Place in a greased bowl, turn over, and top with waxed paper and a tea towel. Set in a warm place to rise for 60 minutes.

Pound down dough, cut into four pieces, shape into loaves, and place in pans. Allow to rise until doubled in bulk, about 25-30 minutes. Bake in a preheated oven at 375°F for 30-33 minutes.

Kimberley's Salad

(makes about 12 cups)

2 cups cooked rice

1/2 cup green onions, sliced

1/2 cup raisins

1 cup cashews

1 cup bean sprouts or sugar peas, chopped

1 red pepper, chopped

1 cup mushrooms, sliced

3 stalks celery, chopped

4 (or more) cups fresh spinach, chopped

1/4 cup fresh parsley, chopped

Combine all ingredients.

Dressing:

1/4 cup soy sauce

1/4 cup olive oil

1 clove garlic, grated

Shake ingredients in a small jar until well blended. Add to salad and mix.

Lincoln's Burgers

(makes 4 big burgers)

1 pound ground beef

1 small onion, chopped

1 egg

1 slice whole wheat bread, crumbled

1 1/2 teaspoons soy sauce

1/4 teaspoon salt

1/4 teaspoon pepper

1 tablespoon fresh parsley, chopped (or 2 teaspoons dried)

Combine all ingredients and form into patties. Grill.

Jake's Coleslaw

(makes about 6 cups)

4 cups red cabbage, shredded

1 cup carrots, shredded

1/4 cup celery, minced

1/4 cup onion, minced

1/4 cup radishes, thinly sliced and minced

Combine all ingredients.

Dressing:

1/4 cup mayonnaise

1/4 cup sour cream

1 tablespoon dill pickle brine

1 tablespoon apple cider vinegar

1 teaspoon prepared mustard

1 1/2 teaspoons maple syrup

1/8 teaspoon paprika

Salt and pepper to taste.

Combine dressing ingredients and pour over salad, mixing well.

To all who helped ...

I could never have completed *Braver Than You Know* to the best of my ability without your assistance. Special thanks to my beta readers—Anna, Dainis, Mary Jean, Jānis, Emma, Velta, Mary Jean, Alvina, Dianne—for volunteering your time to read the manuscript and offer suggestions for improvement. Two anonymous judges of the Catherine Contest 2018 provided insightful comments as to changes needed for the novel as a whole. My editor, Nancy Cassidy at TheRedPenCoach, gently but firmly nudged me to streamline the story's plot and make the characters and their motivations consistent. Cover designer Kim Killion at The Killion Group took my image ideas and transformed them into a cover that captures the essence of *Braver Than You Know*. Last but never least, thanks to my husband, Vilis, for his unfailing support for this novel and my other writing endeavors. You are my best friend and the hero of *my* love story.

Made in the USA
Lexington, KY
06 November 2019

56669776R00216